A Night In

*

Flossie: A Venus Of Sixteen

*

Maudie

Anonymous

NEXUS

A Nexus Book
Published in 1988
by the Paperback Division of
W. H. Allen & Co. Plc
Sekforde House, 175/9 St. John Street,
London, EC1V 4LL

Reprinted 1988, 1989.

Printed in Great Britain by
Cox & Wyman Ltd, Reading, Berks.

ISBN 0 302 32245 4

A NIGHT IN A
MOORISH HAREM

Preface

Lord George Herbert is universally acknowledged to be the handsomest man in the English nobility. His form is tall and muscular, but of a perfect symmetry. His features are handsome but manly and of a ruddy bronze colour acquired at sea. His short and curly brown hair shades a broad and white forehead beneath which sparkle large hazel eyes. He wears a heavy beard and moustache, but they are not able to conceal his handsome mouth.

His courage and talents together with the powerful influence of his family had procured for him, at the early age of twenty-three, the command of one of the finest ships in the English navy.

The following strange but true narrative is from his pen and it may be imagined that he did not intend to have it copied. But he left it in possession of a fair and frail lady who thought it too good to be kept secret, and so the reader has the benefit of it.

3

CHAPTER ONE

Abdallah Pasha's Seraglio

Her British Majesty's ship 'Antler', of which I was in command, lay becalmed one afternoon off the coast of Morocco. I did not allow the steam to be raised for I·knew the evening breeze would soon make toward the land.

Retiring to my cabin I threw myself upon the sofa. I could not sleep for my thoughts kept wandering back to the beautiful women of London and the favours which some of them had granted me when last on shore.

Months had elapsed since then and months more would elapse before I could again hope to quench, in the lap of beauty, the hot desire which now coursed through my veins and distended my genitals.

To divert my mind from thoughts at present so imperative I resolved to take a bath. Beneath the stern windows which lighted my cabin lay a boat, into which I got by sliding down a rope which held it to the ship. Then I undressed and plunged into the cool waves. After bathing I redressed, and, reclining in the boat, fell asleep. When I awoke it was dark and I was floating along near the shore. The ship was miles away.

The rope which held the boat must have slipped when the breeze sprang up, and the people on the ship being busy getting underway had not noticed me. I had no oars and dared not use the sails for fear the Moorish vessels in sight would discover me. I drifted towards a large building which was the only one to be seen; it rose from the rocks near the water's edge. The approach to the place on which it stood seemed to be from the land side, and all the windows which I could see were high above the ground.

The keel of my boat soon grated on the sand and I hastened to pull it among the rocks for concealment, for it was quite possible I might be seized if discovered and sold into slavery. My plan was to wait for the land breeze just before dawn and escape to sea. At this moment I heard a whispered call from above. I looked up and saw two ladies looking down on me from the high windows above, and behind these two were gathered several others whom I could just see in the gloom.

'We have been watching you,' said the lady, 'and will try to assist you. Wait where you are.'

She spoke in French, which is the common medium of communication among the different nations inhabiting the shores of the Mediterranean, and which had become familiar to me. I now thought this isolated building was a seraglio and I resolved to trust the ladies, who would run even more risk than myself in case of discovery.

After waiting some time, a rope of shawls was let down from the window and the same voice bid me climb. My discipline when a midshipman made this easy for me to do; I rose hand over hand and safely reached the window through which I was assisted by the ladies into the perfumed air of an elegant apartment richly furnished and elegantly lighted.

My first duty was to kiss the fair hands which had aided me, and then I explained the accident which had brought me among them and the plan I had formed for escape before dawn. I then gave my name and rank.

While doing this I had an opportunity to observe the ladies; there were nine of them and any one of them would have been remarked for her beauty. Each one of them differed from all the others in the style of her charms: some were large and some were small; some were slender and some plump, some blonde and some brunette, but all were bewitchingly beautiful. Each, too, was the most lovely type of a different nationality, for war and shipwrecks and piracy enable the Moorish Pashas to choose their darlings from under all the flags that float on the Mediterranean.

A lady whom they called Inez and whom, therefore, I took to be a Spaniard, answered me by bidding me in the name of all of them the warmest welcome. 'You are,' she said, 'in the seraglio of Abdallah, the Pasha of this district, who is not expected until tomorrow, and who will never be the wiser if his ladies seize so rare an opportunity to entertain a gentleman during his absence.' She added, 'We have no secrets or no jealousy between ourselves' smiling very significantly.

'That is very unusual,' said I. 'How can any of you know whether he has any secrets with the one he happens to be alone with?'

'But one of us is never alone with him,' said Inez. The blank look of consternation I had set them all laughing.

They were brimful of mischief and were evidently bent on making the most of the unexpected company of a young man. Inez put her hand on my sleeve. 'How wet you are,' said she. 'It will not be hospitable to allow you to keep on such wet clothes.'

My clothes were perfectly dry, but the winks and smiles that the young ladies exchanged as they began to disrobe me led me cheerfully to submit while they proceeded to divest me of every article of clothing.

When at length my shirt was suddenly jerked off they gave little affected screams and peeped through their fingers at my shaft, which by this time was of most towering dimensions. I had snatched a hearty kiss from one and all of them as they had gathered round to undress me.

Inez now handed me a scarf which she had taken from her own fair shoulders. 'We can none of us bear to leave you,' she said, 'but you can only kiss one at a time; please throw this to the lady you prefer.' Good heavens! Then it was true, that all of these beautiful women had been accustomed to be present when one of them was embraced.

'Ladies,' said I 'you are unfair. You have stripped me, but you keep those charms concealed which you offer to my preference. I am not sure now if you have any imperfections which you wish to keep covered.'

The ladies looked at one another, blushed a little, then nodded and laughed, then began undressing. Velvet vests, skirts of lawn and silken trousers were rapidly flung to the floor. Lastly, as if at a given signal, every dainty chemise was stripped off and some of the most lovely forms that ever floated throughout a sculptor's dream stood naked before me. Was I not myself dreaming, or had I been suddenly transported amid the houses of the seventh heaven?

For a while I stood entranced, gazing at the charming spectacle. 'Ladies,' said I at last, 'it would be immodest in me to give preference when all are so ravishingly lovely. Please keep the scarf, fair Inez, and when I have paid a tribute to your fair charms, pass it yourself to another, till all have been gratified.' 'Did he say all?' cried a little brunette. 'All indeed!' cried the rest in chorus, bursting into laughter.

'Every one,' said I, 'or I will perish in the attempt.' Inez was standing directly in front of me; she was about nineteen, and of that rarest type of Spanish beauty, partly derived from Flemish blood. Her eyes were sparkling brown, but her long hair was blonde. It was braided and coiled round the top of her head like a crown which added to her queenly appearance, for she was above the ordinary stature; her plump and well-rounded form harmonised with her height. Her complexion had the slight yellow tinge of rich cream, which was set off by the rosy nipples which tipped her full breasts and the still deeper rose of her lips and mouth.

She happened to be standing on one of the silken cushions which, singly and in piles, were scattered about the room in profusion. It made her height just equal to my own. As soon as I had made the speech last recorded, I advanced and folded her in my embrace.

Her soft arms were wound round me in response; and our lips met in a delicious, and prolonged kiss, during which my shaft was imprisoned against her warm, smooth belly. Then she raised herself on tiptoe, which brought its crest amid the short, thick hair where the belly terminated. With one hand I guided my shaft to the entrance which welcomed it; with my other I held her plump buttocks toward me. Then she gradually settled on her feet again, and, as she did so, the entrance was slowly and delightfully effected in her moist, hot and swollen sheath. When she was finally on her feet again I could feel her throbbing womb resting on my shaft.

The other ladies had gathered round us; their kisses rained on my neck and shoulders, and the presence of their bosoms and bellies was against my back and sides—indeed they so completely sustained Inez and myself that I seemed about to mingle my being with them all at once. I had stirred the womb of Inez with but a few thrusts—when the rosy cheeks became a deeper dye, her eyes swam, her lips parted and I felt a delicious baptism of moisture on my shaft.

Then her head sank on my shoulder, the gathered sperm of months gushed from my crest so profusely that I seemed completely transferred with waves of rapture into the beautiful Spanish girl. Her sighs of pleasure were not only echoed by mine, but by all the ladies in sympathy gathered around us. They gently lowered us from this sustaining embrace to a pile of cushions. As they did so, with hardly any aid on our part, my diminished shaft was drawn out of Inez and, with it, some of my tributary sperm, which splashed on the floor.

11

'It was too bad of you, Inez to take more than you can keep,' said one of the others. She said it in such a pitiful tone it convulsed us all with laughter. As for me, I now realised the rashness of the promise I had made them all, but they gaily joined hands round Inez and myself and began a circling dance, their round, white limbs and plump bosoms floated in the lamplight as they moved in cadence to a Moorish love song, in which they all joined. With my cheeks pillowed against the full breasts of Inez I watched the charming circle, which was like a scene in fairy land. Bracelets and anklets of heavy fettered gold glittered on their arms and legs; rings, necklaces and earrings of diamonds and rubies, which they had in profusion, glistened at every movement.

Each one had her hair elaborately dressed in the style peculiarly becoming to herself and there were no envious garments to conceal a single charm. I urged them to prolong the bewitching spectacle again and again, which they obligingly did. Then they gathered around me, reclining to rest on the cushions as near as they could get, in attitudes which were picturesque and voluptuous.

When we were thus resting I frequently exchanged a kiss or caress with my fair companions, which I took care to do impartially. Then it occurred to me that I would like to hear from the lips of each the most

12

interesting and voluptuous passage from their
lives. Again these interesting ladies, after a little
urging, consented, and Inez commenced.

CHAPTER TWO

The Spanish lady's story

We lived in Seville. When at the age of sixteen my parents promised me in marriage to a wealthy gentleman, whom I had seen but twice and did not admire. My love was already given to Carlos, a handsome young officer who had just been promoted to a lieutenant for bravery. He was elegantly formed, his hair and eyes were as dark as night and he could dance to perfection. But it was for his gentle, winning smile that I loved him.

On the evening of the day that my parents had announced their determination to me, I had gone to be alone in the orange grove in the farthest part of our garden, there to sorrow over my hard fate. In the midst of my grief I heard the voice of Carlos calling me. Could it be he who had been banished from the house and whom I never expected to see again?

He sprang down from the garden wall, folded

15

me in his embrace and covered my hair with kisses for I had hidden my blushing face on my bosom. Then we talked of our sad lot. Carlos was poor and it would be impossible to marry without the consent of my parents; we could only mingle our tears and regrets.

He led me to a grassy bank concealed by the orange trees and rose bushes, then he drew me on his lap and kissed my lips and cheeks and eyes. I did not chide him, for it must be our last meeting, but I did not return his kisses with passion. I had never felt a wanton desire in my life, much less now when I was so sad.

His passionate kisses were no longer confined to my face, but were showered on my neck, and at length my dress was parted and revealed my little breasts to his ardent lips. I felt startled and made an attempt to stop him in what I considered an impropriety, but he did not stop there. I felt my skirts being raised with a mingled sensation of alarm and shame which caused me to try to prevent it, but it was impossible—I loved him too much to struggle against him, and he was soon lying between my naked thighs.

'Inez,' he said, 'if you love me, be my wife for these few moments before we part.'

I could not resist the appeal. I offered my lips to kisses without any feeling save innocent love and lay passive, while I felt him guide a stiff, warm object between my thighs. It entered where nothing had ever entered before and no sooner was it entered than he gave a fierce thrust which

16

seemed to tear my vitals with a cruel pain. Then he gave a deep sigh and sank heavily upon my bosom.

I kissed him repeatedly, for I supposed it must have hurt him as much as it did me, little thinking that his pleasure had been as exquisite as my suffering had been. Just at that moment the harsh voice of my duenna resounded through the garden, calling, 'Inez! Inez!'

Exchanging with my seducer a lingering, hearty kiss, I extracted myself from his embrace and answered the call. My duenna eyed me sharply as I approached her.

'Why do you straddle your legs so far apart when you walk,' said she, and when I came closer, 'Why is the bosom of your dress so disordered and why are your cheeks so flushed?'

I made some excuse about climbing to get an orange and hurried past her to my room. I locked the door and prepared to go to bed that I might think uninterruptedly of Carlos, whom I now loved more than ever. When I took off my petticoat I found it all stained with blood. I folded it and treasured it beneath my pillow to dream upon, under the fond illusion that Carlos' blood was mingled there with my own.

For weeks afterwards I was so closely watched that I could not see Carlos. The evening preceding my marriage I went to vespers with my duenna. While we were kneeling in the cathedral a large woman, closely veiled, came and knelt close beside me. She attracted my attention by plucking my dresss, and, as I turned, she momentarily lifted the corner of her mantel and I saw it was Carlos in disguise. I was now all alert and a small package was slipped into my hand. I had just time to secure it in my bosom when my duenna arose and we left the church.

As soon as I regained the privacy of my own room I tore open the package and found it contained a silken rope ladder and letter from Carlos requesting me to suspend it from the window that night after the family was at rest.

The note was full of love. There was much more to tell, it said, if I would grant the interview by means of the ladder. Of course I determined to see him. I was very ignorant of what most girls learn from each other, for I had no companion. I supposed when a woman was embraced as I had been she necessarily got with child, and that such embraces therefore occurred at intervals of a year or so. I expected, consequently, nothing of the kind at the coming interview. I wanted to learn of Carlos if the child, which I supposed to be in my womb, would be born so soon as to betray our secret to my husband.

When the family retired I went to my room and dressed myself elaborately, braiding my hair and putting on all of my jewellery. Then I fastened one end of the rope ladder to the bedpost and lowered the other end out of the window; it was at once strained by the ascending

18

step of Carlos. My eyes were soon feasted with the sight of my handsome lover, and we were soon locked in each other's arms.

Again and again we alternately devoured each other with our eyes and pressed each other to our hearts. Words did not seem to be of any use; our kisses and caresses became more passionate, and for the first time in my life I felt a wanton emotion. The lips between my thighs became moistened and torrid with coursing blood; I could feel my cheeks burn under the ardent gaze of my lover; I could no longer meet his eyes—my own dropped in shame.

He began to undress me rapidly, his hand trembling with eagerness. Could it be that he wanted to pierce my loins so soon again, as he had done in the orange garden? An hour ago I would have dreaded it; now the thought caused a throb of welcome just where the pain had been sharpest.

Stripped to my chemise, and even that unbuttoned by the eager hand of my lover, I darted from his arms and concealed my confusion beneath the bedcover. He soon undressed and followed me—one kiss on my neck and one on each of my naked breasts, then he opened my thighs and parted the little curls between. Again I felt the stiff, warm object entering. It entered slowly on account of the tightness, but every inch of its progress inward became more and more pleasant.

When it was fully entered I was in a rapture of delight, yet something was wanting. I wrapped my arms around my lover and responded passionately to his kisses. I was almost tempted to respond to his thrusts by a wanton motion of my loins. My maidenhead was gone and the tender virgin wound completely healed, but I had still some remains of maiden shame.

For a moment he lay still and then he gave me half a dozen deep thrusts, each succeeding one giving me more and more pleasure. It culminated at last in a thrill so exquisite that my frame seemed to melt. Nothing more was wanting. I gave a sigh of deep gratification and my arms fell nerveless to my sides, but I received with passionate pleasure two or three more thrusts which Carlos gave me, at each of which my sheath was penetrated by a copious gush which soothed and bathed its membranes.

For a long time we lay perfectly still; the stiff shaft which had completely filled me had diminished in size until it slipped completely out. Carlos at last relieved me of his weight by lying at my side, but our legs were still entwined.

We had not time to converse. My lover explained to me all the sexual mysteries which remained for me to know, then we formed plans which would enable us after my marriage to meet often alone. These explanations and plans were mingled so freely with caresses that before my lover left me we had melted five times in each others' arms. I had barely strength to drag up the rope ladder after he departed.

The day had now begun to dawn. I fell into a dreamless sleep and was awakened by my duenna pounding on the door and calling that it was nearly ten o'clock and that I was to be married at eleven. I was in no hurry but they got me to church in time. During the whole ceremony I felt my lover's sperm trickling down my thighs.

We all applauded Inez as she thus finished her story. While she was telling the story one of the ladies, whom I noticed to be the most fleshy of the number, cuddled up close to my side and suffered me to explore all her charms with my hand. During the description of the scene in the orange garden my fingers toyed with the curls between her thighs, and, as the story went on, parted the curls and felt of the lips beneath. She was turned partly on her belly against me so that this by-play was not observed.

My fingers were encouraged by the lady's hand until two of them made an entrance and were completely enclosed in the hot, moist tissue. The little protuberance which all women have within the orifice, and which is the principal seat of sensation, was in her remarkably developed. It was as large as the end of my little finger. I played with it and squeezed it and plunged my fingers past it again and again; she manifested her pleasure by kissing me on the neck, where she had hidden her face.

When Inez described her first thrill in the bedroom scene my fingers were doing all in their power to complete the other lady's gratification, and this, too, with success, for they were suddenly bathed with moisture, and, at the same time, the lady drew a deep sigh, which was not noticed, for all supposed it to be in sympathy with Inez's story. Then she withdrew my hand and lay perfectly still. Inez was about to give her the scarf, but she lay so motionless that she handed it to another.

'This,' said Inez, 'is Helene, a Grecian lady. She will tell you a story and then she will do anything you wish.'

My head was still pillowed on Inez's breast. Helene smiled, then stooped and kissed me. She was about medium height, very slender, but graceful and well rounded, and her skin was as white as alabaster. Her features were of the perfect antique mould and were lighted with fine grey eyes. Her glossy black hair was all brushed back to a knot just below the back of the neck, from which but a single curl escaped from either side and toyed with her firm but finely rounded bosom.

The deep vermilion of her lips compensated for the faint colour of her cheeks, whose tinge was scarcely deeper than that of her finely cut ears. She was about twenty-two, and ripe to yield a charming embrace. I drew her down to a seat on my loins and begged her to begin her story.

CHAPTER THREE

The Grecian lady's story

I entered the bridal bed a virgin. When the bridesmaid left me I trembled with apprehension and covered up my head under the bedclothes. It was because I had heard so many stories of the trials and hardships of a virgin on her marriage night and not because I had any antipathy for my husband. On the contrary I liked him.

His courtship had been short, for he was a busy man on the diplomatic service of the Greek government. He was no longer young, but he was goodlooking and manly, and I was proud that he had selected me from all the other Athenian girls. My heart beat still more violently when he entered. He came to the side of my bed and, turning down the clothes from my head, he saw how I was agitated. He simply kissed my hand, and then went to the other side of the room to undress. This conduct somewhat reassured me.

When he got into bed and took me in his arms

my back was turned towards him. He took no liberties with any part of my person, but began to converse with me about the incidents of the wedding. I was soon so calm that I suffered him to turn me with my face towards him, and he kissed me first on the forehead and then on the lips.

After a while he begged me to return his kisses, saying that if I did not it would prove that I disliked him; thus encouraged I returned his kisses. When I had so long lain in his arms that I began to feel at home, he turned me upon my back and unfastened the bosom of my chemise and kissed and fondled my breasts. This set my heart beating wildly again, but I kept exchanging kisses till he suddenly lifted the skirt of my chemise and lay between my thighs.

Then I covered my face with my hands for shame, but he was so kind and gentle that I soon got so accustomed to the situation that I suffered him to remove my hands and fasten his mouth to mine in a passionate kiss. As he did so I felt something pushing between my thighs. It entered my curls there and touched the naked lips beneath. I felt my face grow hot with shame and lay perfectly passive.

He must have been in bed with me two hours before he ventured so far. He had his reward, for a soft desire began to grow in my brain, the blood centred on my loins and I longed for the connection which was so imminent. I returned him a kiss as passionate as he gave; it was the signal for which he had been waiting. I felt a pressure on the virgin membrane, not hard enough, however, to be painful. The pressure slackened and then pushed again and again.

By this time I was wanton with desire and not only returned the passionate kisses, but I wound my arms around him. Then came the fateful thrust, tearing away the obstruction and reaching to the very depths of my loin. I gave a cry of mingled bliss and agony, which I could not help repeating at each of the three deep thrusts that followed. Then all was still, an effusion like balm filled my sheath in the place of the organ that had so disturbed it. A delightful langour stole over my frame and I went to sleep in my husband's arms.

In less than six months circumstances compelled me to deceive him. After we had been married awhile our position required us to go a great deal in company. Card playing was very fashionable and the stakes got higher and higher. One night the luck ran terribly against me; I proposed for the party to double.

My husband had gone on a journey a few days before and had left a large sum of money in my charge. It was nearly all his fortune. A portion of this money I now staked, thinking that the luck could not possibly go against me again, but it did. I was rendered desperate. Again I proposed to double—it would take all I had left if I lost.

The ladies who were playing withdrew; the gentlemen were too polite to do so. The cards went against me. I felt myself turn dreadfully pale. The French ambassador, Count Henri, who was sitting beside me, was disposed to conceal my terrible embarrassment. He was a handsome man, but, unlike my husband, he was very stalwart. His manners were very engaging. He kept up a stream of small talk till the others had dispersed to other parts of the room, then he offered to bring me on the morrow the amount I had lost.

I turned as crimson as I had before been pale. I knew the price of such assistance. I made him no reply, my look dropped to the floor and I begged him to leave me, which he politely did. All next day I was nearly distracted; I hoped Count Henri would not come. My cheeks would burn as on the evening before and the blood all rush back to my heart.

At 3 o'clock he came; the valet showed him into the parlour, closed the door and retired. Count Henri must have known he was expected, for I was elegantly dressed in blue silk and my shoulders were set off with heavy lace. I was so weak from agitation that I could not rise from the sofa to greet him.

'May I have the happiness,' he said, 'of being your confidant?' as he seated himself beside me, holding in one hand a well-filled purse and dropping the other around my waist. I could not reject the purse. If I kept the purse I could not ask him to remove his arm. I was giddy with contending emotion.

'For God's sake, spare me,' I murmured. My head dropped, he caught it to his heart—I had fainted away. When I again became conscious I was lying on my back upon the sofa in the arms of the Count, the lace on my bosom was parted, my heavy skirts were all turned up from my naked thighs and he was in the very ecstasy of filling my sheath with sperm.

It was this exquisite sensation which had restored me to consciousness, but I was too late to join in the ecstasy. His shaft became limber and small and I was left hopelessly in the lurch. Then I beseeched him to go as it was no time or place for this.

'Will you receive me in your bedroom tonight?' asked the Count, kissing my bare bosoms.

He had so excited my passions that I no longer hesitated. 'The front door will be unfastened all night,' I replied, 'and my room is directly over this.'

Then he allowed me to rise. I adjusted my disordered dress as quickly as possible, but it was not quick enough. The valet opened the door to bring in the card of a visitor. He saw enough to put me in his power.

After the Count had gone I found the purse in my bosom; it contained more than I had lost, but my thoughts were not of money. My lips had tasted the forbidden fruit; I was no longer the same woman; my excitement had culminated in lascivious desire. I could hardly wait for night to come.

When finally the house was still I unfastened the front door, retired to my room, undressed and was standing in my chemise with my nightgown in my hand read to put on when the door of my room opened and Alex, the valet, stood before me with his finger on his lips. He was a fine looking youth of seventeen, a Hungarian of a reduced family, who acted half in the capacity of secretary and half in that of valet for my husband. I could not help giving a faint scream, while I concealed my person as well as possible with the nightgown I held in my hands.

'My lady,' said he, 'I know all but I shall be discreet. I only ask you to give me the sweetest proof of your confidence.'

There was no help for it. With a murmured 'For shame,' I sprang into bed and hid under the bedclothes. He quickly undressed and followed me. My object was to dismiss him before the Count came; I therefore suffered him to make rapid progress. He took me in his arms and kissed my lips and breasts and, as he raised my chemise, our naked thighs met. He was much more agitated than myself. I had been anticipating a paramour all the afternoon and he

28

could not have known what reception would be accorded him. He could hardly guide his shaft to the lips that welcomed it.

As for myself, I began where I had left off with the Count. My sheath with wanton greediness devoured every inch that entered it and at the very first thrust I melted with an adulterous rapture never felt in my husband's embrace. Just at that moment I heard the front door softly open and shut. I pushed Alex away with force that drew his stiff shaft completely out of me.

'Gather up your clothes quickly and get into the closet,' I said. Madly eager as he must have been to finish, he hurried with his clothes into the closet as the Count entered.

The Count came up and kissed me. I pretended to be asleep. He undressed hastily, and, getting into bed, took me in his arms. But I delayed his progress as much as possible. I made him tell me everything that had been said about my losses at cards. I used every artifice to keep him at bay until his efforts should arouse my passions.

Then he mounted me and his stalwart shaft distended and penetrated me so much deeper than that of young Alex that it was more exquisite than before. Again the wild, adulterous thrill penetrated every part of my body. I fairly groaned with ecstasy. At that moment the front door loudly opened. It must be my husband unexpectedly returning.

'Good heavens, Count!' I cried, 'under the bed with you.' He pulled his great stiff shalf out of me with a curse of disappointment that he could not finish and scrambled under the bed, dragging his clothes after him.

My husband came in all beaming with delight that he had been able to return so soon. I received him with much demonstration. 'How it flushes your cheeks to see me,' he said.

When he had undressed and come to bed I returned his caresses with so much ardour that he soon entered where Alex and the Count had so hastily withdrawn. I felt pleasant, but feigned much more rapture than I felt.

To console the Count I dropped one of my hands down alongside the bed, which he was so polite as to kiss, and, as my husband's face was buried in my neck, while he was making rapid thrusts I kissed my other hand to Alex, who was peeping through the closet door. Then I gave a motion to my loins which sent my husband spending and repeated it till I had extracted from him the most copious gushes. It was too soon for me to melt with another thrill; my object was to fix him for a sound sleep, but the balmy sperm was so grateful to my hot sheath after the two fierce preceding encounters that I felt rewarded for my troubles.

He soon fell sound asleep. Then I motioned for the Count to go. With his clothes in one hand and his stiff shaft in the other he glided out.

Soon after we heard the front door shut and the disconsolate Alex cautiously came forth. With his clothes under his arm and both hands holding his rigid shaft, he too disappeared.

Here Helene finished. During her story I lay on my back with my head resting on Inez' bosom. Helen sat astride my loins with her face towards me, which gave me a fair view of her most secret charms. She somehow or other let the scarf fall over her thighs and beneath it her little tapering fingers began to play with my limber shaft.

As the story proceeded it began to stiffen, and while she was describing the bedchamber scene she contrived to enter it into the crevice so directly above it. It rose and rose until it was almost rigid, vivified as it was by the close retreat in which it was hidden. She kept undulating her loins as the story went on till, just as she finished, I was nearly ready to spend. At the same moment I felt my shaft moistened with the moisture of the pretty Greek girl and she fell fainting in the arms of a lady close by.

My shaft drew out of her with a sucking noise which set all laughing. She hurriedly gave the scarf to the lady in whose arms she lay and in whose bosom she held her face.

'It is with you, Zuleika,' they all cried in chorus. Zuleika looked very much embarrassed. About eighteen years of age, she was formed very much like Inez, whom she equalled in height, but she was more muscular and her skin was of a dark bronze.

Her large, lustrous eyes were dark as night. So was her curly hair, which was set off with a snowy turban on which gleamed a crescent of burnished silver. The colour deepened in her dusky cheeks as she timidly began.

CHAPTER FOUR

The Moorish lady's story

'Ladies,' she said, 'you all know I am three months gone with child. You have now to learn what is equally true. I am a virgin still.'

'A virgin and with a child,' they all echoed, several of them crossing themselves as they exclaimed.

'Listen and you shall hear,' proceeded Zuleika. 'I was purchased from my parents in Fez, where we lived, by a young Moorish merchant. They, as well as myself, were delighted at the prospects which he promised of transferring me to the harm of some great Moorish pasha. The price paid was very high, as I was warranted a virgin.

The next morning we joined the caravan for Morocco; mounted on my camel I enjoyed the trip in the highest spirits. Ali, my master, rode beside me on a fine horse which he managed with grace and vigour. His person was slender and his features, which were at the same time bold and amiable, captured my fancy. His attentions to my company were unremitting. His tent every night was pitched near my own to guard me from intrusion.

The last night that we were on the road I had retired early and was just sinking to sleep as the darkness fell when Ali appeared in my tent. 'What is your will, my lord?' I asked.

He bent down and kissed me. It was the first time he had done so. 'My wish is to make you my wife,' he replied.

'And why should you not my lord?' I asked.

Then he told me all his fortune was invested in my purchase and that it would only bring poverty and misery on us both. We mingled our regrets with caresses which grew more and more ardent, until I found myself lying beneath him with my bosom bared to his kisses and my naked thighs parted. Beneath them I felt a gentle pressure which penetrated the hair and touched the more sensitive lips beneath.

I hoped that Ali had determined to marry me. I knew he would if he despoiled me of my virginity, for then my great market value would be gone. I lay passive with my eyes shut. A soft desire ran through my frame centring at the lips where Ali was pressing and making the pressure delightful. The longer he continued in this position the more I wished for a deeper and more satisfying thrust. But the gentle pushes he gave barely parted the outside lips. I could feel that they were stopped by the virgin membrane that barred any further entrance.

I grew wild with desire—I strained him to my bosom, and, pressing my mouth to his, I was relieved of a melting thrill. At the same moment I felt Ali's answering throb and a gush of his sperm penetrated to the depths of my loins, far within the still unbroken curtain of my virginity.

For a long time after we lay in a voluptuous but motionless repose. Then Ali tore himself from my arms. 'I must go,' he said, 'I cannot resist another such temptation.'

'It is three months since that sweet but imperfect connection, which it is now certain will result in my being a mother.'

'And has no man touched you since?' I asked with deepest interest, as I took the splendid Moorish girl blushing in my lap.

'I can tell you,' replied Inez, 'why the Pasha, who never before suffered a woman to remain a virgin a single night in his harem, has spared her.'

He purchased her from Ali the day she arrived in Morocco. After having her examined by the old woman in his employ, she was brought here, and the same evening as soon as he had finished his supper he threw his handkerchief to her. She retired to receive him in her room alone, as only a virgin in this harem has the privilege of doing, for, as you already know, it is customary for us to receive the Pasha's embraces when we are all present.

I noticed Zuleika looked very reluctant—she was doubtless thinking of Ali, from whom she had so recently parted. I overtook her at the door of the bridal chamber. 'Let me take your place for tonight,' said I. 'We are the same size, and complexions will not show in the dark. The Pasha shall never know.'

'Can you indeed manage it?' she asked. 'If so, you are welcome.'

Then she hurried away and I entered the bridal chamber in her place, undressed, extinguished the light and got into bed.

Before a great while the Pashe came. He kissed me on the back of the neck, for I buried my face in the pillow like a bashful girl. Then he hurriedly undressed, and, stretching himself beside me, took me in his arms. My heart was beating violently for the success of my bold scheme, but this agitation he took for virgin fright. I answered in whispered monosyllables to his questions and shrank from every caress he bestowed on my bosom and thighs. He came, as I intended he should, only the more eager.

When at length he mounted me, I covered my face with both hands as if in a paroxysm of shame, and wrapping one of my legs over the

36

other, held them tightly together. He had to lie with his thighs parted over mine. In this position he guided his crest between them, which worked its way between the hair and began to enter the tightly squeezed lips beneath. My passions had become so thoroughly aroused by this time that I could scarcely help opening my thighs and letting him have free entrance.

My monthly period was just passing off, in the latter part of which a woman is peculiarly susceptible to desire, but I made him gain his way by the hardest pushing. Not only were my thighs locked, but I tightly contracted the muscles of my sheath at the lips. He would give a fierce but ineffective thrust, then he would squeeze and suck my breasts, until at last my wantonness became uncontrollable and I gave way with a feeling that unnerved me, letting his shaft plunge into the hilt. He spent profusely with a long sigh of triumphant satisfaction.

I gave a sigh equally profound; I could not help it. But it only completed his delusion, for he thought it was caused by pain I suffered at the rupture of my maidenhead. He petted and consoled me with kisses and caresses till we were both ready for another embrace. This time he did not expect me to be especially coy at his embrace. Then he fell asleep.

I knew he would awake in the morning with a stiff shaft, so just before dawn I went and took a bath and put on my most seductive apparel, adorned myself with all my jewellery and perfumed myself with musk. Soon I heard him call, 'Zuleika, Zuleika!'

I hastened to his bedside. 'Zuleika begs that you will excuse her my lord,' said I. 'Pray have some mercy on the poor girl.' Then I turned down the sheet and exposed the blood stains occasioned by my monthly period. 'See' said I, 'you have butchered her.'

'Then you must come to bed with me,' said he. This was just what I sought and I lost no time in doing so and for the third time I got all I wanted.

Inez ended amid the hearty laughter of the ladies. As for me, I had been caressing Zuleika; her plump bosom, her smooth belly and her grand thighs passed in review under my hand. She concealed her face on my bosom but she made no resistance. Perhaps she no longer thought of Ali.

I ventured even to insert my forefinger between the lips which concealed her maidenhead. It stretched from side to side of her entire sheath, save the little orifice that is never closed. She raised her face, which was overspread with crimson blush; her eyes were shut, but her mouth pouted for the kiss which my lips fastened upon it.

The voluptuous stories and the wanton situation had done their work upon her. My intrusive finger perceived the throbbing of the lips between which it was inserted. My shaft had become as rigid as bone. The glands clung to the base all ready for action.

As soon as Inez finished speaking I laid Zuleika on her back upon the cushion, spread her thighs wide open and mounted her. My crest was at once buried where my finger had lately explored. I gave a push that strained the virgin membrane, but it had the strength which characterised the rest of her splendid physique, and bounded back like India rubber. Her whole form quivered at the touch.

Furious with lust I wrapped my arms around the small of her back and braced my whole strength for another thrust. My crest went plunging in, tore through the curtain of her virginity and rammed against her pregnant womb.

'Allah! Allah!' she cried, tossing her arms wildly upwards and rolling her eyes towards heaven. Whether her pain or her pleasure was most exquisite I did not know, but my whole being seemed to centre in my loins and gush into the superb Moor. Then I sank prostrate and exhausted on her bosom with everything gratified.

'The baby has been fed,' said Inez, which caused another laugh among the ladies.

'See Zuleika,' said another in an alarmed tone, 'she has fainted.'

Zuleika had indeed become very pale. One gave her a glass of water and bathed her forehead; another took the scarf from her hand and staunched the blood which was flowing from between her thighs. I supported her head on my arm and gave her kisses which before long she began to return. Then she threw one of her thighs over me to conceal the trace of her wound, saying to the lady who had been using the scarf that she bequeathed it to her.

This lady's name was Laura, and she was an Italian. It was the same who had melted at the touch of my fingers during the first story. She was about twenty-four and the most fleshy lady in the room. Her immense bosom and buttocks quivered as she moved, but rounded out again in perfect contour when she was still. She had dimples on her cheeks and chin, dimples at her elbows and knees and dimples at her hips.

Her features were very pleasing, with a rosy mouth, a saucy retroussé nose and eyes that were dark in expression and shaded by long lashes. She wore her long hair in puffs supported by a tall shell comb—perhaps to add to her height, which was only medium, notwithstanding her enormous weight. Still her waist was not overgrown, and her wrists and ankles were pretty.

'I think I shall have time to tell a long story,' she said, glancing ruefully at the diminished little object between my legs. Amid the titters caused by this remark, she seated herself on the opposite side of me from Zuleika, where she could caress my genitals with one of her hands while she proceeded with her story.

CHAPTER FIVE

The Italian lady's story

I am sorry to confess that I did not possess a maidenhead when I was married. It caused a jealousy and suspicion on my husband's mind which I could not eradicate. When I was a girl of sixteen at school in a convent, one of my companions handed me an improper book. It contained the amours of the ancient gods and goddesses. They were painted so minutely that it left nothing to be imagined, and it so fascinated me that I at once began it.

I retired to my room and bolted my door to devour it undisturbed. I took off my clothes, and, putting on my dressing gown, lay on my bed to read at my ease. Alone as I was, my cheeks burned at the lascivious descriptions in the book. Then I longed to be in the place of one of the goddesses or nymphs in the wanton adventures.

The blood coursed hotly through my veins. I felt the need of something which I never had before, something to quench the seething heat for the first time generated in my loins. I put my hand on the seat of desire; the young hair which grew there had not yet become thick enough to protect the lips beneath from the most casual touch.

They grew sensitive under my hands, and, after I read of the rape or seduction of one goddess after another, my fingers slipped in betwen the lips, and by a gentle movement, they afforded me some pleasure. The motion to be satisfactory had to be constantly increased until I came to the raptures of Venus in the arms of Mars. My wantonness became uncontrollable, a sensation such as was described in the book partially thrilled me, I plunged my fingers in the whole length to complete it and away went my maidenhead.

It hurt me cruelly, but I did not care for that. I knew the irreparable injury which my folly had caused. I was disgusted with my folly and flung the book away. I never put my fingers on that same place again, much less let any man touch me. One night I told my husband all the pitiful truth, but he was still suspicious.

We lived in Naples. He was a professor in the university. He seemed to think of nothing but science. For two or three weeks together he would go to bed with me and rise again without even having put his hand under my chemise, and still more rarely gave me the marital embrace.

But I did not suffer myself to care for that.

One day I accompanied him on a journey to another town to look for some rare manuscripts of which he had heard. We were going on a lonely road through a forest when a large and gaily dressed brigand stepped from the woods and stopped the horse.

'Resist at your peril,' he said, pointing a cocked pistol and leading the horse and vehicle into a lonely side path. When we had got some distance from the main road he stopped and ordered us to get out. He fastened the horse to a tree and then procured some cord from his pocket with which he firmly bound my husband's hands behind his back; and, having also tied his feet together, he bound him to a tree and searched him for valuables. 'Now, my fair lady,' said he, approaching me, 'it is now your turn.'

'Take my jewellery—it is all I've got—and let me go.'

'Thank you for the present,' he said, 'but you have got something else I prize still more.' Then he put his arm around my waist and attempted to kiss me. I struggled to get free, while my husband alternately cursed and entreated him, but all to no purpose. I tried to get close to my husband, but it only served to make him a nearer witness of what followed.

I was suddenly tripped and thrown on the grass with the brigand on top of me. He held both of my hands on the ground above my head with one of his own; with the other he tore open the front of my dress and explored my bosoms, which he rifled with his hand and sucked with his mouth. Then he pulled up the skirts of my dress and petticoat.

I redoubled my exertions and even got one of my hands loose; but by this time he had forced open my thighs with his knee and lay between them. He pinioned both of my hands as before, leaving one of his hands free to get out his shaft and enter it into me. Then every struggle I made seemed to work him in further. I could only sob with rage and shame. The brigand, with his Herculean strength, did his will with me right before my husband's eyes, who had by this time howled himself hoarse with curses.

Angry and mortified, as I was, it began to feel good. To escape this crowning humiliation I made one tremendous effort to get free. I was pinioned to the ground by a fierce thrust of my ravisher, and then I felt the cream of his strength entering my loins. The sensation almost thrilled me, but his powerful grasp so relaxed that by a great effort, I extracted myself from beneath him.

I ran to my husband and began untying him, but the brigand seized me by the wrists and dragged me some distance up the pathway. Then he suddenly thrust his hand into my bosom and gave it a parting squeeze, kissed my averted face and let me go.

I ran back trembling and sobbing to my husband, whom I unbound as rapidly as possible. He unfastened the horse without saying a word or even helping me into the vehicle and drove home in silent and sullen gloom.

It was too cruel. I had been able to endure his suspicions with regard to the loss of my maidenhead, because it had been the result of my own folly. But this dreadful rape had been committed without any fault of mine. He never afterward lay with me or held me in his embrace, although we continued to live together. A young women in the bloom of vigour and just well enough initiated with the mysteries of matrimony, I was condemned to celibacy. Wanton thoughts occupied my mind until my sheath would throb and its lips moisten and swell with desire for hours together.

I reverted to the means that had despoiled me of my maidenhead, but it was a little more than constant agitation. My husband suspected me; I determined to give him a cause. It seemed as if no one man could satisfy me now; I longed for an opportunity to give reins to my passions.

At this time a Russian fleet came into the harbour. My sister's husband was a naval officer in the harbour and it devolved on him to help entertain the Russian officers. So my sister gave a masked ball to which they were invited. My husband would not go but he made no objections to my attending and staying all night at my sister's house.

My room opened—from the passage that connected the ballroom with the conservatory and then into my room—without being noticed. I procured a long and ample nun's robe which covered me from my throat to my toes; it had also a cowl which concealed my head and face. Under this disguise I had the dress—or rather the undress—of a dancing girl; a vest of cloth of gold and a skirt of the thinnest lawn were absolutely the only articles of which it consisted, besides my stockings and slippers. The vest had no sleeves or shoulders and exposed my bosom clear to the nipples. If I moved quickly the short and gauzy skirt showed my naked thighs.

As soon as the guests began to mingle on the floor I touched the arm of a stalwart Russian officers; he, like all the other guests, was masked, but I knew he was a Russian by his fair hair. 'Follow me,' I whispered. We entered the passageway described, and finding it clear I led him to my room.

'What a dainty bower!' he said in French. 'Will its sweet-voiced occupant be pleased that we both unmask?' He removed his mask and disclosed one of those ruddy countenances with bright eyes and fair hair which always so bewitch an Italian lady.

I flung back my nun's disguise and stood revealed to him in the costume of a lascivious young dancing girl. The young Russian seemed to admire my dark Italian complexion as much as I admired his northern hue. He knelt and kissed my hand.

'Can you pity a bride,' said I, 'whose husband neglects her?'

A flush of pleasure crossed the officer's face which made my looks seek the floor. 'It would be the supremest happiness,' he said, 'to pity and console you.' Clasping his arms around me our lips met.

The moment I had so long desired for had now come. I was borne in his strong arms to the bed, where I lay palpitating with desire while he stripped off his outer garments.

Then the fervour of our kisses and caresses showed the length of time we had both suffered without an embrace. My dress formed no obstacle to his caresses, either to my bosom, which he fairly seemed to devour, or to my thighs, which he squeezed and patted. I guided his shaft with one hand while with the other I parted the hair encircling the lips to receive it.

How stiff it was, and yet how full of life and warmth! How tight, and yet how soft and lubricated was the place it was entering! I was so eager I had not even affected to be coy. 'How delicious!' he exclaimed.

'How exquisite!' I replied.

He gave a thrust which enabled me to take his shaft into the hilt. Then he gave another and another, each successive one more greedily swallowed. Flesh and blood could no longer endure the rapture that was concentrated at my very loins! I thrilled from my womb to my very fingertips! I melted and bathed his hot crest; his responsive gush drenched my glowing womb. It seemed as if we were being fused together at the point of contact. Then our muscles relaxed closely in the moisture and we engaged for awhile in voluptuous repose.

'Now kiss me and go,' said I, 'and if you value the favour I have granted you, leave this house at once.' My object was to fill his place with another handsome Russian, who might come fresh to the encounter, and whose genitals my wanton hands might explore and my wanton desire ravish. Months of longing were to be supplied by one night of boundless lust. Six times more before the ball broke up I took a Russian officer to my room and dismissed him as before—and each time a different one. Each time I was completely melted, and my Italian moisture mingled with the Russian sperm. The next morning my glass showed me that I had dark and sunken circles around my eyes and I was somewhat languid, but for a few days at least I was not troubled with desire.

The fat and charming Italian lady had been gently fondling my genitals all the while she had been speaking and my shaft had begun to rise at the delicate attention. When she finished her story she knelt before me with her forehead on the carpet, laughingly saying, 'Salaam, alirkoum,' which was the Moorish to signify she was at my service.

Her large, round buttocks were elevated in the air and looked so temptingly smooth and soft that I mounted her in that position as a stallion would mount a mare. She seemed nothing loth and my half stiffened shaft worked its way in past the swollen lips—past the extraordinary protuberance within, which my fingers had first discovered, and buried itself amid the moist and clinging folds of her sheath.

My loins sank into her fat buttocks, which yielded as I pushed, till my stones were hidden in her hair like eggs in a nest. Still I kept pushing into the yielding mass without once drawing back till my shaft grew stiff with the delightful sensation, and my crest exchanged a wanton desire with her womb. I held her firmly by clasping her great, soft breasts in either hand. A few minutes more and I would have paid tribute to her voluptuous loins, but Laura could not wait.

With a sigh of satisfaction her frame became limp, her knees gave way and she sank flat upon her belly. My shaft drew out of her far more stiff than it went in. The same accompanying sucking noise that ended my connection with Helene set them all to laughing.

'I must take a measurement,' said one of them and, taking off her bracelet, she clasped it around my shaft, but the clasp would not fasten. The bracelet was not large enough. Then they all tried their bracelets on with the same result.

'How shall we measure its length,' said one of them.

'Four of you have that measure already,' said I, 'and you know I promised it to all of you. Please let me take some measurements now,' I added, unwinding the garter from the leg of the nearest lady. It was a piece of strong tape and suited my purpose admirably. I measured the height of all their bosoms and the circumference of their thighs, and then, amid laughing protestations I parted the hair between each of their thighs and measured the length of their slit.

In the last measurement they all seemed to be desirous of being the smallest, as in the other they each wished to be the largest in size. A young Persian who was introduced later in the evening bore off the palm in the last contest. Her diminutive slit looked all the more cunning that the hair around it was hardly long enough to curl. Zuleika had the largest bosoms, while the thighs of Laura defied competition.

'Here, Anna, take the scarf,' interrupted the Italian, 'and tell the Captain something about Circassia.'

The lady thus addressed was about nineteen years of age and she was very tall and slender. Her limbs were finely tapered; so was her round waist, which I could have spanned with my two hands. Her nicely cut breasts were as erect as if they had been carved from alabaster, which her skin resembled in whiteness. The hair on her small head was of the palest blonde, but that at her loins was fiery red, which I had read was a sign of uncontrollable wantonness.

If so, this lady's face gave no indication of it. Her large blue eyes looked at you with the innocence of childhood, and the delicate rosette hue of her cheeks varied at every changing emotion. She did not seem sensible, however, of the privilege conferred upon her by the scarf. She stretched herself between my thighs, where she leaned with her elbow on the cushion supporting her graceful head with her hand. Her bosom rested on my loins and my shaft was imprisoned by her snowy breasts from between which its red crest peeped out while she looked me in the face and told her lascivious story.

CHAPTER SIX

The Circassian lady's story

The powerful old chief to whom my mother was
married had no children of his own. I was her
only child by a former marriage and her fondness
was all centred on me. Our religion, which was
the Greek, forbade a plurality of wives. The old
chief was not likely to have a direct heir, and, as
he was now seventy, her great object was to have
him confer on me the succession of principality;
this last he consented to do if she would
countenance his amours with other women.

She consented to do so and the strange
compact was formed. I was present as witness,
but unknown to either of them, I had been in the
habit, for a long time, of frequenting a little
alcove in their bedroom where a few books were
kept. It was separated by a curtain from the rest
of the room and communicated also with my
chamber by a sliding panel. This secret panel,
which I had accidentally discovered, was a kind

often met in such old castles as we inhabited. It was known to me alone, or, if the old chief knew it, he never thought of it.

I had there witnessed all the secrets of the marriage chamber, and of course my passions were rapidly developed. My mother was still plump and handsome; she enjoyed keenly the marriage embrace, but always had to work very hard in order to finish the tardy rapture of the old chief. On the occasion of the compact I heard her tell him she could give him all he wanted. He could only reply that a man liked a variety.

'Very well,' said she, 'make out the deed for Anna's succession and I will not only countenance but assist in your amours. We can in that way at least secure secrecy and avoid scandal, for no one will suspect a wife of conniving at her husband's amours.' The old chief then confided to her that the present object of his desire was Leuline; the handsome of the steward of the castle.

The next evening I was at my post early. My mother had already managed with Leuline. She was a large and voluptuous looking woman with dark hair and blue eyes; her bosoms were not much developed, but her thighs were immense. She got into bed with my mother and pretended to be asleep when the old chief came in.

He undressed and got into bed with them and mounted Leuline, who lay with her head on my mother's arm, close to her bosom. An expression of pleasure stole over Leuline's face, which became

54

more ineffable at every thrust. At last their mingled sighs and the stillness that followed gave proof that the embrace had been mutually satisfactory.

('You can imagine,' said Anna, smiling at the other girls, 'how I longed for the embrace of a man.')

Plans for future meetings and jokes at the expense of Leuline's husband filled up the time, together with explorations of Leuline's charms, till the shaft of the old chief grew again stiff. He plunged it into Leuline's great loins, and she enjoyed it so highly that she finished and left him in the lurch.

I could hardly restrain myself, I so longed for the thrusts that were now wasted on Leuline. My mother must have felt the same way, for she asked the old chief to let her finish him. He had more that once sucked her fine bosoms during this onset. He now transferred his crimson crest dripping with Leuline's moisture.

The energy with which my mother received him made me fairly wriggle my loins in sympathy. She wound her arms around him and played up her loins to meet his descending thrusts, then their frames were convulsed for a few moments with the culminary rapture and they subsided into perfect repose.

I had often before felt wanton emotion at my post of observation; I now left the alcove in a frenzy of lust. I wanted a man, and that immediately, I was about to seek one of the sentinels at his post and confer my virginity on the first rude soldier I met on the cover of the ramparts when I remembered Tessidor, a young priest, who was attached to the chapel of the castle. He was a delicate looking youth of about seventeen, with a countenance which indicated the purity of his character. I went to his room and timidly knocked on the door.

To my timid knock the answer was delayed; when at last he said 'come in,' I saw that he had employed the interval by slipping on a nightgown, for he had been just about to retire. He looked astonished, and well he might when he saw me.

'I have come to make a confession and ask your counsel,' said I.

'Had we better not go to the chapel?' he asked.

'It is better here,' I said, 'for the subject is a worldly one, though of much importance to me. I love a young man who is indifferent to my preference, nay, he is even insensible to my love. I would have my parents hint to him that his addresses would be accepted; but I shall have to marry a soldier and he is not a soldier. What shall I do?'

'Strive to forget him, my lady,' was the reply. I stood a moment with my look cast on the ground and my cheeks burning. 'Cruel man,' I said, 'it is you who have my heart.'

My head dropped forward, I seemed about to

fall, but I put up my mouth for the kiss which he bent over to impress upon it. Regrets were then mingled with kisses, while I allowed my wrapper to part open and expose my bosoms. He ventured to timidly kiss them; his kisses became more and more ardent. I had got him at last where a man has no conscience. He stretched himself on the bed beside me, took me in his arms: our lips were glued together.

As much by my contrivance as his own, but he did not know it, my wrapper and dressing gown opened, and a skirt and chemise was all that separated a stiff little object from my thighs. Fired by lust as I was, I had shame enough left to leave the removal of these slight little objects to himself. I could hardly wait upon his timidity. I must have been the first woman he had ever entered, for he was very awkward in guiding his crest to the lips that yearned to close upon it. It was a little thing, but very stiff.

At last it penetrated me a little way and I felt the touch of his crest against my maidenhead like an electric shock; it set all my nerves tingling with pleasure, and expectant of the coming connection. I could no longer even feign modesty. I involuntarily wrapped my arms around him and he gave the fateful thrust.

His little crest pierced through my maidenhead with a cutting pain which I felt no more than a bulling heifer would have felt the stroke of a switch. The pain was drowned in overwhelming pleasure. The thrill swept over every fibre in my frame, not only at the first thrust, but three times successively, and at each plunge I gave a sigh of rapture. Then my tense muscles relaxed and I received with pleasure at least a dozen more thrusts.

Something was still wanting. It was the gush of sperm that Tessidor at last poured into my heated sheath like balm. He sank heavily upon me for a few minutes with his face buried in my neck. I was enjoying a voluptuous languour, when I felt his little shrunken crest floating out of my sheath with the mingled blood and sperm.

Remorse had already seized him. He raised himself on his elbow and gazed pitifully into my face. I was past blushing so I covered my face with my hands. 'I have ruined you,' he said, 'wretch that I am, heaven forgive me!' He got up from the bed without even giving me another kiss and knelt before his crucifix. 'Will you join me in asking heaven for mercy on my sin?' he added.

I made some excuse and fled from the room. The next morning I heard that he had gone to join a convent in the mountains. By this time I had come to the conclusion that I had let him off too quickly. I had not had enough. Perhaps a warm bath would help to soothe me.

There was a large bath half the size of a room and deep enough when full to cover my breasts; it had a door into my room, also into my mother's who was busy at this time in the morning with her servants. It was the old chief's time to take a bath and he always had the warm water; I determined to share it with him. I had heretofore doubted whether the old chief would want to touch his wife's daughter, but my success with the young priest gave me courage.

I took off all my clothes in my room and peeped through the door. He was floating on his back playing with his shaft, which dangled limber in the water. I had most always seen it stiff, and I promised myself the pleasure of getting it in that position, which I preferred. Pretty soon he came to the side towards me, where he could not be seen by me; now was the time for me to come in as if I had not known he was there.

I opened my door suddenly and ran and jumped into the water. I swam across the bath, turned around and became the picture of astonishment at seeing him. I first covered my face with my hands, then covered by bosom with one hand and my loins with the other. I did not scream; that might bring my mother.

Then I turned my back on him. The side of the bath where I stood was perpendicular. He stood by the sloping side where we got out—of course I had to stay. 'It's all right, Anna,' he said, 'we will have a nice bath together.'

I started to dodge past him, but of course he caught me. 'I shall scream,' said I, but of course I did not scream. I was fast in his arms, his stiffening shaft crushing against my buttocks, and each of his hands squeezed one of my bosoms. My apprehensions of reluctance on his part were all departed, so I kept up more show of resistance. I struggled to get away, but only struggled harder to get around in front of him. This brought my back to the sloping side of the bathtub, against which he pressed me.

Half standing and half lying my head was still above water. The wantonness of the situation and the warmth of the water made the bath seem like a voluptuous sea. Of course I had put both arms around him to keep from sinking; his hands were thus both at liberty. He needed them both to work his half-stiffened shaft into me. Leuline and my mother only the night before had taken the starch out of it; nothing but the excitement of such a kind of rape would have stiffened it at all.

Half limber as it was, it completely filled me, paining me a little at first, but gradually feeling better and better, pervading all through me with the most lascivious sensation. The warm water churned in and out of my sheath at every thrust with a feeling like gushing sperm. All the water in the bath seemed to be of the male gender, and all of it embracing me and administering to my lust.

For fully five minutes I abandoned myself to the delicious dissolving feeling, not as thrilling as the young priest's had caused the night before, but more prolonged. Even after it had subsided and died away, the plunges of the old chief were still pleasant. Finally his shaft became for a moment rigid deep within me, he gave a throb or two which deprived him of his strength and he no longer supported me.

I scrambled from his arms up the side of the bath and, regaining my own room, shut the door and sank exhausted on the bed. We never pursued the intrigue, as the terror of my mother was too much before our eyes. Besides I was in a few days after engaged in an amour with Rudolf, the handsome young captain of the guards, while the old chief had been supplied with a fresh bed-fellow by my mother. This time it was a young maid, who timidly blushed, in the place of Leuline, for I still amused myself occasionally peeping through the alcove.

A short time afterward the old chief was slain in battle and the sagacity of my mother was rewarded, for I succeeded peaceably to the principality, but my mother swayed the real power. I was willing she should do so, provided she did not interfere with my amours. It was by her advice that I did not marry. 'A virgin chieftain will be popular with the people, and you can control men,' she would say, 'far better unmarried.'

In fact, Rudolf, captain of the guards, was my abject slave, and so were Cassim and Selim, two of the bravest young chiefs in the army. I admitted them all to my bed in turn, Rudolf the most frequently, for he was powerfully built and had genitals correspondingly large. When I wished to be tickled deeply, the tall and slender Selim received the secret summons to my chamber. Cassim was short and stout—it was agreeable sometimes to be stretched without being deeply penetrated. Each of these suspected that the other also enjoyed my favour, but they were not certain of it.

One evening I invited them all to my secret apartments. The sideboard had been replenished, the servants had been dismissed for the evening and the doors locked. I was dressed in a purple velvet bodice with a petticoat of red silk. I had on my richest lace and jewellery and the crown of the principality was on my brow. The handsome young officers glittered in their splendid uniforms; suspense and curiosity were mingled in their countenances.

I waited until several toasts had been drunk in my honour and my wanton eyes devoured the fine proportions of the young men, and I thus addressed them: 'Should not a Circassian princess have as many privileges as a Turkish pasha?'

'Certainly,' they all replied.

'Should she not be entitled to a harem as well as he?' They hesitated but answered, 'Yes.'

'You then, shall be my harem,' said I, rising. 'You Cassim, should be lord of the lips.' The polite young officer set the example of devotion by coming to my side and kissing the lips that I had committed to his charge.

'You, Selim, are the lord of the bosom.' He came up on the other side of me and kissed the bosom which peeped out above the lace front of my bodice.

'You, Rudolf, shall be the lord of the thighs.' He knelt before me, and, raising my skirts, planted a kiss on the hairy mouth they concealed.

Then I felt his tongue penetrate the lips beneath; it caused a flush of desire to mantle through my frame. 'Let us divest ourselves of this clothing which makes mortals of us and become like the ancient gods,' I said.

My example, together with the champagne, now broke down all reserve. We stripped entirely naked and amused ourselves by imitating the attitude usually given by art to the most celebrated heathen divinities. It was not enough for me to compare the forms of the young men by observation. I freely caressed and handled their genitals with my hands until they lost all restraint and gathered so closely about me that I was squeezed in their joint embrace.

I flung my arms around Cassim and bid him lie down on his back with me on top of him; his loins were elevated higher than his head by the piles on which he lay. I worked backward while he guided his shaft completely into me.

My buttocks presented a fair mark for Selim, who mounted me behind and slowly worked his shaft into the same orifice that Cassim had already entered. It was the tightest kind of a fit.

The first entrance had stirred my desire to a flame and made me welcome the second with great greediness. Cassim's position was such that he could hardly stir, but Selim plunged his long and slender shaft into me again with thrusts that required all his strength. My sheath was stretched to its utmost tension by the two shafts, but all its distended nerves quivered with lust.

Rudolf now knelt close in front of me, with his knees on either side of my head. I lay for a moment with my flushed cheeks on his genitals, then I grasped his shaft in my hand and played rapidly up and down it.

Cassim, with his arms wrapped around my waist, was sucking my bosoms. Selim squeezed my thighs in his grasp at every thrust he gave. I felt my crisis coming, overwhelming in three-fold intensity. In very wild abandonment I sucked Rudolf's crest in my mouth, then I thrilled and melted with a groan which resounded through all the room. All three of the young men followed me to the realms of bliss where I soared.

My sheath was overflowed with the double tribute which jetted and spurted and gushed into it. My mouth was filled with Rudolf's sperm. Both pairs of my lips were dripping. My whole frame seemed saturated with the fecund moisture. When the mingled sighs of the young men, which echoed to my prolonged groans of rapture, had died away, I sank into a semi-conscious state from which I did not rise that evening.

It was a deep, dreamy, voluptuous repose which an occasional smarting sensation in my strained sheath did not disturb. The wine and profuse organs had done their work. The young men put me to bed and quietly dispersed. It was the only time I had my harem. The next day our troops lost a battle, the castle was taken by the enemy, and I was on my way to the slave market.

Anna finished her story. My shaft still peeped out from between her bosoms, but it was now stiff with desire. The fat Italian had aroused it to vitality, though she had failed to exact any tribute from it. My stones had again filled while I listened to the innocent Circassian's passionate tale.

Still holding her between my thighs I turned so as to bring her on her back beneath me. Then, changing and adjusting my thighs between hers, I parted the fiery red hair that concealed lips equally fiery and commenced the onset. The delicious heat and moisture set the blood dancing in my veins. My crest lingered a moment at the lips, then glided past them into the clinging folds of her sheath. When I was completely entered, it gave a convulsive contraction around my shaft and Anna melted—indeed the ladies were all ripe to the melting point, while I had to meet their fresh successive ardour.

Anna became passive, but she still seemed to enjoy the deep and rapid thrusts which for several moments I continued to thrust into her white loins. At every thrust I became more and more furious. I buried my hilt again and again in the vain attempt to touch her womb. I felt that if my crest could only reach so far up in her long slender person, I could consummate the exquisite connection. She seemed to divine my wish; she opened her thighs and, drawing her knees upward, wrapped her long, slender legs around my waist with a strength I had not thought her capable.

Fixing my look on her sweet face I gave another plunge. She was so fairly exposed to my thrust that I rammed her womb clear up her belly. The sperm gushed from my crest in consecutive jets and I gave a sigh of perfect satisfaction. I was completely exhausted; my nerveless frame stretched itself at full length upon her and I sank into a voluptuous languor that gradually turned into sleep.

I slept fully an hour, the ladies told me on waking and I felt my vigour returning. They brought me some sherbet and confections which further refreshed me; and one of them was so considerate as to point out to me where to make water. Then I heard that Anna had thrown the scarf so that it fell on the shoulders of two young girls and would not tell them which was to keep it but mischievously referred it to me.

Leaving the disorder to the chapter of incidents, I begged them both to favour us with a story. It was a Portuguese girl named Virginia who began. She was a pretty little creature not more than seventeen, and very small for that age. Her slight limbs were beautifully rounded and tapered to the cunningest little hands and feet. Her pretty bosoms, though small, were perfect hemispheres.

Her hair was very dark and braided into strands which were carefully coiled up under a round comb. Her complexion was dark but her large fiery eyes indicated some nothern blood. She and her little companion sat on either side of me, each encircled by one of my arms, while the story was in progress.

CHAPTER SEVEN

The Portuguese lady's story

My father was an English wine merchant in Lisob and my mother was a Portuguese lady. I was the only child, but there was a little boy named Diego, two years older than myself, who came to reside with us when I was fifteen. I subsequently found that he was the fruit of my father's amours before his marriage, but as Diego's mother was dead, my mother naturally let him have a home with us.

Diego and I were the best of friends; among other amusements a favourite play with us was getting married. Diego knew enough to play this when no one was by, and always finished by getting on me. His organ could hardly get stiff enough to penetrate me, but he must have gradually obliterated all trace of a maidenhead, for I can never remember of ever having one. There was no consummation in our connections, neither of us were ripe enough for that, but there was a charm about it which made us keep it up at intervals for a year or two.

One evening Diego proposed, and I agreed, that we should postpone being together after our little ceremony of marriage until we went to bed. This occurred the day after I had first noticed the appearance of some marks of my first monthly period on my shirt. Our rooms were joining and after I had got nearly asleep that night, for I had forgotten all about it, Diego came in. He crept into bed and getting on top of me inserted his organ as usual.

Being both undressed it seemed much nicer than ever before, and we both explored each other's naked forms with our hands, my bosoms for the first time attracting Diego's attention; they were quite little, but it gave me as much pleasure to have them fondled and kissed as it seemed to give him to do it, for the Portuguese blood matures young. Our lips now met with more fervour than ever before, and I began to have a feeling in my sheath.

Diego's little shaft being in so still did not satisfy, and I gave a push upwards with my loins. He returned it with a thrust which felt pleasant. He kept thrusting incessantly for many minutes, and all the time I felt more delightful, yet I longed for the thrust to become more deep and rapid.

'Isn't it splendid,' I whispered, 'do it harder.'

'It's perfectly splendid,' he answered in a voice

rendered almost inarticulate by rapture. For two or three minutes we kept up the rapid motion when I felt Diego's shaft growing stiffer than ever before.

The delight he afforded me was so exquisite that I culminated in a long, sweet, refreshing thrill. Diego must have melted at the same moment and paid the first tribute of his scanty drops. We both fairly whined with the excitement and delight of our unexpected success.

The noise brought my mother to the room. She caught us lying exhausted in each other's arms. She took off her slipper and scourged Diego back into his room. Then she turned down the bedclothes and spanked my bottom thoroughly, and, having locked the door between my room and his, left me to my tumultuous reflections.

The next morning Diego was sent to Brazil. My parents at once began to look around for a suitable match for me, fearing, doubtless, that I might seek another opportunity to gratify my precocious passions. They fixed upon a young nobleman who was attracted by my father's wealth and promised him my hand. He had been dissipated, but so were all the young men of family in Lison. He was quite good looking, and, though I had seen him but a few times, I looked forward to the marriage night with pleasure, for I longed for such another delightful experience as I had with Diego.

At length the bridal evening came. The

ceremony was completed in the presence of many guests and was followed by dancing and the popping of champagne corks to a late hour. When the bridesmaids put me to bed I did not have to wait long for my husband. He came in somewhat under the influence of wine, hurriedly took off his clothes and hardly waited to kiss and embrace me before he exercised his marital rites. I was penetrated by a little object not as big as Diego's.

Before I recovered from my surprise and disappointment he had completed his purpose and sank down beside me to sleep. I shed bitter tears of chagrin. Several times every night for two or three weeks the same strange connection took place, differing only in that he was not immediately overcome with wine and sleep.

Only once during that time did my constantly aroused and disappointed passions succeed in culminating quick enough for me to melt, and that only partially. I dared not question him, for that would betray the experience I had. One night I purposely left the lamp burning and waited for him to get in a sound sleep. Then I turned the bedclothes down and examined his organ. It was a mere scarred remnant which had evidently been eaten away by disease. It was only capable by weakness of any excitement. No wonder it was constantly subjected to the torture of his disappointed desire!

After this I shunned him as much as possible,

finding no solace in his company and constantly tormented with desire. 'Oh, for an entire man,' I sighed! He took himself nearly every night to the gaming table.

Early one evening he went off as usual. I retired to my bedroom, looking out through the window blind. Our house, like most others in Lisbon, was built in a quadrangle, the rear of which was the stable. If I sat on one side of the window I could only see one side of the stable wall, and I could only be seen from it. There was only one window in it, which served for Pedro the coachman, and he was rarely in his room.

It was the fashion at that time in Lisbon to have large fine looking Negroes for coachmen, who were admitted to many privileges, for there is no prejudice against colour in Portugal. Pedro was the most gigantic coachman in the city; indeed he was the largest well-proportioned man I had ever seen in my life.

As I looked out through the blind I indistinctly saw him gazing towards my window. I at once determined to have some sport. Standing before the glass beside the window I lighted the lamp as if unconscious of observation—indeed I could not have been seen from any other quarter except Pedro's window, and that was small and higher than mine.

I threw open the blind as if for air and began slowly to undress. Then I stood in my chemise and petticoat lazily brushing my hair before the glass, which displayed my naked arms and bosoms to good advantage. Then I sat down to take off my shoes and lifted my foot to my knee for convenience in untying. My hidden observer must have seen under my petticoat up to my loins, and perhaps indeed an inch inside of them, for my legs were stretched very wide apart.

I grew wanton with the thought of the influence I made by this time on his passions. If his desires were not thoroughly aroused it was no fault of mine. I stood before the glass again and let my petticoat and chemise fall to the floor, but delayed putting on my nightgown. I yawned and fondled my breasts with my hands as a woman does, giving as I did so an undulating motion to my loins. Soon I heard a soft and heavy tread coming from the coachroom stairs towards my door. I might have locked it but I did not. Was this not just what I had been praying for?

The door opened and Pedro entered. I held up my nightgown before my naked form. 'If I am too bold,' he said, in great agitation, 'bid me go and I will cast myself in the Tagus.' He need not have been half so tragic.

'Pedro,' said I, 'have you no more politeness than to keep your clothes on when a lady's undressed?'

His anxious countenance relaxed at once into a reassured smile. He gallantly kissed my hand—my lips he did not presume to kiss at all—and then undresed himself without stopping

74

till his Herculean form stood entirely naked before me in all its gigantic but complete proportions. His immense shaft was proudly erect and huge even for such a giant. Pendant from it hung stones which seemed to my somewhat startled eyes as large as a coconut. He lifted me without an effort till my bosoms were opposite his mouth, into which he almost entirely sucked one of them. My legs wound themselves around his waist and I found myself sitting on the crest of his great stiff shaft, which was so directly underneath the lips of my sheath that it slowly entered them.

At last I was penetrated by an organ which I could hardly accommodate; the effort to do so, however, was attended with the extremest pleasure. I relaxed my legs and suffered myself to settle down with all my weight upon it till I thought his whole shaft must have entered. Then I looked in the mirror before which we were standing. At least half his great shaft was plainly visible below my buttocks. He appeared like a great statue of ebony bearing at his bosom one of ivory. I worked my loins, and I could see plainly by the mirror that his shaft was now further entered by the motion, but I had so much of it in me that I was progressing rapidly to a blissful consummation.

At this moment he laid me upon my back on the bed without losing our connection and, bracing his feet upon the footboard, gave an irresistible plunge.

It seemed to ram my womb clear under my bosoms. My whole body seemed only a sheath quivering with lascivious gratification. I bore without flinching two more such plunges and then came the overwhelming thrill. In the midst of it I felt the gushing sperm spurting like a fountain in my belly. We subsided simultaneously with a long-drawn breath and Pedro at once considerately relieved me of his great weight.

Twice more before he left I was spurred on by desire to court the brunt of his tremendous onset; then I made him go. I was completely gorged and sated. Three days afterwards we had to fly together to escape imminent discovery threatened by my maid. We safely reached the African coast.

When the pretty little Portuguese finished her story I exchanged kisses with her and with her companion on the other side of me. My crest was rising, but another story would give it time to be fully ready. 'My friend's name is Myrzella and she is a Persian,' said Virginia, receiving another kiss for her information.

Myrzella of course was kissed when she was thus named. She was younger than Virginia. The pink slit between her thighs was set off by the faintest trace of hair; it looked like a delicate sea shall. She was quite plump. Her thighs were nearly twice the size of Virginia's. Her bosoms were developed as much as those of a northern girl several years later in life.

Her hair was black and glossy as a raven's wing; it descended in two large braids to the calves of her legs when she stood erect. Her eyes were as black as her hair, large and sparkling, but full of tenderness. Her cheeks had little colour, except under emotion, but her lips were crimson red.

CHAPTER EIGHT

The Persian lady's story

My home, till two months ago, was on the banks
of the Tigris. I was captured by Turks when on a
journey to meet my affianced husband, whom I
had never seen. Our party was on horseback
proceeding along the bank of the river when the
Turkish bandits pounced upon us. There was a
flash of sabres and a volley of pistol shots which
dispersed my friends, and my horse was seized by
the bridle and hurried to the bank of the river.
There was a boat in waiting which conveyed us
over to the Turkish shore.

I soon found myself an inmate of the harem of
the fierce bandit who had captured me. There
were four other women in the harem among
whom I was allowed to rest and refresh myself
with supper, though I could eat but little. The
Turk then came into the apartment. He was a
man of middle age on whose countenance was
written the most brutal passions.

I fairly loathed the sight of him and hoped I would soon be ransomed. He put his arm around me and attempted to kiss me, but I shrank from his embrace.

'She should prefer to have you undress her,' he said to the women, who seemed to enjoy the spectacle of my unwilling exposals. They soon took everything off me but my chemise while the Turk himself stripped perfectly naked, and for the first time and under such uninteresting circumstances I saw the genitals of a man. They were excited by lust to a size which added to my plight.

He again tried to take me in his arms, but I struggled so that my chemise was torn off and I cowered naked on the floor. He bid the women hold me. Each of my feet and each of my hands were seized by one of the four and I lay on my back with my arms and legs stretched apart panting with my struggles. He got upon me and entered me with one fierce and brutal thrust which tore away my maidenhead with a pang of excruciating agony.

With a tremendous effort I got my hand loose from one of the women who held it and seized the Turk's dagger which lay near upon the pile of clothing he had taken off. The women all let go of me and the Turk jumped off before he had time to repeat his thrust. I sprang to the corner of the room in an agony of shame and rage, ready to kill the first who touched me.

The Turk stood grasping his stiff shaft all stained with my blood; his baffled lust sought the first object on which to vent itself. 'Lie down, Achmet,' he said, 'I must have a tight place to finish what I have begun on that girl.' The person addressed lay belly downward and then the Turk turned up the female petticoats which had heretofore concealed the male sex of the wearer.

It was indeed a boy, doubtless a eunuch whom the Turk kept to supplement the services of the three women of his harem. On the prostrate form of this boy the Turk mounted, and the grunts of satisfaction soon proclaimed that he had satisfied his brutal lust. I thanked heaven that I had not suffered him to gender on me.

After awhile he arose and pulled down the petticoat over the boy's buttocks and he again appeared in the semblance of a women.

'Lock up that little tigercat in a room by herself,' said the Turk, pointing to me. I was glad to be alone and went into the room indicated without any opposition. I looked around for something to put on. The only article I could see was a rich suit of the boy's clothing which doubtless belonged to the one in the next room. I dressed myself in these, completing my disguise by concealing my hair under the boy's turban. Then I looked from the window to see what were the chances for escape.

Though I was on the second storey, it was not

very high from the ground. I leapt. Then I made my way to the river and jumped into a boat that was moored at the bank. Casting it loose I floated down the stream. The night was very dark and my boat was nearly run down by a passing vessel, but I called loudly for aid and was taken on board. Then I breathed free.

The vessel sailed down the Persian Gulf, and, crossing over to the Red Sea, proceeded to Egypt. I found my way to Alexandria in company with some merchants, one of whom took a fancy to me and engaged me as an attendant. He was trading between Alexandria and Morocco and owned the ship on which we sailed from the former port. We were the only occupants of the cabin. He was a handsome young man and he won my heart by his uniform kindness, and I did not reveal the secret of my sex.

The day before we reached Morocco, he called me into his cabin to assist him in a bath. He stripped unconcernedly before me; his form was manly and graceful but I was fascinated with the organs peculiar to his sex. They hung drooping at his loins, unconscious that a woman was looking at them—nay, touching them, for I contrived to touch them as often as I could while I bathed him.

When I had finished sponging him he lay extended on the sofa for me to rub him dry. My hands explored all parts of his person, but lingered longest at his thighs—so much so that his shaft began to rise at the friction. 'Take care little fellow,' said he, 'you will arouse a passion which you cannot gratify.'

I felt my cheeks burning, a soft desire came through my veins, and I was about to open my bosom and reveal my sex, but the thought of the terrible pang in the Turkish harem restrained me. I stooped and kissed his thighs; my cheeks brushed his genitals. Then I sat down and watched him while he dressed until the object which had so attracted me was concealed by his clothes.

The next day we were in port a dour Pasha Abdallah came on board. When his business was finished conversation turned on me. 'I will make you a present of him,' said the young merchant. 'Poor little fellow! It is too bad to keep him at sea.' He did not know how dejected I looked at this change of masters, but it was no time for explanations.

Abdallah took me with him and confined me to his chief eunuch to whom I sought the first opportunity to confide my sex and misfortune. I have now been with these amiable people a week, but the Pasha has not touched me yet. I suppose I owe my exemption to the fact I am not a virgin.

'But you are to all intents and purposes a virgin, my charming Myrzella,' said I, tightening my arm around her waist and kissing her as she finished speaking. She eluded my grasp and seized Virginia by the hands, 'Come,' she said, 'let's have a waltz.'

The two pretty little creatures floated round and round the room in each other's arms, while Inez took up a lute and played a suitable accompaniment Virginia, at every complete turn of the dance, held Myrzella in a close grasp, and their loins were pressed together. This wanton motion was kept up till their already excited passions were completely aroused.

They suddenly finished the dance and lay on the cushions in each other's embrace with their thighs locked so that the lips between them were pressed together. The lips at their loins were not only kissed, but their mouths were glued together in this barren embrace. I was on top of them both in a twinkling, and guided my stiff shaft between them.

My nap after Anna's exhaustive embrace had restored my vigour. The stories of the young girls had aroused my passions. The thought of conferring on Myrzella her first rapture made me feel like a war horse going to battle. My shaft glided between them entering neither, but it was deliciously moistened with the dewy lips at the loins of both. As I gave another thrust Virginia slyly put her hand behind her and guided it into her own sheath.

She was on top of Myrzella, between whom and myself she was pinioned. My loins were no sooner crushed against her little buttocks than I felt my crest bathed in her melting shower. To me the sensation was exquisite; to her it was final. She sank with a long-drawn sigh, perfectly limp on top of Myrzella.

I drew out my shaft and plunged it all dripping with Virginia's moisture into the pretty Persian girl. Moist as it was, it entered with difficulty the orifice which was so tight, but it entered to the hilt. Virginia's thin buttocks were but little in the way. My hand could fondle with both their bosoms at once. My crest, vivified with the moisture of them both, was battering at Myrzella's womb; my kisses were showered on the neck of one and then the other. I was transported with a double rapture which my overwrought nerves could endure no longer, and the gushing sperm came blissfully to a termination.

While it was gushing the pretty Persian melted with a thrill at her first rapture. Her screams of delight were so loud and prolonged that the ladies had to hush her for fear it would alarm the guards at the gates. I had just strength to turn Virginia over on her back close beside Myrzella. Then clasping them both in my arms, I stretched a leg between the thighs of each and we lay in a voluptuous repose, my forehead resting on the cushion and each appropriating one of my cheeks for kisses.

'Do tell us how your maidenhead was taken,

Captain, said one of the ladies after I had recovered from the exhaustion of my double embrace.

'Sure enough, why not?' they cried in chorus. So, setting myself into a luxurious position more convenient for storytelling, I was clasped in the arms of Virginia and Myrzella.

CHAPTER NINE

The Captain's first story

When I was a boy there was a beautiful girl named Rosamond whose family estate in Yorkshire adjoined our own. Though she was some years older than I, a close but innocent feeling sprang up between us. I was her companion in horseback rides, nutting excursions and country pleasures. This intimacy was kept up till suitors began to appear for her hand, to one of whom she was finally married and went to live in London. Soon after I was sent away to school. Rosamond, who had now been married some time, kept a standing invitation for me to visit her.

Accordingly I stopped at her house one night on my road through London. Her husband was away and we had full leisure to talk over old times. She had now expanded into an elegant woman with a form well developed and was a fine type of blonde, rosy-cheeked, blue-eyed English matron. My boyish admiration grew more confirmed than ever. After dinner was over and we were sitting on the sofa together we grew so confidential that she at last unfolded her troubles to me. Her husband, she said, was unfaithful; he had even then left the city so that he might be with another woman. It was probably the first occasion on which she had confided her troubles to anyone.

I hardly understood what she meant. I was as green and innocent as it was possible for a country boy to be, but when I saw her tears I knew she was unhappy and I drew her head to my shoulder and kissed her. 'Do let me console you,' I said.

My meaning was innocent but she took it otherwise, I know, for the crimson mantled over her neck and cheeks. She seemed to come to some sudden determination, for she returned my caresses and kisses again and again.

It was bedtime; the servants had retired. Rosamond began slowly to loosen her dress at the neck, as if making what preparations she might downstairs before retiring. I got a glimpse of two plump, white bosoms. Little more was said. We both sat deeply thinking; my thoughts were still innocent. Then she drew up her skirts as ladies sometimes do before retiring and warmed her ankles at the fire. I got a glimpse of two plump calves that were twice as big as when we used to romp through the woods in the country, but I sat profoundly still.

'George,' she said, at length rising, 'I feel lonesome tonight and you may sleep with me if you will.'

'If you will not tell on me,' said I, thinking I was too big a boy to sleep with a woman any more.

'You can trust me for that,' she replied, and led the way upstairs. I told her I thought I would undress in my own room, which I did and then sheepishly came and got into bed with her.

She received me in a close embrace; my frame was clasped in her soft, white arms. Two thicknesses of linen only separated it from her glowing form and our lips met in a long, delicious kiss. Then, for the first time, desire shot through my marrow and I felt my shaft stiffen against her belly. I knew now what she wanted.

What a triumph it would be to gratify her and mingle my thin blood with the beautiful woman in my embrace, for such as my ignorant idea of the sexual connection; but to mingle with her, to pour my whole being into her was what nature impetuously demanded of me. I no longer hesitated to lift her chemise and get on top of her.

My naked loins sank between her naked thighs; my face was buried in her bosoms. How it got in I do not know, but my shaft was taken in to the hilt with a sensation more sweet than had ever entered my imagination to conceive. I tried to get it in deeper; there was plenty of depth unsounded, but, though she helped me with her clasped arms, it would reach no further. I pushed and pushed with all my might to do something. I knew not what, when Rosamond gave a deep sigh and lay perfectly still.

'Have I hurt you, dear Rosamond?' I anxiously asked.

She burst into a merry laugh. 'Get off for a while,' she said, 'and let us rest.' I did not want to get off at all, but I did so and lay by her side with my moist and rigid shaft squeezed up against her plump thigh.

It was half an hour before she would let me get in again. I spent the time in passionately kissing her cheeks, lips and bosoms and exploring all the secrets of her person with my hands. She gave the signal by partially lifting me, and again I sank upon her voluptuous form. My shaft was enguled at the first thrust, I rapidly plunged it in again and again, now guiding it against one side and then against the other side of her gaping sheath. The heat and the moisture were more delicious than before. I felt something leaving my loins; it jetted from my crest and was lost in the profuse moisture that rose up in Rosamond. I gave a groan of ecstasy which explained to me the deep sighs she again heaved, and then I knew no more.

When I became conscious again she was standing over me sprinkling water in my face.

'How you have frightened me,' she said. 'You lay so still and you looked so pale.'

'I only want to lie quiet in your arms,' I said.

She folded me tenderly in her arms and I went directly to sleep with my head pillowed on her bosom and my hand between her thighs. We were virtuous next morning. She had plucked the fruit before it was ripe and none had grown in the night to replace it. My shaft would not stiffen at the bidding of her warmest kisses.

After breakfast the coach drove up for me and I went off to school. I visited Rosamond's house many times after that but she never again would allow me to take the slightest liberty with her, not even a kiss at meeting or parting. Her husband had reformed and she had no more wrongs to goad her into retaliation.

'I think,' said Inez, 'it was a shame for a married woman to seduce an innocent boy.'

'How nice it must have been,' said Anna, 'to take a sweet young fellow's maidenhead.'

'Do tell another story, Captain,' said Helene. 'Do,' echoed all the others.

CHAPTER TEN

The Captain's second story

When I arrived at the age of sixteen I was still a slender stripling, but, having an intrigue with a lady's maid, I fancied myself quite a man of the world. One evening I attended the theatre with several other young noblemen.

The character of Cleopatra was splendidly sustained by an actress of Irish birth whom I will call Charlotte. She was of colossal size, but of perfect proportions. The dark complexion of her lovely face made her a good representation of the Egyptian queen, whose voluptuous person and amorous nature she delineated so finely that every man in the house was carried away; yet this magnificent woman was nearly fifty. Her powerful organisation had triumphed over time.

After the play was over we went into the green room and I was introduced to her. The charm of her person and form lost nothing on a near approach, though I detected one or two silver threads in her glossy hair. Her eyes had the brilliant sparkle of youth, her lips were plump and red and her teeth were as white as pearls. As soon as she heard my name she manifested deep interest; a tender light came into her eyes and her colour heightened in her cheeks as she began to talk of my father.

Now I had heard of the trouble my father gave his friend in his youth by his infatuation for an actress. I could no longer doubt that she stood before me. Charlotte's name was free from scandal—remarkably so for an actress. Perhaps her liaison with my father had been her only folly.

'Do give a little supper party after the theatre which will meet in my room,' she asked me.

I promised to do so, and accordingly met there a few actors and patrons of the theatre. We had a modest supper where wit, not wine, reigned. I sat next to Charlotte who seemed hardly able to take her eyes off me.

When the guests left to go I lingered at the door, and they went without noticing that I remained. The impulse was mutual to clasp each other in our arms.

'Oh, how I wish that you had been my son! It ought to have been so.'

I was in no mood to be made a baby of. The grand voluptuous form of the queenly actress aroused far other emotions when it was folded to mine.

'Is this your bedroom?' said I, drawing her towards the door.

'For shame, Georgie,' she said, as a crimson blush spread from her cheeks to her splendid bosoms. She was in the costume of Cleopatra, over which she had thrown a long mantle after the play. This mantle had fallen off. It was evident that she had intended no assignation for she moved reluctantly to the door—but she returned the passionate kiss I planted full on her mouth. So commanding was her height that she had to stoop slightly to do it.

As soon as we entered the bedroom she sat down on the bed and covered her face with her hands. I took the opportunity to divest myself of most of my clothes and then I stole up to her and kissed her naked and massive shoulder. She rose to her feet and, taking me in her strong arms as if I were an infant, she walked back and forth across the room with me.

'Oh! Georgie, Georgie,' she cried. 'This is almost incest, but I can deny you nothing—I, who have allowed no man to embrace me since those delicious days of long ago.'

She still carried me in her arms, walking to and fro. My face was in contact with her great bosoms, each of which was as large as my head. As I passionately kissed them, my right hand dropped to her thighs, from which it parted the loose oriental drapery and found in it a shaggy mass of curls. Searching to the bottom of these it found a pair of moist, warm lips. I lifted my face from her bosom, and meeting hers, we exchanged a kiss. It differed from those she had heretofore given me. It was as voluptuous as my own and was prolonged until I felt her other lips, which my hand was searching, begin to swell and grow hot.

Charlotte carried me rapidly to the bed. Her mood was changed from maternal tenderness to fiery passion. She lay me upon my back and sprang upon me. She folded me in her great muscular arms; her ponderous thighs settled on my own. Immense as they were, they were as a young girl's. It was her hand which guided my rigid shaft amid the thick profusion of hair till it was fairly entered and rammed to the hilt by the vibration of her powerful loins. So firmly was I pinned to the bed by her great weight that I could not move. I felt as if I were about to be ravished like a woman. It was a novel sensation and charming as it was novel.

Charlotte suddenly turned over on her back without relaxing her hold in the least upon me. I found myself on top of her, but she was still master of the situation. Her arms and legs were wrapped so tight around me that my bones fairly cracked. It was the rapid undulation of her loins alone that moved our closely joined forms. Her mouth was fastened on mine as if she was about to devour me; her big womb pressed against my crest.

I felt the crisis coming overwhelmingly in the powerful embrace in which I was held. At this moment her muscles began to relax with her profuse melting shower. I spent, not with a stinted jet, but with profuse gushes that made a suitable tribute to the magnetism of her massive beauty. The rapture lasted me some time, even after I became nerveless, and at length died imperceptibly away.

'Now, you must go, you naughty boy,' said Charlotte tenderly, kissing and spanking me. 'In ten minutes more my maid will come to undress me.'

I was scarcely able to rise from her arms after such a long and exhaustive orgasm. I was like a squeezed and sucked orange; my vigour was all gone. It was fortunate that my ship was to sail the next day—I was a midshipman under my first orders and I had to go. If the intrigue had been pursued it would have ruined her reputation and my health.

'And now, Captain, tell us another,' was the persistent petition of all the ladies.

CHAPTER ELEVEN

The Captain's third story

After I had grown to manhood, I began, I was one summer at a place of public resort in the highlands of Scotland. One night after I had gone to bed I heard voices close beside me. Then I noticed that my head lay close to a door which separated my room from the one adjoining it. The voices were evidently those of a young married couple in bed and, like myself, close to the door which separated my room from theirs.

I heard kisses and then the sound as if the lady's buttocks were being spanked Then there was a struggle, and then the young man's voice in a coaxing tone. 'Please, dear Alice, do let me.'

'No, Charlie, you ought to be ashamed of yourself. I am right in the midst of my period and I have been bleeding all day. Wait till you come next week and you shall have some, and be sure and bring some condoms with you. There are none left and it would be dreadful to make a baby so soon. Now lie on your side of the bed and go to sleep—don't squeeze my thighs that way; it only makes you worse.'

The sweet voice of Alice now begn to grow angry. I heard Charlie turn over and they both soon went to sleep. My passions were aroused and my shaft grew rigid, but I lay perfectly quiet during the conversation so as to keep them in ignorance that they had a listener.

The next morning they were near me at the breakfast table. Alice was a little blonde, the smallest and youngest bride I ever saw in Great Britain. She was so slender and had such large innocent blue eyes that she looked like a child in woman's dress. Charlie was a young surgeon; he was about my own age and his size and appearance resembled my own. After breakfast he started for Edinburgh, where he practised through the week, returning to his bride to pass Sundays.

During his absence I paid assiduous attention to Alice, hoping to engage her in an intrigue. She was a lively little thing, but her life was all for Charlie, with whom I could see she was yet dead in love. I became enamoured of her artless beauty. I longed to possess her, if only for one embrace. Her indifference only made me long for her more madly. All the week I went to bed with a stiff and hot shaft, close to the little beauty but unknown to her.

Saturday night brought Charlie, all radiant

with the promise I had overheard Alice make him the week before. I sat in my room reading when at early bedtime they came to their room. The kisses they exchanged when the door was shut were very aggravating to me. My shaft became perfectly rigid. Just at this moment there came a call for Charlie to go to a neighbouring hamlet to set a broken limb; with a muttered curse he reluctantly obeyed the call.

I knew it would take him three hours at least. I listened to Alice undressing; then I heard the tinkle of a little stream of water in crockery; then she put out the light and went to bed. Night after night the little bride had gone to sleep unconscious that she was near me, and now she fell asleep I could hear by her regular breathing—but tonight her door was unlocked, waiting for Charlie.

Would it be possible for me to impersonate him? The risk would be a terrible one, but the rigidity of my shaft put an end to reason and conscience. If I could fill those graceful little loins of hers the world might come to an end for all I cared.

I stole softly in my shirt and drawers out in the and into Alice's room. I crept carefully into bed with her and took her in my arms. I caressed her cunning round bosoms and felt of her plump and polished thighs. They were much larger than I imagined they were seeing her dressed. She had a few little curls between them, which I was daintily fingering when she woke up.

'So you have come, Charlie,' she said. For reply I fastened my mouth to hers and we continued uninterruptedly to exchange kisses. She was honestly ready to give Charlie what she had promised him. She opened her legs for the expected charge and I did not disappoint her. My crest entered with delicious tightness.

'What a great clumsy condom you have on,' she said. From this I inferred that my naked shaft was much bigger than Charlie's with condom on.

I gave a plunge that drove my crest far in among the quivering membranes, far up in her loins. I was in rapture. The burning moments repaid me for my longing—any, for a possible retribution to come. She enjoyed it as much as I did, judging from the increased ardour of knees and the motion of her thighs. I gave another plunge so deep that my shaft seemed to disturb her slender waist and my crest to upheave her bosom.

'Oh, Charlie,' she said, with a dying sigh. Another plunge and the sheath of the young bride was flooded with mingled gushes.

A moment of perfect stillness followed. To me it was a moment of ineffable satisfaction and perfect bliss. Then she suddenly scrambled from beneath me. 'The condom must have burst!' she said, hastily pouring water in the basin and washing away.

Pretty soon she came back to bed and nestled

in my arms. I pretended to be overcome with drowsiness and languour and answered two or three of her questions with an inarticulate, 'Eh?'

The completeness with which she had melted was soon evident from the deep sleep of exhaustion into which she sank. Then I stole silently from her bed back into my own, but did not go to sleep. I awaited anxiously Charlie's return. In due time he came. While he was undressing, Alice awoke. I heard her ask him drowsily, 'Why did you go out?' meaning why had he got up and gone out, after he had gone to bed with her.

'I had to go out,' he replied, meaning he had had to go and attend a professional call. She must have thought he had a necessary occasion to go into the yard. I heard her yawn and turn over as he got into bed with her and then the more significant sound of the creaking of the bed made me more jealous. This was followed by Charlie's deep sigh; then all was still save the regular breathing of the two sleepers.

It made me happy to think Alice had not joined in the sighing. I believe this gave me more pleasure than my successful escape from discovery. The next morning at breakfast Alice looked me right in the eye with her large, innocent eyes, perfectly unconscious that but a few hours before she had rapturously melted in my arms.'

* * *

'What a shame!' said Inez.

'There was no harm done after all,' said Anna.

'Well, then,' said I, 'listen to another story. Perhaps this will please you all.'

CHAPTER TWELVE

The Captain's fourth story

During one of my stays in port, my uncle, who was a member of the ministry, needed a confidential messenger to one of the German courts. I accepted the mission with pleasure. The business took me but a few days, during which I mingled in the festivities of the court. The sovereign was very gracious to me; his spouse I did not see, though it was said she was in the gallery of the dining hall during one of the state dinners at which I was present.

It was known to all when I was to return and on the evening before I started, I had declined several invitations that I might get ready to go. Just at nightfall I received the following singular note:

'A lady sends her compliments to Lord George Herbert and begs that he will call at No. 300, ------- street.'

I hesitated what to do all the time I was

enjoying my after-dinner cigar, but I finally put a pistol in my pocket and proceeded to the place named. It was a neat house in a respectable street. I was received at the door by a nice elderly lady and ushered into a well but plainly furnished room. She thanked me for being so kind as to come.

'I have received you at the door myself,' she said, 'because I thought best to have my servant away. It is a strange request I have to make of you, but your reputation for gallantry is known to me. May I rely on your honour to keep it secret whether you grant it or not?'

I assured her she might.

'My foster daughter, whom I dearly love,' she said, 'is married, but the union has not been blest with children. Her husband is very desirous of having an heir. He blames her very unjustly and is making her life wretched, for she loves him. She can endure his reproaches no longer. I have known it was not her fault and I have advised her to do what is necessary to get an heir. Now, my lord, have I advised her rightly?'

'Perhaps so,' said I, 'but what have I got to do with it? I am about to leave this city tomorrow, probably never to see it again.'

That is the very reason,' she said, 'that I have invited you to come here to meet her. She has seen you and wishes that heir to inherit your noble blood and handsome person and, this once accomplished, never to see or be seen again by

106

its sire—for the desire of an heir and not wantonness has influenced her. Do you consent?'

'I must see the lady,' I replied.

'She would die of mortification if you should see her and reject her,' said the old lady, 'but there is no fear of that. If you are pleased with her, go up and kiss her hand when I present you.' She then conducted me upstairs and opened the chamber door.

A lady was standing in the centre of the room looking timidly at me as I entered. As soon as I saw the lady I loosened my grasp on the pistol which I had in my pocket. All fear of treachery vanished from my mind and another sentiment immediately took its place. I approached her and kissed her hand. The old lady shut the door and retired.

I was alone with a woman not indeed beautiful, but very interesting. Her figure was fine and her features, though irregular, were pleasing. Her look fell to the carpet; the ensign of modesty warmed on her cheeks, receded and paled, then showed again more rosy than before. Her hand trembled in mine. Her attire made no accession to her appearance. She was dressed in plain muslin without an ornament; her hair was plainly brushed, but there was that in her air which convinced me that she was a lady, and that too in an embarrassing position.

'Fair lady,' said I, 'your choice has fallen on

one who can appreciate your delicacy, notwith-standing the strange circumstances which brought you to this.' A grateful smile lighted for an instant her fine face, but she involuntarily averted her cheek from the kiss I pressed upon it. She did not reply, nor did she speak once during the whole interview.

By this time I felt that the task of getting her with child would be the most agreeable one that had ever fallen to my lot to perform. She stood passive in a deep reverie, looking almost unconscious while I fastened her dress and let it fall to the floor. Her undergarments were of the finest lawn and lace. The stud that fastened her chemise was a large diamond, which only confirmed my opinion she was a lady of high station.

I kissed her beautiful white bosoms which were now disclosed. She awoke from her reverie with another deep blush and, going to the other side of the bed, she took off her shoes with her back to me, so that I did not get a glimpse of one finely turned ankle. Then she dropped off her petticoat and got into bed, covering herself up, face and all.

I soon undressed and followed. I took her in my arms and kissed her tenderly. Though she suffered my lips to revel on her ripe mouth, her lips did not move to return my kisses. My hands wandered over all parts of her fine form. As long as they lingered on her bosoms she was passive, but when I played too wantonly with the curls at her loins, she grew restless. I was excited by her modesty to the highest pitch of desire.

I drew her unresisting form beneath me and, parting her thighs, my crest entered the Elysian Fields—at least the promised joy of the Elysian Fields would not have tempted me to withdraw it. It entered where it was surrounded by moist, clinging tissues alive with affinity to its sensitive touch. Still she lay passive.

I put my arms under the small of her back and, holding her firmly, gave a plunge which sent my crest until it touched her womb. She could no longer refrain from manifesting her delight; she wrapped her arms around me. I gave another thrust which unsealed the fountain of my glands, and then another which planted the gushing sperm in the midst of her loins.

She held my face between her hands and gazed entranced with her eyes while the life giving fluid dashed against her womb. She melted while she gazed and put up her lips for the first and only kiss she exchanged with me. Our lips were glued together till the last drop trickled from my crest, and the thrilling rapture slowly faded and left me nearly lifeless in her arms.

The life which she had ravished from me could hardly fail to vivify in her womb, and her melting gaze as she reviewed it could hardly fail to stamp the nascent life with my features. We lay perfectly still for a long time, when the door opened and the old lady called me. I got up to see what she wanted.

'You must go now,' she said. I told her I could not bear to leave my charming companion. 'You will undo what I hope you have done if you stay longer.' Then she whispered, 'I do not wish to startle her, but there is danger of discovery. Lie perfectly still on your back, darling,' she added to the lady in bed, 'and it will be a fine boy.'

I dressed and stepped to the bedside. The sheet was drawn; her forehead alone was visible. I kissed it and withdrew. The old lady soon followed me and put a ring into my hand as she dismissed me hastily from the front door. 'She begs you to accept it in token of her admiration and respect. Her love is all for her husband.'

I should not have accepted it if I had seen, as I did on reaching home, that it was a diamond worth thousands. On the inside of the ring was engraved the words, 'in honour . . .'

'I left the city, as had been announced, on the first morning train. Before proceeding far we met with an accident. No one was injured, but we would have to wait for the afternoon train. I took a carriage and rode back to the city rather than wait for the afternoon train. As we approached the main street we could not cross. We had to await, as the cortege of the sovereign was passing. By his side was sitting his august spouse.

It was the lady with whom I had lain the night

before. She supposed me far on my journey or she would not have left the seclusion of her palace. She rode unconscious of the presence of the man whose seed was even then germinating in her womb. It is six months since then. The newspapers which we received at port a few days ago announce that there was great rejoicing in a certain capital city. The august spouse of the sovereign was in an interesting condition.

'You see what you have got to expect, Inez,' said Anna. 'You and I, Myrzella, what will the black-eyed pasha say if three blue-eyed babies are born the same night in the harem?'

The ladies laughed and then began teasing for another story. 'One of you must tell it then,' said I. When they found that I would tell no more, enquiries were made for the scarf.

Virginia produced it and threw it to a lady she called El Jelis, from Arabia. She, like Anna, was very tall and slender, but there all resemblance between them ceased. The Arab girl had hair and eyes as black as jet, and skin the colour of rich cream. She took the scarf and shook it out to its full length, displaying the spots where Zuleika's blood had stained it.

'You will excuse me if I give you a dance instead of a story,' she said, springing lightly to her feet and waving the long thin fabric high over her head. She accompanied the waving motion with the most beautiful dancing I ever saw.

Her slender, but firmly rounded limbs seemed to float through the air. Her little feet came to the carpet with a touch too light to crush a rose leaf. Her shining black hair was unbound and reached to her ankles; it floated from side to side as she danced like a cloud. Her motion without losing its grace became more rapid; the colour came to her cheeks; her large, lustrous, black eyes flashed from under the dark lashes.

Still the dance became more rapid. Her round bosoms did not even quiver, so free from any jar was every graceful spring. At last her whole form seemed to float in the air, then one toe lightly touched the carpet and the other pointed to the ceiling directly over her head.

For an instant between her naked thighs was disclosed a long, crimson gash and the parted curls. In another instant she was standing upright and motionless before me. Her hands were folded on her bosoms and her head bowed in oriental submission. Her hair slowly ceased to wave and fell to her ankles in a veil.

'It was very graceful, my charming El Jelis,' said I, 'but I cannot let you off from your story.'

'My story is so disgraceful that I cannot look you in the face and tell it,' she said and, turning with her back towards me, the beautiful girl told the following story.

CHAPTER THIRTEEN

The Arabian lady's story

I was born in the dominions of the Iman of Yemen. When I was sixteen years old I was selected by one of his emissaries for the Iman's harem. My parents were well pleased with my preferment, and I set out from home with girlish glee. On being introduced to the harem I was bathed and elegantly dressed; then I was led to a room where the Iman was sitting conversing with his ladies.

He was an old man with a countenance indicating a feeble character. The conversation showed the supremacy which was exercised over him by his wife, Ayesha, a very fat lady, whose corpulence seemed to be her only charm. After a while the Iman began to look at me a great deal, which I could see she noticed.

At last he called me to his side, where I stood with his bare arm around my waist, answering his questions. His arm gradually lowered and I felt his hand under my petticoat. I suppose he thought the other ladies did not see him, for I was standing very close to his side The eyes of Ayesha, however, were on the alert; they flashed with anger.

The Iman's hand explored my thighs, and at last his finger entered a place where no man had ever before touched. It felt its way carefully in and soon met with an obstruction. The pressure upon it, though slight was very disagreeable to me, but I did not dare to repulse the Iman.

What I did not dare to do Ayesha did. 'Your Highness,' said she, 'has promised to present a virgin to the Sultan of Muscat; I think this one will do in default of any better.' 'Yes, she is a virgin,' he said, partly answering her and partly giving vent to his own thoughts.

'Shall I order the chief eunuch to see to her?' said Ayesha. The Iman gave a long look at me, then he looked at the black thunder cloud on the brow of Ayesha, from beneath which her eyes were flashing.

'Yes,' he said, 'you may give the order.' I suppose the graceful charm which rewarded his obedience was in the possession of some state secret which controlled him, or it may have been her temper.

The next day I was on the road to Muscat, where, after several days' journey, I was duly presented. The Sultan received his present very gracefully. I heard him say a bale of rich goods should be returned to my former lord. Then he ordered the female slaves to care for me very tenderly. They bathed me and perfumed me and dressed me in the richest apparel and jewellery, then they led me to sumptuous repast—they could not do too much for me, whom their lord delighted to honour.

After supper the Sultan came into the women's apartments. I had learned from the slave girls that Fatima was his favourite wife. She was a beautiful woman, but I found afterwards that she had a cruel and pitiless heart. She did not seem to care for the attentions the Sultan lavished on me. I eeven thought there was a gleam of satisfaction on her countenance as he led me to a remote part of the harem.

We passed through two or three doors until nothing could be heard of the sounds of music or conversation we had just left. We were now in a rich apartment with an elegant bed. As I was somewhat agitated the Sultan sat on a sofa beside me and began to soothe me. His person was agreeable and I began to enjoy his conversation. I knew what was coming, but I neither desired nor dreaded it much.

'Now please undress yourself,' he said. I obeyed at once, taking off everything but my chemise; in the meantime he had stripped stark naked. It made my heart beat violently as I looked for the first time on a man's shaft ready for action. He came and unbuttoned my chemise and let it drop to the floor. I covered my face with my hands.

He lifted me and laid my back on the bed close to the edge of it and knelt on the floor beside me. Then he spread my thighs wide apart and opened the lips between them and made a critical examination of my virginity. 'By Allah!' he exclaimed, 'a crescent-shaped maidenhead. It brings good luck to the captor!'

'I am glad it pleases you, my lord,' said I, timidly.

The Sultan gave a sudden cry of agony and fell across me. I took my hands from my face and saw Fatima holding a shawl tightly around his head while a man whom I had never seen was driving a dagger into his body with repeated blows. I tried to call out, but my voice was frozen with horror.

'Dare to make a noise,' said Fatima, 'and you shall share his fate.' I knelt to plead for my life, but they took no further notice of me till they had satisfied themselves that the Sultan was dead. Fatima flung the covers over the body.

'Let me be the first to congratulate you as Sultan of Muscat,' she said, turning to her companion.

'The most beautiful woman in Muscat has the right to congratulate me,' he said. Then he turned towards me, let his eyes rove over my naked form and addressed some soothing words to me.

'Have the decency to put on your clothes and follow me, hussy,' said Fatima. While I was dressing the Sultan parted with Fatima, first giving her some instructions about the harem to cary out while he went to confirm his authority with the troops.

The conspiracy at the crowning act, at which I was present, was perfectly successful, and the new Sultan reigned without opposition. Fatima was absolute in the harem. She kept me as much as possible out of sight of the new Sultan, though she allowed him to have free access to the other women. He took every opportunity to speak to me, but I avoided him with horror. I could not forget the scene of the assassination.

One evening after he had been more persistent in his attentions, Fatima called me into a room alone. She told me to lie down on the bed, and, when I had obeyed her, she turned my petticoats up over my head. I was so afraid of the beautiful tigress that I dared not stir; I only begged for mercy.

'Lie still, I shall not hurt you,' she said, and, having pulled by thighs apart, she opened my sheath with her fingers. I heard the 'click' of scissors and felt a slight but keen pain. I put my hand involuntarily to the place and felt that my maidenhead was gone.

'Now,' she said, 'you will not play your arts on the Sultan any more on pretence of being a virgin.' I burst into tears of mortification and anger and went into my room with the blood trickling down my thighs.

The next evening the Sultan came into the women's apartments. She hastily ordered me from the room on some errand. 'Don't be too harsh with the poor maid,' he said. 'Maid!' she retorted, contemptuously. 'She has lain with half the young men in Yemen.'

'I will match your wager on that,' he said.

'Very well,' she said. 'If you are right you shall lie with her tonight. If I am right I will dispose of her.'

This conversation was carried on in a low tone, but I overheard it. She arose and bade me follow her. The Sultan came after us to the bedroom.

'Now feel the hussy,' she said, 'and satisfy yourself.'

The Sultan, brute as he was, was very much embarrassed. But he drew me towards him, put his hands under my clothes and with his finger satisfied himself that my maidenhead was gone. I was then dismissed with my cheeks flaming with rage and shame, and then the two devils passed the night together. Once more after this the Sultan sought an opportunity to be alone with me, which I baffled. Fatima's keen eyes detected him and my fate was sealed.

That evening I was seized in my room by the eunuchs, bound and gagged and sewn in a sack. After being carried a short distance in silence the creaking of a boat and the rippling of water

118

revealed to me the awful doom to which I was to be consigned. I could not move; I could not call. I was lifted and flung into the water and heard a boat row away.

I settled slowly under the waves, and, as my clothes became saturated, the water reached my nostrils. I made in hopeless agony a prayer to Allah; as if in answer to it I heard the stroke of oars. They became louder and louder till the water settled over me and I knew no more.

I returned to consciousness lying in the bottom of a boat, the sweet moonlight streaming in my face, and the eyes of a young man were gazing earnestly into my own. He must have been pleased with what he saw there. 'Sweet houri of paradise, she lives,' he said in a tender and manly tone.

His attentions were unremitting until I was fully restored and my lungs freed from water. Then he arranged me in the bottom of the boat with his coat for a pillow. 'Lie close, we may be observed,' he said.

He rowed silently to shore in the suburbs of the city where he had a little dwelling, which we reached without observation and to which he made me welcome. He offered me in the most delicate manner some clothing of his own until mine could be dried. Then he cooked me a nice meal, and after I was thus refreshed we conversed without reserve.

He listened to my story with his face beaming

with compassion; it lighted with joy when I allowed him to infer that my person as well as heart was still to be disposed of as far as any *man* was concerned. I emphasised man for I thought of the fiendish and jealous rape Fatima had accomplished.

Hassan, for that was his name, soon told his story. He had come into the city to seek his fortune and had been driven to smuggling to obtain a livelihood. It was while on the alert at this vocation that he had been able to save me. 'We must fly before morning,' he said, 'if we would be safe.'

He would be the happiest man in the world if I could suffer him to take me to his desert home. So much kindness after so much cruelty completely won by heart. He read my assent in my eyes, and kissing me tenderly, went out to make his preparations to go. We were soon both mounted on a single horse and miles away from Muscat.

We had been an hour on the road and were still borne along at the same unflagging gallop. Hassan held me in front of him like a baby in his arms, often kissing me, his kisses constantly growing more ardent, and then I felt his stiff shaft pressing against my person. He suggested that I should ride astride awhile and rest myself by a change of position.

I obeyed his suggestion, turning with my face towards his, putting my arms around his neck, while my thighs were wide open over Hassan's. He let the bridle drop over the horse's neck, whose headlong pace subsided into a gentle canter which was like the rocking of a cradle. Hassan put his arms around my loins and lifted me a little; his other hand was busy clearing away the petticoats and then I felt the crest of his naked shaft knocking for entrance between my naked thighs.

I was willing to yield to Hassan anything that he wished but no sooner had the lips of my sheath been penetrated than I involuntarily clung more tightly around his neck; and, sustaining myself in that way prevented him from entering further. I found the sensation entirely different, however, from that which I had experienced when the fingers of the Iman explored the same entrance. Now the organ seemed adapted to the place and excited a sensation of pleasure.

I offered my mouth to Hassan and returned his ardent kisses with an ardour equally warm. A desire to secure more of the delightful intruder overcame my dread of the intrusion. I loosened my hold on Hassan's neck; my weight drove his shaft so completely home, notwithstanding the tightness of the fit, that his crest rested on my womb. It felt so unexpectedly good that I gave a murmur of delight. The motion of the horse kept partially withdrawing and completely sent it in again at every canter. The first thrust, good as it was, was completely eclipsed by each succeeding one. I could have murmured with delight still louder, but kept still for very shame. What would Hassan think of a girl so wanton?

But he was in no condition to think. He was fiercely squeezing and kissing me, while at every undulating motion of the cantering horse he seemed to penetrate me more deeply. The pleasure was too exquisite to be long endured. It culminated in a melting thrill, and my moisture mingled with the sperm that gushed from Hassan's crest. He reeled in the saddle but recovered himself.

The cantering motion drove his shaft less deeply in as it became more limber. It finally dropped out of me, a little limp thing drowned in the descending moisture. 'What a conquest for a slender girl to achieve over such a formidable object,' I thought. Exhausted, but triumphant, I dropped my head on Hassan's shoulder.

'Poor girl,' said he, 'how it makes you bleed!'

'Never mind,' I whispered. He always remained under the innocent delusion, for the trying scenes of that eventful night brought on my period prematurely and my petticoats before morning were stained with blood. Twice more during the night he slacked the speed of his horse, and each time we completed an embrace equally satisfactory. At dawn we were beyond the reach of pursuit, safe and free.

* * *

El Jelis finished as she began, with her back towards me, while I was leaning back against Myrzella and Virginia. The graceful Arabian was astride my thighs, partly kneeling on the carpet and partly lying on my loins. She played with my genitals all the time she was telling her story and my shaft got so stiffened that she inserted it.

It was sufficiently excited to enjoy the charming retreat where it was cherished. My glands relaxed and my pendant was fondled in her tapered fingers and caressed by the soft hair which hung down from her loins. I lay luxuriously quiet, but El Jelis had been longing all the evening for the connection and she could not keep still. She made little wanton motions with her loins all the while she was speaking, and at every move the moist, warm tissues where my crest was hidden quivered with life and imparted their vitality to me.

I would have summoned energy to give her the thrusts for which she longed but I postponed it from moment to moment, revelling passively in the lascivious situation. El Jelis could no longer restrain herself. She finished her story and began to play her loins up and down my shaft, which though erect to its full size, was not entirely rigid, and it bent with her vigorous motion. Her position was favourable to the play of her loins and she moved them with greater and greater rapidity.

I seemed to have changed my sex and to be a

woman actually enjoying the thrusts of her paramour. In a few moments I would have been ripe to melting, but El Jelis could not wait; her buttocks settled heavily upon me, her sheath loosened and her moisture flushed my genitals. She sank back with a deep sigh into my arms, which drew my shaft completely out of her and exposed it like a tower rising tempest beaten from the waves.

It subsided at once when the stimulating efforts of El Jelis were withdrawn. I was not ready for another onset. The ladies were too polite to laugh; I had exerted myself too much on their behalf. El Jelis threw the scarf and then nestled quietly in my arms.

It fell to the ninth lady. She was a Parisian and her name was Renée. the others had done well to leave her to the last for she was the most beautiful woman in the room. The sweetness and vivacity of her expression and the grace of her manner lent additional charms to her perfect features and her splendid form.

She was of medium height with full contours, graceful as a fawn yet voluptuous in the bold roundness of her bosoms and the grand swell on her thighs. Her complexion was wonderfully clear. Her snow-white skin was so transparent that a delicate pink tinge showed plainly beneath it, especially at the little ears and the small tips of her fingers. The rosy tinge was deep on her lips and her mouth was like an opening red rose. Her large hazel eyes were clear and full and the long lashes that partially veiled them could not conceal their lustre.

Her hair was of a dark chestnut colour, but if the light fell full upon it, it was of a golden auburn; it began to curl at the centre of her head where it was parted, and would have descended in a luxuriant mass to her knees if it had not been carefully confined by combs. The hair at her loins was dark but had a ruddy tinge.

After she had exchanged a kiss with me she reclined in a graceful position at my feet where I could uninterruptedly feast my eyes on her marvellous beauty while she told her story.

CHAPTER FOURTEEN

The French lady's story

When I arrived at the age of sixteen I was still at
a convent boarding school in Paris. Lisette, my
room-mate, was my most intimate friend. I
confided to her all my secrets and supposed she
did the same to me, especially what we could
learn about marriage and sexual intercourse, a
subject which had a strange fascination, even for
a girl like myself who had never engaged in it,
but who looked forward to an early marriage
with eager satisfaction.

One evening Lisette came into the room with a
triumphant expression. She had something in a
small box which she mysteriously produced. It
was labelled: 'One Superfine Dildo'.

She locked the door and, opening the box,
revealed an India rubber article about the size of
a man's shaft ready for action. She explained to
me what it was and said she had got it from her
milliner as a great favour and had paid her five

hundred francs for it. She was all eagerness to try it.

'But, Lisette,' said I, 'if we do, and if we should ever get married, our husbands would know it.'

'Oh!' she said, 'we could easily fool them.' Having filled the dildo with warm water and fastened it upon my loins with the straps attached to it, she prevailed upon me to act the man's part. She pulled me into bed and seemed perfectly familiar with the proper manner for me to mount her. So far from being hurt by the thing, Lisette seemed to enjoy every movement of it, from the time I thrust it into her till she gave a dying sigh and subsided.

After a while she was ready to perform the same office for me. When she had got it adjusted I felt the warm thing enter in a little way with a sensation not unpleasant. Then she gave a thrust with all her might which tore away my maidenhead. It pained me so cruelly, that I pushed her off me and burst into tears while the blood trickled from the wound and down my thighs. I was terribly enraged with Lisette. I finally forgave her when she told me that my brother had taken her maidenhead when she was on a visit to me.

Both Lisette and myself were married soon after leaving school, she to a country gentleman and I to an officer. Lisette had not been long married when I had too good reason to suppose that she had kept up a liaison with my brother. I wrote to her hinting my painful suspicion and begging her to make a visit that I might persuade her to break off a connection so dangerous to both herself and my brother.

She replied saying that she could not visit me now, but she would be glad if I would receive a visit from her unmarried sister, adding that she was a shy, timid girl and that a visit to Paris would do her good. Her sister Amie accordingly came in due time and was cordially welcomed by me, though I had never seen her before.

She was a handsome girl, but very masculine in appearance, although she appeared to be very modest. Her features were pleasing but rather large, and she was broad shouldered and tall, though her bosoms seemed to be flat and her thighs small. She wore her hair very short, even for the clipped style then prevailing for young ladies. My husband was at this time off with his regiment, and I thought it would be kind to allow Amie to sleep with me.

When we retired she seemed to be very awkward about retiring, but finally followed me to bed. I took her in my arms and kissed her affectionately. She returned the kisses and caresses with so much ardour that I wished Louis, my husband, was in her place. He had been absent long enough for my desires to become like tinder, ready to flame up at a spark.

So we lay locked tightly in each other's embrace with our lips glued together. I felt something squeezed up against my thigh which could not be Amie's arm, for both of her arms were around me. I put my hand down and felt that it was a man's warm, throbbing shaft. I gave a scream and pushed my bedfellow violently from me. 'You are not Lisette's sister!' was my absurd exclamation.

'True, charming Renée, but I am her brother, and no one will ever know of this but her. Will you now allow Aramond to have one sweet kiss like those you have just given to Amie?' He drew me towards him as he spoke, with the fire of passion on his handsome face.

I hesitated, but my sheath was still swelling with wanton emotion and I suffered him again unresisted to take me in his arms. This was not the moral lecture I had prepared for Lisette. Desire was coursing through all my veins; I returned Aramond's kisses; I opened my thighs to facilitate the connection. The touch of his crest under the hair was like the first taste of some delicious fruit unexpectedly presented to the lips of a thirsty traveller. I took it in so greedily and swallowed it with a sensation so much more pleasurable that I was ashamed of myself. Aramond would think he was not the first who had taken advantage of my husband's absence.

But I could not help it; my person had been seduced before my consent had been won. It was too late now for virtue to erect a barrier. I was penetrated to the secret and sensitive depths where wantonness reigned supreme.

The rapidity and strength of Aramond's thrusts showed the vigour of seventeen. I was transported to the seventh heaven, carrying the amorous boy in his arms. When I finally returned to the consciousness of earthly things we lay so still that for a few moments there was not a motion in the bed, save that Armond's diminished shaft was slowly sinking from my sheath with the balmy flow that filled it.

Aramond's visit was prolonged to a week and no suspicion was excited on the part of my friends and servants, nor was the intrigue known in any quarter save Lisette, who rallied me without mercy. It was a week of abandonment to unrestrained wantonness. I would sometimes ask Aramond, when in the privacy of my room to take his male attire from his trunk and put it on. He then seemed like a slender and effeminate youth, a mere fair-faced boy, entirely different from the amazon he appeared in girl's clothes.

But if I rallied him on his effeminacy, he would at once proceed to give most convincing proof of his virile power. No married embrace ever conferred such rapture. Fornication, that becomes so insipid when lawful, is so delicious when stolen. The lascivious nights were not enough; we retired every afternoon on the pretence of taking a nap. At every embrace his fresh enthusiasm bewitched me and I was melted by his fervent ardour.

But dark and sunken circles came around

Aramond's eyes, his flesh fell rapidly away, and, when at last he tore himself away from me to return home, a hectic fever was consuming him. As for me, I grew plump as he grew thin, and my cheeks bloomed with stolen pleasure.

When my husband returned home on leave of absence, he had no occasion to reproach me for want of ardour. It had, however, begun to be monotonous, when we received an invitation from Lisette, seconded by her husband, Adolphe, to visit their country seat, which we accepted. We sat up late the first evening. There was much to converse about, and, besides, the champagne flowed freely. I enjoyed conversing with so agreeable a man as Adolphe; besides he was fat and jolly. The change was agreeable from being continually with my husband, who was thin and earnest.

Lisette and I talked on after our husbands had retired. We finished another bottle of wine, which they had merely opened, and we grew very confidential. We concluded to undress by the stove and carried our clothes upstairs in our hands. Standing in our chemise we compared our forms; as of old, they were very similar. We pressed our bosoms together and we squeezed together the little mouths at our loins.

'Why do we stand here,' I said, 'when we can go to bed and get all we want?'

'Suppose,' she said, 'we should make a mistake going to our rooms and exchange husbands?'

I looked at Lisette to see if she had divined my own adulterous thoughts and to see if she was really in earnest. She smiled and nodded; so did I. Wine and wantonness combined to put us up to that mad frolic. It was agreed she was to take my clothes along with her and that I should take hers with me, in case of the necessity of suddenly escaping to our room. As she put her hand on the doorknob of my husband's room I felt a pang of jealousy, but I let that disappear and entered Adolphe's room.

He was sleeping quietly. I laid Lisette's clothes on a chair and got into bed with him. I waited a few moments for the violent beating of my heart to still and then nestled close up and put my arms around him. I put aside his moustache and kissed him on the lips. Still he did not wake. Then I pulled up his shirt and felt his massive thighs and played with his genitals. They grew under my hand and he awoke and put his arms around me. I returned his kisses and caresses.

'Why, Lisette,' he said, 'how good you are tonight.' I replied with kisses. Then he got upon me and I soon felt his shaft enter me. It was larger than I had been accustomed to, but very soft. It was a dainty morsel to the gluttonous lips through which it passed; they closed upon it with the keenest zest. Adolphe's ponderous loins settled down on mine till the hair between was matted into one mass and his shaft was caressed by every membrane in my sheath. Before he could give another thrust I was overtaken by the melting thrill.

Adolphe had not yet reached his climax. He gave two or three more lazy thrusts while mine was subsiding. 'I was dreaming of Renée,' he said, 'when I awoke.' Exerting all my strength, I pushed him on me jealously as Lisette would have done if she had been in my place. Then I turned my back to him. He now realised what a foolish confession he had made. 'Sweet Lisette,' he said, 'I don't care a straw for Renée; she is not half so pretty as you are.'

I obdurately shrugged my shoulders. The Lisette I impersonated would not be pacified. He snuggled up to my back and held me struggling in his arms. I could feel his stiff shaft pressed against my buttocks. He squeezed my thighs and fondled my bosoms and kissed the back of my neck, but I would not turn over.

He was so excited with desire from his half-finished embrace that at last he communicated his wantonness to me. I was now ready for another onset, so I turned my head and kissed him. He quckly turned me on my back and mounted fiercely to the charge. Plunge after plunge in rapid succession again woke all sensibilities of my sheath.

My mouth was buried under his moustache and the kisses kept time to the rapid play. The glow of the friction became more and more intense, spreading from the place of contact in electric waves all over my frame, and the stolen and guilty pleasure culminated in another melting thrill. Adolphe was ravished at the same time and paid me a tribute as profuse as his excitement had been long. His ample person seemed to be dissolving in my loins.

The he sank down upon me, too weak, for some moments to relieve me of his great weight. He soon fell sound asleep, his hand still grasping one of my bosoms and one of his heavy thighs on my own. Cautiously and by degrees I extricated myself and stole from the room dripping at every step. Lisette was awaiting me with jealousy and impatience depicted on her countenance.

'What have you been doing all the time?' she said.

'The same as you have, I suppose,' said I, laughing. 'I have been standing here this hour and a half,' said she. 'I was sobered up by the danger as soon as I got into Louis' room, and I dared not get into bed with him.'

We went to our chambers, Lisette almost crying and I almost bursting with laughter. During the rest of our visit, she watched me narrowly to see that I was not a moment alone with Adolphe. She need not have been so suspicious as he was perfectly unconscious and, as for me, the curiosity of wantonness was satisfied with regard to him.

When we returned to Paris, Louis rejoined the army. I had now acquired such a taste for variety that I felt much pleased at the attentions of a young duke. He sought my company on every public occasion. At last he called at my house. He had sent me a magnificent diamond necklace the day before, and it was now necessary for me to return it if I were unwilling to pursue the intrigue.

In expectation of the interview I dressed myself as attentively as possible. A dress of elegant pink silk cut low in the neck displayed my bosoms to advantage and I wore the diamond necklace. The duke saw it with a smile of pleasure the moment I entered the parlour. He came and knelt at my feet and kissed my hand, then he arose and our lips met.

I consented to meet him later in the day, at a safe place of assignation, and if he had then taken his leave, all would have gone smoothly, but the duke kept kissing me and prolonged the interview. Though my husband was not expected for a day or two, still a servant was liable to enter the parlour. I rose to have him go, but he still kept his chair.

With his arm around my waist, he drew me towards him and transferred his kisses from my neck to my bosoms. I bent down and kissed him on his white forehead. Desire was getting control over us both. The duke's hand stole under my skirts and explored all the mysteries they hid. Then he lifted one of my legs over his lap and I found myself sitting astride of his thighs clasped in his embrace and our lips glued together.

We were infatuated to risk ourselves there in that position when a few hours later we could safely revel in each other's embrace. The duke produced his stiff shaft and I felt it pleading for entrance between my thighs. I half rose to tear myself from his arms, but with such feeble purpose that he pulled me down again.

I sat directly upon his crest and my weight entered it. It filled me with a sensation of such exquisite pleasure that I abandoned myself to my uncontrollable passions. He could not move freely, but my loins undulated to assist him, which made my crisis culminate. My ecstasy was prolonged and I had not finished melting when my husband opened athe door and stood thunderstruck at the sight. I jumped backwards from the duke's arm and my skirts fell and covered my nakedness. But the duke was in the very act of spending. The sperm from his rampant crest splashed upon my dress and skirts.

For a single moment I stood still and my brains whirled with incongruous thoughts, one of which was that my beautiful pink dress was spoiled by the splashes. Only a moment I stood, and then I darted from the room. I wrapped myself in a long cloak and hood as I fled through the lower hall and gained the front door. As I passed through it, I heard the trampling of feet and the crash of furniture in the parlour above. It must have been my husband and the duke in a deadly struggle.

What the issue of it was, I never knew. I reached the station of a Marseilles railway just as a train was about to leave. I got in it and reached Marseilles. Even then I did not feel safe till I had put the Mediterranean between myself and France.

CHAPTER FIFTEEN

Conclusion

Renée concluded. She now expected her reward. It was her turn at last. The loins of eight of those beautiful women hd been stirred to the depths by me and they had melted in my embrace. To four of them I had paid tribute to return. The night would be fittingly crowned by a tribute to the loveliest and last.

She lay back at length on the cushions with Laura's back for a pillow. The charming French girl then shot a seductive glance at my face from beneath her long eyelashes and opened her graceful tapering legs.

I knelt between them and kissed the grand snow-white thighs close to the thick ruddy hair that adorned them. I planted another kiss on her smooth, round belly just over her womb. From the pink nipples of each of her plump bosoms, I sucked voluptuous kisses, and then my lips fastened on her rosebud mouth. She wound her soft white arms around me as I stretched myself on her lovely form, and with her lily fingers she guided my crest to the heaven it sought.

I pushed my way slowly in. It was deliciously tight and elastic and hot and juicy. I had to thrust more than once before my shaft was completely entered, which was no sooner accomplished than I felt Renée's frame shudder beneath me and then become limp and nerveless. Her arms relaxed their grasp and her sheath became loose and was flushed with moisture.

'Lie still, as you are, for a minute,' she whispered, 'and I shall be able to finish you.' I was in no hurry. I lay luxuriantly upon her with my crest soaking in the most inward recesses of her loins.

Laura's waist still served her as a pillow and my mouth occasionally wandered from Renée's rosy mouth to kiss Laura's fat bosoms, which were so conveniently near, and my fingers searched Laura's equally convenient sheath.

Inez nestled close up to us and hid the fingers of my other hand deep between her thighs.

Helene, kneeling on the other side, gently fondled my glands with her slender fingers.

Zuleika, Myrzella and Virginia kissed the small of my back, shoulders and neck.

My feet were abandoned to Amie and El Jelis, who sat each holding a foot between their thighs so that my toes searched their crevices.

The wanton touch of nine charming and

amorous women infused me rapidly with some of their own superfluous vigour. My shaft became perfectly rigid.

Renée awoke to the responsibility that rested chiefly on her. As a signal that she was again ready she darted her tongue into my mouth while I was sucking her lips. Her sheath again grew tight and I felt its inmost membranes convulsively contract and lasciviously seize my crest. I responded by giving her a deep, prolonged thrust, then I braced my toes in the hot crevices where they rested and rammed my shaft completely home again and again. Renée surged up her loins to meet each descending thrust. I felt the crisis approaching. The very marrow of my bones seemed to be distilling into my empty glands. My plunge became more rapid, until the very nerves of my shaft seemed to be laid bare to the friction.

Renée redoubled her exertions. As her loins rose to meet me she gave them a rotary motion, which made her womb circle round my crest. The supreme moment which had been coming, came at last, and I was completely ravished. My very life blood seemed to gush. I gave a deep, long groan of ecstasy and sank, an almost inanimate mass, on the panting and glowing form of Renée. She kept squeezing my shaft to complete her own rapture, and extracted a few more drops from me after I was too far gone to groan. I heard several of the ladies mingle their sighs with hers and my fingers and toes were bathed with moisture that had melted in sympathy with ours. I lay for a long time unable to stir, perfectly triumphant.

'That will make another blue-eyed boy,' said Myrzella.

'I feel as if I were with twins,' said Renée, giving one more squeeze to my diminished shaft.

When I recovered sufficiently to be able to move, my first look was at the clock. It was near dawn, and it was necessary for me to go. The ladies helped me to dress, for I had not the strength of a kitten. Each exchanged with me a tender kiss, then I got upon the window where the rope of shawls hung, but I felt too weak to climb. I fastened the rope around under my arms, and all the ladies taking hold together, lowered me safely down.

I pushed my boat from the strand and set sail. The land breeze was just setting in and I gained the offing, when I descried my ship beating up and down looking for me. In an hour more I was safely on board.

FLOSSIE:
A VENUS OF SIXTEEN

Preface

In presenting to a critical public this narrative of a delightful experience, I am conscious of an inability to do justice to the indescribable charm of my subject.

A true daughter of the Paphian goddess, Flossie added to the erotic allurements inherited from her immortal mother a sense of humour which is not traceable in any of the proceedings on Mount Ida or elsewhere. Those of my readers, who have had the rare good fortune to meet with the combination, will not gainsay my assertion that it is an incomparable incentive to deeds of love.

If some of those deeds, as here set down, should seem to appertain to a somewhat advanced school of amatory action, I beg objectors to remember that Flossie belongs to the end of the century, *when such things are done*, to the safety, comfort and delight of vast numbers of fair English girls, and to the unspeakable enjoyment of their adorers.

* *Credo experto.* *

So, in the words of the City toastmaster:—

'Pray silence, gentlemen, for your heroine, Flossie: a Venus of Sixteen.'

J.A.

Postscript—Flossie has herself revised this unpretending work, and has added a footnote here and there which she trusts may not be regarded as painful interruptions to a truthful tale.

All thine the new wine of desire
   The fruit of four lips as they clung
Till the hair and the eyelids took fire;
   The fan of a serpentine tongue,
The froth of the serpents of pleasure,
   More salt than the foam of the sea,
Now felt as a flame, not at leisure
        As wine-shed for me!

They were purple of rainment, and golden,
   Filled full of thee, fiery with wine,
Thy lovers, in haunts unbeholden,
   In marvellous chambers of thine.
They are fled and their footprints escape us
   Who appraise thee, adore, and abstain,
O daughter of Death and Priamus!
        Our Lady of Pain.
A. C. Swinburne

CHAPTER ONE

'My love, she's but a lassie yet'

Towards the end of a bright sunny afternoon in June, I was walking in one of the quieter streets of Piccadilly, when my eye was caught by two figures coming in my direction. One was that of a tall, finely-made woman about twenty-seven years of age, who would under other circumstances, have received something more than an approving glance. But it was her companion that rivetted my gaze of almost breathless admiration. This was a young girl of sixteen, of such astounding beauty of face and figure as I had never seen or dreamt of. Masses of bright, wavy, brown hair fell to her waist. Deep violet eyes looked out from under long curling lashes, and seemed to laugh in unison with the humourous curves of the full red lips. These and a thousand other charms I was to know by heart later on, but what struck me most at this view, was the extraordinary size and beauty of the girl's bust, shown

149

to all possible advantage by her dress which, in the true artistic French style, crept in between her breasts, outlining their full and perfect form with loving fidelity. Tall and lithe, she moved like a young goddess, her short skirt shewing the action of a pair of exquisitely moulded legs, to which the tan-coloured open-work silk stockings were plainly designed to invite attention. Unable to take my eyes from this enchanting vision, I was approaching the pair, when to my astonishment, the elder lady suddenly spoke my name.

'You do not remember me, Captain Archer.' For a moment I was at a loss, but the voice gave me the clue.

'But I do,' I answered, 'you are Miss Letchford, who used to teach my sisters.'

'Quite right. But I have given up teaching, for which fortunately there is not longer any necessity. I am living in a flat with my dead little friend here. Let me introduce you,—Flossie Eversley—Captain Archer.'

The violet eyes laughed up at me; and the red lips parted in a merry smile. A dimple appeared at the corner of the mouth. I was done for! Yes; at thirty-five years of age, with more than my share of experiences in every phase of love, I went down before this lovely girl with her childish face smiling at me above the budding womanhood of her rounded breasts, and confessed myself defeated!

A moment or two later, I had passed from

them with the address of the flat in my pocket, and under promise to go down to tea on the next day.

At midday I received the following letter:

'Dear Captain Archer,

I am sorry to be obliged to be out when you come; and yet not altogether sorry, because I should like you to know Flossie very well. She is an orphan, without a relation in the world. She is just back from a Paris school. In years she is of course a child, but in tact and knowledge she is a woman; also in figure, as you can see for yourself! She is of an exceedingly warm and passionate nature, and a look that you gave her yesterday was not lost upon her. In fact, to be quite frank, she had fallen in love with you! You will find her a delightful companion. Use her *very* tenderly, and she will do anything in the world for you. Speak to her about life in the French school; she loves to talk of it. I want her to be happy, and I think you can help. Remember she is only just sixteen.

Yours sincerely,
Eva Letchford'

I must decline any attempt to describe my feelings on receiving this remarkable communication. My first impulse was to give up the promised call at the flat. But the flower-like face, the soft red lips and the laughing eyes passed before my mind's eye, followed by an instant vision of the marvellous breasts and the delicate shapely legs in their brown silk stockings, and I knew that fate was too strong for me. For it was of course impossible to misunderstand the meaning of Eva Letchford's letter, and indeed, when I reached the flat, she herself opened the door to me, whispering as she passed out, 'Flossie is in there, waiting for you. You two can have the place to yourselves. One last word. You have been much in Paris, have you not? So has Flossie. She is *very* young—*and there are ways*—Good-bye.'

I passed into the next room. Flossie was curled up in a long chair, reading. Twisting her legs from under her petticoats, with a sudden movement that brought into full view her delicately embroidered drawers, she rose and came towards me, a rosy flush upon her cheeks, her eyes shining, her whole bearing instinct with an enchanting mixture of girlish coyness and anticipated pleasure. Her short white skirt swayed as she moved across the room, her breasts stood out firm and round under the close-fitting woven silk jersey; what man of mortal flesh and blood could withstand such allurements as these! Not I, for one! In a moment, she was folded in my arms. I rained kisses on her hair, her forehead, her eyes, her cheeks, and then, grasping her body closer and always closer to me, I glued my lips upon the scarlet mouth and revelled in a long and maddeningly delicious kiss—a kiss to be ever remembered—so well remembered now, indeed, that I must make some attempt to describe it. My hands were behind Flossie's head, buried in her long brown hair. Her arms were round my body, locked and clinging. At the first impact, her lips were closed, but a moment later they parted, and slowly, gently, almost as if in the performance of some solemn duty, the rosy tongue crept into my mouth, and bringing with it a flood of the scented juices from her throat, curled amorously round my own, whilst her hands dropped to my buttocks, and standing on tiptoe, she drew me to her with such extraordinary intimacy that it seemed our bodies were already in conjunction. Not a word was spoken on either side—indeed, under the circumstances, speech was impossible, for our tongues had twined together in a caress of unspeakable sweetness, which neither would be the first to forego. At last, the blood was coursing through my veins at a pace that became unbearable and I was compelled to unglue my mouth from hers. Still silent, but with love and longing in her eyes, she pressed me into a low chair, and seating herself on the arm, passed her hand behind my head, and looking full into my eyes, whispered my name in accents that were like the sound of a running stream. I kissed her open mouth again and again, and then, feeling that the time had come for some little explanation:

153

'How long will it be before your friend Eva comes back?' I asked.

'She has gone down into the country, and won't be here till late this evening.'

'Then I may stay with you, may I?'

'Yes, do, do, *do*, Jack. Do you know, I have got seats for an Ibsen play to-night, I was wondering . . . if . . . you would . . . take me!'

'Take *you*—to an Ibsen play—with your short frocks, and all that hair down your back! Why, I don't believe they'd let us in?'

'Oh, if *that's* all, wait a minute.'

She skipped out of the room with a whisk of her petticoats and a free display of brown silk legs. Almost before I had time to wonder what she was up to, she was back again. She had put on a long skirt of Eva's, her hair was coiled on the top of her head, she wore my 'billycock' hat and a pair of blue pincenez, and carrying a crutch-handled stick, she advanced upon me with a defiant air, and glaring down over the top of her glasses, she said in a deep masculine voice:

'Now, sir if you're ready for Ibsen, *I* am. Or if your tastes are so *low* that you can't care about a play, I'll give you a skirt dance.'

As she said this, she tore off the long dress, threw my hat on to a sofa, let down her hair with a turn of the wrist, and motioning me to the piano, picked up her skirts and began to dance.

Enchanted as I was by the humour of her quick change to the 'Ibsen woman,' words are

154

vain to describe my feelings as I feebly tinkled a few bars on the piano and watched the dancer.

Every motion was the perfection of grace and yet no Indian Nautch-girl could have more skilfully expressed the idea of sexual allurement. Gazing at her in speechless admiration, I saw the violet eyes glow with passion, the full red lips part, the filmy petticoats were lifted higher and higher; the loose frilled drawers gleamed white. At last breathless and panting, she fell back upon a chair, her eyes closed, her legs parted, her breasts heaving. A mingled perfume came to my nostrils—half *'odor di faemina,'* half the scent of white rose from her hair and clothes.

I flung myself upon her.

'Tell me, Flossie darling, what shall I do *first?*

The answer came, quick and short.

'Kiss me—*between my legs!'*

In an instant, I was kneeling before her. Her legs fell widely apart. Sinking to a sitting posture, I plunged my head between her thighs. the petticoats incommoded me a little, but I soon managed to arrive at the desired spot. Somewhat to my surprise, instead of finding the lips closed and barricaded as is usual in the case of young girls, they were ripe, red and pouting, and as my mouth closed eagerly upon the delicious orifice and my tongue found and pressed upon the trembling clitoris, I knew that my qualms of conscience had been vain. My utmost powers were now called into play and I sought, by every means I possessed, to let Flossie know that I was no halfbaked lover. Passing my arms behind her, I extended my tongue to its utmost length and with rapid agile movements penetrated the scented recesses. Her hands locked themselves under my head, soft gasps of pleasure came from her lips, and as I delivered at last an effective attack upon the erect clitoris, her fingers clutched my neck, and with a sob of delight, she crossed her legs over my back, and pressing my head towards her, held me with a convulsive grasp, whilst the aromatic essence of her being flowed softly into my enchanted mouth.

As I rose to my feet, she covered her face with her hands and I saw a blue eye twinkle out beteen the fingers with an indescribable mixture of bashfulness and fun. Then, as if suddenly remembering herself, she sat up, dropped her petticoats over her knees, and looking up at me from under the curling lashes, said in a tone of profound melancholy.

'Jack, am I not a *disgraceful* child! All the same, I wouldn't have missed *that* for a million pounds.'

'Nor would I, little sweetheart; and whenever you would like to have it again—'

'No, no, it is your turn now.'

'What! Flossie; you don't mean to say—'

'But I *do* mean to say it, and to *do* it too. Lie down on that sofa at once, sir.'

'But, Flossie, I really—'

Without another word she leapt at me, threw her arms round my neck and fairly bore me down on to the divan. Falling on the top of me, she twined her silken legs round mine and gently pushing the whole of her tongue between my lips, began to work her body up and down with a wonderful sinuous motion which soon brought me to a state of excitement bordering on frenzy. Then, shaking a warning finger at me to keep still, she slowly slipped to her knees on the floor.

In another moment, I felt the delicate fingers round my straining yard. Carrying it to her mouth she touched it ever so softly with her tongue; then slowly parting her lips she pushed it gradually between them, keeping a grasp of the lower end with her hand which she moved gently up and down. Soon the tongue began to quicken its motion, and the brown head to work rapidly in a perpendicular direction. I buried my hands under the lovely hair, and clutched the white neck towards me, plunging the nut further and further into the delicious mouth until I seemed almost to touch the uvula. Her lips, tongue and hands now worked with redoubled ardour, and my sensations became momentarily more acute, until with a cry I besought her to let me withdraw. Shaking her head with great emphasis, she held my yard in a fimer grasp, and passing her disengaged hand behind me, drew me towards her face, and with an unspeakable clinging action of her mouth, carried out the delightful act of love to its logical conclusion, declining to remove her lips until, some minutes after, the last remaining evidences of the late crisis had completely disappeared.

Then and not till then, she stood up, and bending over me, as I lay, kissed me on the forehead, whispering:—

'There! Jack, now I love you twenty times more than ever.'*

I gazed into the lovely face in speechless adoration.

'Why don't you say something?' she cried. 'Is there anything else you want me to do?'

'Yes,' I answered, 'there is.'

'Out with it, then.'

'I am simply dying to see your breasts, naked.'

'Why, you darling, of course, you shall! Stay there a minute.'

Off she whisked again, and almost before I could realise she had gone, I looked up and she was before me. She had taken off everything but her chemise and stockings, the former lowered beneath her breasts.

Any attempt to describe the beauties thus laid bare to my adoring gaze must necessarily fall absurdly short of the reality. Her neck, throat and arms were full and exquisitely rounded, bearing no trace of juvenile immaturity.

---

* 'This is a fact, as every girl knows who has ever gamahuched and been gamahuched by the man or boy she loves. As a *link*, it beats fucking out of the field. I've tried both and I *know*.' *Flossie*

Her breasts, however, were of course the objects of my special and immediate attention. size, perfection of form and colour, I had never seen their equals, nor could the mind of man conceive anything so alluring as the coral nipples which stood out firm and erect, craving kisses. A wide space intervened between the two snowy hillocks which heaved a little with the haste of her late exertions, I gazed a moment in breathless delight and admiration, then rushing towards her, I buried my face in the enchanting valley, passed my burning lips over each of the neighbouring slopes and finally seized upon one after the other of the rosy nipples, which I sucked, mouthed and tongued with a frenzy or delight.

The daring little girl lent herself eagerly to my every action, pushing her nipples into my mouth and eyes, pressing her breasts against my face, and clinging to my neck with her lovely naked arms.

Whilst we were thus amorously employed, my little lady had contrived dexterously to slip out of her chemise, and now stood before me naked but for her brown silk stockings and little shoes.

'There, Mr. Jack, now you can see my breasts, and everything else that you like of mine. In future, this will be my full-dress costume for making love to you in. Stop, though; it wants just one touch.' And darting out of the room, she came back with a beautiful chain of pearls round her neck, finishing with a pendant of

159

rubies which hung just low enough to nestle in the Valley of Delight, between the wonderful breasts.

'I am, now,' she said, 'The White Queen of the Gama Huchi Islands. My kingdom is bounded on this side by the piano, and on the other by the furthest edge of the bed in the next room. Any male person found wearing a *stitch* of clothing within those boundaries will be sentenced to lose his p . . . but soft! who comes here?'

Shading her eyes with her hand she gazed in my direction:—

'Aha! a stranger; and, unless these royal eyes deceive us, a man! He shall see what it is to defy our laws! What ho! within there! Take this person and remove his p . . .'

'Great Queen!' I said, in a voice of deep humility, 'if you will but grant me two minutes, I will make haste to comply with your laws.'

'And we, good fellow, will help you. (*Aside*.)

'Methinks he is somewhat comely*. (*Aloud*.)

'But first let us away with these garments, which are more than aught else a violation of our Gama Huchian Rules, Good! now the shirt. And what, pray, is *this?* We thank you, sir, but we are not requiring any *tent-poles* just now.'

'Then if your Majesty will deign to remove your royal fingers I will do my humble best to

---

*Don't believe I ever said anything of the sort, but if I did, 'methinks' I'd better take this opportunity of withdrawing the statement.   *Flossie*

160

cause the offending pole to disappear. At present, with your Majesty's hand upon it—!'

'Silence, Sir! Your time is nearly up, and if the last garment be not removed in twenty seconds . . . So! you obey. Tis well! You shall see how we reward a faithful subject of our laws.' And thrusting my yard between her lips, the Great White Queen of the Gama Huchi Islands sucked in the whole column to the very root, and by dint of working her royal mouth up and down, and applying her royal fingers to the neighbouring appendages, soon drew into her throat a tribute to her greatness, which, from its volume and the time it took in the act of payment, plainly caused her Majesty the most exquisite enjoyment. Of my own pleasure I will only say that it was delirious, whilst in this, as in all other love sports in which we indulged, an added zest was given by the humour and fancy with which this adorable child-woman designed and carried out our amusements. In the present case, the personating of the Great White Queen appeared to afford her especial delight, and going on with the performance, she took a long branch of pampas-grass from its place and waving it over my head, she said:—

'The next ceremony to be performed by a visitor to these realms will, we fear, prove somewhat irksome, but it must be gone through. We shall now place our royal person on this lofty throne. You, sir, will sit upon this footstool before us. We shall then wave our sceptre three times. At the

...nees will part and our guest will ...im the royal spot of love. This he will ...eed to salute with a kiss which shall last until we are pleased to signify that we have had enough. Now, most noble guest, open your mouth, *don't* shut your eyes, and prepare! One, two, *three;*'

The pampas-grass waved, the legs parted, and nestling between the ivory thighs, I saw the scarlet lips open and show the erected clitoris peeping forth from its nest below the slight brown tuft which adorned the base of the adorable belly. I gazed and gazed in mute rapture, until a sharp strident voice above me said:—

'Now then, there, move on, please; can't have you blocking up the road all day!' Then changing suddenly to her own voice:—

'Jack, if you don't kiss me at once I shall *die!*'

I pressed towards the delicious spot and taking the whole cunt into my mouth passed my tongue upwards along the perfumed lips until it met the clitoris, which thrust itself amorously between my lips, imploring kisses. These I rained upon her with all the ardour I could command, clutching the rounded bottom with feverish fingers and drawing the naked belly closer and ever closer to my burning face, whilst my tongue plunged deep within the scented cunt and revelled in its divine odours and the contraction of its beloved lips.

The Great White Queen seemed to relish this

particular form of homage, for it was many minutes before the satin thighs closed, and with the little hands under my chin, she raised my face and looking into my eyes with inexpressible love and sweetness shining from her own, she said simply:—

'Thank you, Jack. You're a darling!'—

By way of answer I covered her with kisses, omitting no single portion of the lovely naked body, the various beauties of which lent themselves with charming zest to my amorous doings. Upon the round and swelling breasts, I lavished renewed devotion, sucking the rosy nipples with a fury of delight, and relishing to the full the quick movements of rapture with which the lithe clinging form was constantly shaken, no less than the divine aroma passing to my nostrils as the soft thighs opened and met again, the rounded arms rose and fell, and with this, the faintly perfumed hair brushing my face and shoulders mingled its odour of tea-rose.

All this was fast exciting my senses to the point of madness, and there were moments when I felt that to postpone much longer the consummation of our ardour would be impossible.

I looked at the throbbing breasts, remembered the fragrant lips below that had pouted ripely to meet my kisses, the developed clitoris that told of joys long indulged in. And then . . . And then . . . the sweet girlish face looked up into mine, the violet eyes seemed to take on a pleading expression, and as if reading my thoughts, Flossie pushed me gently into a chair, seated herself on my knee, slipped an arm round my neck, and pressing her cheek to mine, whispered:—

'Poor, *poor* old thing! I know what it wants; and *I* want it too—badly, oh! so badly. But, Jack, you can't guess what a friend Eva has been to me, and I've promised her *not to!* You see I'm only just sixteen, and . . . *the consequences!* There! don't let us talk about it. Tell me all about yourself, and then I'll tell you about me. When you're tired of hearing me talk, you shall stop my mouth with—well, whatever you like. Now sir, begin!'

I gave her a short narrative of my career from boyhood upwards, dry and dull enough in all conscience!

'Yes, yes, that's all very nice and prim and proper,' she cried. 'But you haven't told me the principal thing of all—when you first began to be—naughty, and with whom?'

I invented some harmless fiction which, I saw, the quickwitted girl did not believe, and begged her to tell me her own story, which she at once proceeded to do. I shall endeavour to transcribe it, though it is impossible to convey any idea of the humour with which it was delivered, still less of the irrepressible fun which flashed from her eyes at the recollection of her schoolgirl pranks and amourettes. There were,

164

of course, many interruptions*, for most of which I was probably responsible; but, on the whole, in the following chapter will be found a fairly faithful transcript of Flossie's early experiences. Some at least of these I am sanguine, will be thought to have been of a sufficiently appetising character.

* The first of these is a really serious one, but for this the impartial reader will see that the responsibility was divided.

CHAPTER TWO

'How Flossie Acquired the French tongue.'

'Before I begin, Jack, I should like to hold something nice and solid in my hand, to sort of give me confidence as I go on. Have you got anything about you that would do!'

I presented what seemed to me the most suitable article 'in stock' at the moment.

'Aha!' said Flossie in an affected voice, 'the very thing! How *very* fortunate that you should happen to have it ready!'

'Well, madam, you see it is an article we are constantly being asked for by our lady-customers. It is rather an expensive thing—seven pound ten—'

'Yes, it's rather stiff. Still, if you can assure me that it will always keep in its present condition, I shouldn't mind spending a good deal upon it.'

'You will find, madam, that anything you may

spend upon it will be amply returned to you. Our ladies have always expressed the greatest satisfaction with it.'

'Do you mean that you find they come more than once? If so, I'll take it now.'

'Perhaps you would allow me to bring it myself—?'

'Thanks, but I think I can hold it quite well in my hand. It won't go off suddenly, will it?'

'Not if it is kept in a cool place, madam.'

'And it mustn't be shaken, I suppose, like *that*, for instance?' (Shaking it.)

'For goodness gracious sake, take your hand away, Flossie, or there'll be a catastrophe.'

'That is a good word, Jack! But do you suppose that if I saw a 'catastrophe' coming I shouldn't know what to do with it?'

'*What* should you do?'

'Why, what *can* you do with a catastrophe of that sort but *swallow it?*'

The effect of this little interlude upon us both was magnetic. Instead of going on with her story, Flossie commanded me to lie upon my back on the divan, and having placed a couple of pillows under my neck, knelt astride of me with her face towards my feet. With one or two caressing movements of her bottom, she arranged herself so that the scarlet vulva rested just above my face. Then gently sinking down, she brought her delicious cunt full upon my mouth from which my tongue instantly darted to penetrate the

168

adorable recess. At the same moment, I felt the brown hair fall upon my thighs, my straining prick plunged between her lips, and was engulfed in her velvet mouth to the very root, whilst her hands played with feverish energy amongst the surrounding parts, and the nipples of her breasts rubbed softly against my belly.

In a very few moments, I had received into my mouth her first tribute of love and was working with might and main to procure a second, whilst she in her turn, wild with pleasure my wandering tongue was causing her, grasped my yard tightly between her lips, passing them rapidly up and down its whole length, curling her tongue round the nut, and maintaining all the time an ineffable sucking action which very soon produced its natural result. As I poured a torrent into her eager mouth, I felt the soft lips which I was kissing contract for a moment upon my tongue and then part again to set free the aromatic flood to which the intensity of her sensations imparted additional volume and sweetness.

The pleasure, we were both experiencing from this the most entrancing of all the reciprocal acts of love, was too keen to be abandoned after one effort. Stretching my hands upwards to mould and press the swelling breasts and erected nipples, I seized the rosy clitoris anew between my lips, whilst Flossie resumed her charming operations upon my instrument which she gamahuched with ever increasing zest and delight, and even with a skill and variety of action which would have been marvellous in woman of double her age and experience. Once again the fragrant dew was distilled upon my enchanted tongue, and once again the velvet mouth closed upon my yard to receive the results of its divinely pleasurable ministrations.

Raising herself slowly and almost reluctantly from her position, Flossie laid her naked body at full length upon mine, and after many kisses upon my mouth, eyes and cheeks said, 'Now you may go and refresh yourself with a bath while I dress for dinner.'

'But where are we going to dine?' I asked.

'You'll see presently. *Go* along, there's a good boy!'

I did as I was ordered and soon came back from the bath-room, much refreshed by my welcome ablutions.

Five minutes later Flossie joined me, looking lovelier than ever, in a short-sleeved pale blue muslin frock, cut excessively low in front, black openwork silk stockings and little embroidered shoes.

'Dinner is on the table,' she said, taking my arm and leading me into an adjoining room where an exquisite little cold meal was laid out, to which full justice was speedily done, followed by coffee made by my hostess, who produced some Benedictine and a box of excellent cigars.

'There, Jack, if you're quite comfy, I'll go on

170

with my story. Shall I stay here, or come and sit on your knee?'

'Well, as far as getting on with the story goes, I think you are better in that chair, Flossie—'

'But I told you I must have something to hold.'

'You, you did, and the result was that we didn't get very far with the story, if you remember—'

'Remember! As if I was likely to forget. But look at this,' holding up a rounded arm bare to the shoulder. 'Am I to understand that you'd rather not have this round your neck?'

Needless to say she was to understand nothing of the sort, and a moment later she was perched upon my knee and having with deft penetrating fingers enough under her magic touch, began her narrative.

'I don't think there will be much to tell you until my school life at Paris begins. My father and mother both died when I was quite small; I had no brothers or sisters, and I don't believe I've got a relation in the world. You mustn't think I want to swagger, Jack, but I am rather rich. One of my two guardians died three years ago and the other is in India and doesn't care a scrap about me. Now and then, he writes and asks how I am getting on, and when he heard I was going to live with Eva (whom he knows quite well) he seemed perfectly satisfied. Two years ago he arranged for me to go to school in Paris.

'Now I must take great care not to shock you, but there's nothing for it but to tell you that about this time I began to have the most wonderful feelings all over me—a sort of desperate longing for

171

something,—I didn't know what—which used to become almost unbearable when I danced or played any game in which a boy or man was near me. At the Paris school was a very pretty girl, named Ylette de Vespertin, who, for some reason I never could understand, took a fancy to me. She was two years older than I, had several brothers and boy cousins at home, and being up to every sort of lark and mischief, was just the girl I wanted as confidante. Of course she had no difficulty in explaining the whole thing to me, and in the course of a day or two, I knew everything there was to know. On the third day of our talks Ylette slipped a note into my hand as I was going up to bed. Now, Jack, you must really go and look out of the window while I tell you what it said:

' "Chérie,

Si tu veux te faire sucer la langue, les seins et le con, viens dans mon lit toute nue ce soir. C'est moi qui te ferai voir les anges.

Viens de suite à ton
Ylette." ' '

'I have rather a good memory, and even if I hadn't, I don't think I could ever forget the words of that note, for it was the beginning of a most delicious time for me.

'I suppose if I had been a well-regulated young person, I should have taken no notice of the invitation. As it was, I stripped myself naked in a brace of shakes, and flew to Ylette's bedroom which was next

172

door to the one I occupied. I had not realised before what a beautifully made girl she was. Her last garment was just slipping from her as I came in, and I stared in blank admiration at her naked figure which was like a statue in the perfection of its lines. A furious longing to touch it seized me, and springing upon her, I passed my hands feverishly up and down her naked body, until grasping me round the waist, she half dragged, half carried me to the bed, laid me on the edge of it, and kneeling upon the soft rug, plunged her head between my legs, and bringing her lips to bear full upon the *other* lips before her, parted them with a peculiar action of the mouth and inserted her tongue with a sudden stroke which sent perfect waves of delight through my whole body, followed by still greater ecstasy when she went for the particular spot *you* know of, Jack—the one near the top, I mean—and twisting her tongue over it, under it, round it and across it, soon brought about the result she wanted, and in her own expressive phrase "me faisait voir les anges".

'Of course I had no experience, but I did my best to repay her for the pleasures she had given me, and as I happen to possess an extremely long and pointed tongue, and Ylette's cunt—oh Jack, *I've said it at last!* Go and look out of the window again; or better still, come and stop my naughty mouth with—I *meant* your tongue, but this will do better still. The wicked monster, what a size he is! Now put both your hands behind my head, and push him in till he touches my throat. Imagine he is *somewhere else*, work like a demon, and for your life, don't stop until the very end of all things Ah! the dear, darling, delicious thing! How he throbs with excitement! I believe he can *see* my mouth waiting for him. Come, Jack, my darling, my beloved, let me gamahuche you. I want to feel this heavenly prick of yours between my lips and against my tongue, so that I may suck it and drain every drop that comes from it into my mouth. Now, Jack *now* . . .'

The red lips closed hungrily upon the object of their desire, the rosy tongue stretched itself amorously along the palpitating yard, and twice, the tide of love poured freely forth to be received with every sign of delight into the velvet mouth.

Nothing in my experience had ever approached the pleasure which I derived from the intoxicating contact of this young girl's lips and tongue upon my most sensitive parts, enhanced as it was by my love for her, which grew apace, and by her own intense delight in the adorable pastime. So keen indeed were the sensations she procured me that I was almost able to forget the deprivation laid upon me by Flossie's promise to her friend. Indeed, when I reflected upon her youth, and the unmatched beauty of her girlish shape with its slender waist, smooth satin belly and firm rounded breasts, the whole seemed too perfect a work of nature to be married—at least as yet—by the probable consequences of an act of coition carried to its logical conclusion by a pair of ardent lovers.

So I bent my head once more to its resting place between the snowy thighs, and again drew from my darling little mistress the fragrant treasures of love's sacred store house, lavished upon my clinging lips with gasps and sighs and all possible tokens of enjoyment in the giving.

After this it was time to part, and at Flossie's suggestion I undressed her, brushed our her silky hair and put her into bed. Lying on her white pillow, she looked so fair and like a child that I was for saying goodnight with just a single kiss upon her cheek. But this was not in accordance with her views on the subject. She sat up in bed, flung her arms round my neck, nestled her face against mine and whispered in my ear:

'I'll never give a promise again as long as I live.'

It was an awful moment and my resolution all but went down under the strain. But I just managed to resist, and after one prolonged embrace, during which Flossie's tongue went twining and twisting round my own with an indescribably lascivious motion, I planted a farewell kiss full upon the nipple of her left breast, sucked it for an instant and fled from the room.

On reaching my own quarters I lit a cigar and sat down to think over the extraordinary good fortune by which I had chanced upon this unique liaison. It was plain to me that in Flossie I had encountered probably the only specimen of her class. A girl of sixteen, with all the fresh charm of that beautiful age united to the fascination of a passionate and amorous woman. Add to these a finely-strung temperament, a keen sense of humour, and the true artist's striving after thoroughness in all she did, and it will be admitted that all these qualities meeting in a person of quite faultless beauty were enough to justify the self-congratulations with which I contemplated my present luck, and the rosy visions of pleasure to come which hung about my waking and sleeping senses till the morning.

About midday I called at the flat. The door was opened to me by Eva Letchford.

'I am so glad to see you,' she said. 'Flossie is out on her bicycle, and I can say what I want to.'

As she moved to the window to draw up the blind a little, I had a better opportunity of noticing what a really splendid-looking woman she had become. Observing my glances of frank admiration, she sat down in a low easy chair opposite to me, crossed her shapely legs, and looking over at me with a bright pleasant smile, said:

'Now, Jack—I may call you Jack, of course, because we are all three going to be great friends—you had my letter the other day. No doubt you thought it a strange document, but when we know one another better, you will easily understand how I came to write it.'

'My dear girl, I understand it already. You forget I have had several hours with Flossie. It was her happiness you wanted to secure, and I hope she will tell you our plan was successful.'

'Flossie and I have not secrets. She has told me everything that passed between you. She has also told me what did *not* pass between you, and how you did not even try to make her break her promise to me.'

'I should have been a brute if I had—'

'Then I am afraid nineteen men out of twenty are brutes—but that's neither here nor there. What I want you to know is that I appreciate your nice feeling, and that some day soon I shall with Flossie's consent take an opportunity of showing that appreciation in a practical way.'

Here she crossed her right foot high over the left knee and very leisurely removed an imaginary speck of dust from the shotsilk stocking.

'Now I must go and change my dress. You'll stay and lunch with us in the coffee room, won't you?—that's right. This is my bedroom. I'll leave the door open so that we can talk till Flossie comes. She promised to be in by one o'clock.

We chatted away on indifferent subjects whilst I watched with much satisfaction the operations of the toilette in the next room.

Presently a little cry of dismay reached me:

'Oh dear, oh dear! do come here a minute, Jack. I have pinched one of my breasts with my stays and made a little red mark. Look! *Do* you think it will show in evening dress?'

I examined the injury with all possible care and deliberation.

'My professional opinion is, madam, that as the mark is only an inch above the nipple we may fairly hope—'

'*Above* the nipple! then I'm afraid it will be a near thing,' said Eva with a merry laugh.

'Perhaps a little judicious stroking by an experienced hand might—'

'Naow then there, Naow then!' suddenly came from the door in a hoarse cockney accent.

'You jest let the lydy be, or oi'll give yer somethink to tyke' ome to yer dinner, see if oi don't!'

'Who is this person?' I asked of Eva, placing my hands upon her two breats as if to shield them from the intruder's eye.

'Person yerself!' said the voice, 'Fust thing *you've* a-got ter do is ter leave' old of my donah's breasties and then oi'll *tork* to yer!'

'But the lady has hurt herself, sir, and was consulting me professionally.'

There was a moment's pause, during which I had time to examine my opponent whom I found to be wearing a red Tam-o'-Shanter cap, a close fitting knitted silk blouse, a short white flannel skirt, and scarlet stockings. This charming figure threw itself upon me open-armed and open-mouthed and kissed me with delightful abandon

After a hearty laugh over the success of Flossie's latest 'impersonation', Eva pushed us both out of the room, saying. 'Take her away, Jack, and see if *she* has got any marks. Those bicycle saddles are rather trying sometimes. We will lunch in a quarter of an hour.'

I bore my darling little mistress away to her room, and having helped her to strip off her clothes, I inspected on my knees the region where the saddle might have been expected to gall her, but found nothing but a fair expanse of firm white bottom which I saluted with many lustful kisses upon every spot within reach of my tongue. Then I took her naked to the bathroom, and sponged her from neck to ankles, dried her thoroughly, just plunged my tongue once into her cunt, carried her back to her room, dressed her and presented her to Eva within twenty minutes of our leaving the latter's bedroom.

Below in the coffee-room, a capitally served luncheon awaited us. The table was laid in a sort of little annex to the principal room, and I was glad of the retirement, since we were able to enjoy to the full the constant flow of fun and mimicry with which Flossie brought tears of laughter to our eyes throughout the meal. Eva, too, was gifted with a fine sense of the ridiculous, and as I myself was at least an appreciative audience, the ball was kept rolling with plenty of spirit.

After lunch Eva announced her intention of going to a concert in Piccadilly, and a few minutes later Flossie and I were once more alone.

'Jack,' she said, 'I feel thoroughly and hopelessly naughty this afternoon. If you like I will go on with my story while you lie on the sofa and smoke a cigar.'

This exactly suited my views and I said so.

'Very well, then. First give me a great big kiss with all the tongue you've got about you. Ah! that was good! Now I'm going to sit on this footstool beside you, and I *think* one or two of these buttons might be unfastened, so that I can feel whether the story is producing any effect upon you. Good gracious! why, it's as hard and stiff as a poker already. I really *must* frig it a little—'

'Quite gently and slowly then, *please* Flossie, or—'

'Yes, quite, *quite* gently and slowly, so—Is that nice, Jack?'

'Nice is not the word, darling!'

'Talking of words, Jack, I am afraid I shall hardly be able to finish my adventures without occasionally using a word or two which you don't hear at a Sunday School Class. Do you mind, very much? Of course you can always go and look out of the window, can't you!'

'My dearest little sweetheart, when we are alone

together like this, and both feeling extremely naughty, as we do now, any and every word that comes from your dear lips sounds sweet and utterly void of offence to me.'

'Very well, then; that makes it ever so much easier to tell my story, and if I *should* become too shocking—well, you know how I love you to stop my mouth, don't you Jack!'

A responsive throb from my imprisoned member gave her all the answer she required.

'Let me see,' she began, 'where was I? Oh, I remember, in Ylette's bed.'

'Yes, she had gamahuched you, and you were just performing the same friendly office for her.'

'Of course: I was telling you how the length of my tongue made up for the shortness of my experience, or so Ylette was kind enough to say. I think she meant it too: at any rate she spent several times before I gave up my position between her legs. After this we tried the double gamahuche, which proved a great success because, although she was, as I have told you, older than I, we were almost exactly of a height, so that as she knelt over me, her cunt came quite naturally upon my mouth, and her mouth upon my cunt, and in this position we were able to give each other an enormous amount of pleasure.'

At this point I was obliged to beg Flossie to remove her right hand from the situation it was occupying.

'What I cannot understand about it,' she went

on, 'is that there are any number of girls in France, and a good many in England too, who after they have once been gamahuched by another girl don't care about anything else. Perhaps it means that they have never been really in love with a man, because to *me* one touch of your lips in that particular neighbourhood is worth ten thousand kisses from anybody else, male or female and when I have got your dear, darling, delicious prick in my mouth, I want nothing else in the whole wide world, except to give you the greatest possible amount of pleasure and to make you spend down my throat in the quickest possible time—'

'If you really want to beat the record, Flossie, I think there's a good chance now—'

Almost before the words had passed my lips the member in question was between *hers*, where it soon throbbed to the crisis in response to the indescribable sucking action of mouth and tongue of which she possessed the secret.

On my telling her how exquisite were the sensations she procured me by this means she replied:

'Oh, you have to thank Ylette for that! Just before we became friends she had gone for the long holidays to a country house belonging to a young couple who were great friends of hers. There was a very handsome boy of eighteen or so staying in the house. He fell desperately in love with Ylette and she with him, and he taught her

182

exactly how to gamahuche him so as to produce the utmost amount of pleasure. As she told me afterwards, 'Every day, every night, almost ever hour, he would bury his prick in my mouth, frig it against my tongue, and fill my throat with a divine flood. With a charming amiability, he worked incessantly to show me every kind of gamahuching, all the possible ways of sucking a man's prick. Nothing, said he, should be left to the imagination, which, he explained, can never produce such good results as a few practical lessons given in detail upon a real standing prick, plunged to the very root in the mouth of the girl pupil, to whom one can thus describe on the spot the various suckings, hard, soft, slow or quick, of which sit is essential she should know the precise effect in order to obtain the quickest and most copious flow of the perfumed liquor which she desires to draw from her lover.'

'I suppose,' Ylette went on, 'that one invariably likes what one can do well. Anyhow, my greatest pleasure in life is to suck a good-looking boys prick. If he likes to slip his tongue into my cunt at the same time, *tant mieux*.'

'Unfortunately this delightful boy could only stay a fortnight, but as there were several other young men of the party, and as her lover was wise enough to know that after his recent lessons in the art of love, Ylette could not be expected to be an abstainer, he begged her to enjoy herself in his absence, with the result, as she said that 'au bout d'une semaine il n'y avait pas un vit dans la maison qui ne m'avait tripoté la luette*, ni une langue qui n'était l'amie intime de mon con.'

'Every one of these instructions Ylette passed on to me, with practical illustrations upon my second finger standing as substitute for the real thing, which, of course, was not to be had in the school—at least not just then.

'She must have been an excellent teacher, for I have never had any other lessons than hers, and yours is the first and only staff of love that I have ever had the honour of gamahuching. However, I mean to make up now for lost time, for I would have you to know, my darling, that I am madly in love with every bit of your body, and that most of all do I adore your angel prick with its coral head that I so love to suck and plunge into my mouth. Come, Jack, come! let us have one more double gamahuche. One moment! There! Now I am naked. I am going to kneel over your face with my legs wide apart and my cunt kissing your mouth. Drive the whole of your tongue into it, won't you, Jack, and make it curl round my clitoris. Yes! that's it—just like that. Lovely! Now I can't talk any more, because I am going to fill my mouth with the whole of your darling prick; push; push it down my throat, Jack, and when the time comes, spend your very longest and most. I'm going to frig you a little first and rub you under your balls. Goodness! how the

* Uvula

184

dear thing is standing. In he goes now . . . m . . .
m . . . m . . . m . . . m . . . m . . .

A few inarticulate gasps and groans of
pleasure were the only sounds audible for some
minutes during which each strove to render the
sensations of the other as acute as possible. I can
answer for it that Flossie's success was complete,
and by the convulsive movements of her bottom
and the difficulty I experienced in keeping the
position of my tongue upon her palpitating
clitoris, I gathered that my operations had not
altogether failed in their object. In this I was
confirmed by the copious and protracted
discharge which the beloved cunt delivered into
my throat at the same instant as the
incomparable mouth received my yard to the
very root, and a perfect torrent rewarded her
delicious efforts for my enjoyment.

'Ah, Jack! that was just heavenly,' she sighed,
as she rose from her charming position. '*How*
you did spend, that time, you darling old boy,
and so did I, eh, Jack?'

'My little angel, I thought you would never
have finished,' I replied.

'Do you know, Jack, I believe you really did
get a little way down my throat, then! At any rate
you managed the 'tripotage de luette' that
Ylette's friend recommended so strongly!'

'And I don't think I ever got quite so far into
your cunt, Flossie.'

'That's quite true; I felt your tongue touch a

spot it had never reached before. And just wasn't it lovely when you got there! It almost makes me spend again to think of it! But I am not going to be naughty any more. And to show you how truly virtuous I am feeling, I'll continue my story if you like. I want to get on with it, because I know you must be wondering all the time how a person of my age can have come to be so . . . what shall we say, Jack?'

'Larky,' I suggested.

'Yes, "larky" will do. Of course I have always been "older than my age" as the saying goes, and my friendship with Ylette and all the lovely things she used to do to me made me "come on" much faster than most girls. I ought to tell you that I got to be rather a favourite at school, and after it came to be known that Ylette and I were on gamahuching terms, I used to get little notes from lots of other girls in the school imploring me to sleep with them. One dear thing even went so far as to give me the measurements of her tongue, which she had taken with a piece of string.'

'Oh, I say, Flossie, *come now*—I can swallow a good deal but—'

'You can indeed, Jack, as I have good reason to know! But all the same it's absolutely true. You can't have any conception what French school-girls of sixteen are like. There is nothing they won't do to get themselves gamahuched, and if a girl is pretty or fascinating or has particularly

186

good legs, or specially large breasts, she may, if she likes, have a fresh admirer's head under her petticoats every day of the week. Of course, it's all very wrong and dreadful, I know, but what else can you expect? In Franc gamahuching between grown-up men and women is a recognised thing—'

'Not only in France, *nowadays*,' I put in.

'So I have heard. But at any rate in France everybody does it. Girls at school naturally know this, as they know most things. At that time of life—at *my* time of life, if you like—a girl thinks and dreams of nothing else. She cannot, except by some extraordinary luck, find herself alone with a boy or man. One day her girl chum at school pops her head under her petticoats and gamahuches her deliciously. How can you wonder if from that moment she is ready to go through fire and water to obtain the same pleasure?'

'Go on, Flossie. You are simply delicious today!'

'Don't laugh, Jack. I am very serious about it. I don't care how much a girl of (say) my age longs for a boy to be naughty with—it's perfectly right and natural. What I think is bad is that she should *begin* by having a liking for a girl's tongue inculcated into her. I should like to see boys and girls turned loose upon one another once a week or so at authorised gamahuching parties, which should be attended by masters and governesses (who would have to see that the *other* thing was not indulged in, of course). Then the girls would grow up with a good healthy taste for the other sex, and even if they did do a little gamahuching amongst themselves beween whiles, it would only be to keep themselves going till the next 'party'. By my plan a boy's prick would be the central object of their desires, as it ought to be. Now *I* think that's a very fine scheme, Jack, and as soon as I am a little older, I shall go to Paris and put it before the Minister of Education!'

'But why wait, Flossie? Why not go now?'

'Well, you see, if the old gentleman (I suppose he is old, isn't he, or he wouldn't be a minister?)—if he saw a girl in short frocks, he would think she had got some private object to serve in regard to the gamahuching parties. Whereas a grown-up person who had plainly left school might be supposed to be doing it unselfishly for the good of the rising generation.'

'Yes, I understand that. But when you *do* go, Flossie, please take me or some other respectable person with you, because I don't altogether trust that Minister of Education and whatever the length of your frocks might happen to be at the time, I feel certain that, old or young, the moment you had explained your noble scheme, he would be wanting some practical illustrations on the office armchair!'

'How dare you suggest such a thing, Jack!

You are to understand, sir, that from henceforth my mouth is reserved for three purposes, to eat with, to talk with, and to kiss you with on whatever part of your person I may happen to fancy at the moment. By the way, you won't mind my making just one exception in favour of Eva, will you? She loves me to make her nipples stand with my tongue; occasionally, too, we perform the "*soixant neuf*".'

'When the next performance takes place, may I be there to see?' I ejaculated fervently.

'Oh, Jack, how shocking!'

'Does it shock you, Flossie? Very well, then I withdraw it, and apologise.'

'You cannot withdraw it now. You have distinctly stated that you would like to be there when Eva and I have our next gamahuche.'

'Well, I suppose I *did* say.'

'Silence, sir,' said Flossie in a voice of thunder, and shaking her brown head at me with inexpressible ferocity. 'You have made a proposal of the most indecent character, and the sentence of the Court is that, at the first possible opportunity, you shall be *held to that proposal*! Meanwhile the Count condemns you to receive 250 kisses on various parts of your body, which it will at once proceed to administer. Now, sir, off with your clothes!'

'Mayn't I keep my . . .'

'No, sir, you may *not*!'

The sentence of the Court was accordingly

189

carried out to the letter, somewhere about three-fourths of the kisses being applied upon one and the same part of the prisoner to which the Court attached its mouth with extraordinary gusto.

CHAPTER THREE

Nox Ambrosiana

My intercourse with the tenants of the flat became daily more intimate and more frequent. My love for Flossie grew intensely deep and strong as opportunities increased for observing the rare sweetness and amiability of her character, and the charm which breathed like a spell over everything she said and did. At one moment, so great was her tact and so keen her judgment, I would find myself consulting her on a knotty point with the certainty of getting sound advice; at another the child in her would suddenly break out and she would romp and play about like the veriest kitten. Then there would be yet another reaction, and without a word of warning, she would become amorous and caressing and seizing upon her favourite plaything, would push it into her mouth and suck it in a perfect frenzy of erotic passion. It is hardly necessary to say that these contrasts of mood lent an infinite zest to our liaison and I had almost ceased to long for its more perfect consummation. But one warm June evening, allusion was again made to the subject by Flossie, who repeated her sorrow for the deprivation she declared I must be feeling so greatly.

I assured her that it was not so.

'Well, Jack, if you aren't, *I* am,' she cried. 'And what is more there is someone else who is "considerably likewise" as our old gardener used to say.'

'What *do* you mean, child?'

She darted into the next room and came back almost directly.

'Sit down there and listen to me. In that room, lying asleep on her bed, is the person whom, after you, I love best in the world. There is nothing I wouldn't do for her, and I'm sure you'll believe this when I tell you that I am going to beg you on my knees, to go in there and do to Eva what my promise to her prevents me from letting you do to me. Now, Jack, I know you love me and you know *dearly* I love you. Nothing can alter *that*. Well, Jack, if you will go into Eva, gamahuche her well and let her gamahuche you (she *adores* it), and then have her thoroughly and in all positions—I shall simply love you a thousand times better than ever.'

'But Flossie, my darling, Eva doesn't—'

'Oh, doesn't she! Wait till you get between her legs, and see! Come along: I'll just put you inside the room and then leave you. She is lying outside her bed for coolness—on her side. Lie down quietly *behind* her. She will be almost sure to think it's me, and perhaps you will hear—something interesting. Quick's the word! Come!'

The sight which met my eyes on entering Eva's bedroom was enough to take one's breath away. She lay on her side, with her face towards the door, stark naked, and fast asleep. I crept noiselessly towards her and gazed upon her glorious nudity in speechless delight. Her dark hair fell in a cloud about her white shoulders. Her fine face was slightly flushed, the full red lips a little parted. Below, the gleaming breasts caught the light from the shaded lamp at her bedside, the pink nipples rising and falling to the time of her quiet breathing. One fair round arm was behind her head, the other lay along the exquisitvely turned thigh. The good St Anthony might have been pardoned for owning himself defeated by such a picture!

As is usual with a sleeping person who is being looked at, Eva stirred a little, and her lips opened as if to speak. I moved on tiptoe to the other side of the bed, and stripping myself naked, lay down beside her.

Then, without turning round, a sleepy voice said, 'Ah, Flossie, are you there? What have you done with jack? (*a pause*). When are you going to lend him to me for a night, Flossie? I wish I'd

193

got him here now, between my legs—betwe-e-e-n m-y-y-y- le-egs! Oh dear! how randy I do feel tonight. When I *do* have Jack for a night, Flossie, may I take his prick in my mouth before we do the other thing? Flossie—Floss*ee*—why don't you answer? Little darling! I expect she's tired out, and no wonder! Well, I suppose I'd better put something on me and go to sleep too!'

As she raised herself from the pillow, her hand came in contact with my person.

'Angels and Ministers of Grace defend us! What's this? *You*, Jack! *And you've heard what I've been saying?*'

'I'm afraid I have, Eva.'

'Well, it doesn't matter: I meant it all, and more besides! Now before I do anything else I simply must run in and kiss that darling Floss for sending you to me. It is just like her, and I can't say anything stronger than *that*!'

'Jack,' she said on coming back to the room. 'I warn you that you are going to have a stormy night. In the matter of love, I've gone starving for many months. Tonight I'm fairly roused, and when in that state, I believe I am about the most erotic bedfellow to be found anywhere. Flossie has given me leave to *say* and *do* anything and everything to you, and I mean to use the permission for all its worth. Flossie tells me that you are an absolutely perfect gamahucher. Now I adore being gamahuched. Will you do that for me, Jack?'

'My dear girl, I should rather think so!'

'Good! But it is not to be all on one side. I shall gamahuche you, too, and you will have to own that I know something of the art. Another thing you may perhaps like to try is what the French call "*fouterie aux seins*".'

'I know all about it, and if I may insert monsieur Jacques between those magnificent breasts of yours, I shall die of the pleasure.'

'Good again. Now we come to the legitimate drama, from which you and Floss have so nobly abstained. I desire to be thoroughly and comprehensively fucked tonight—sorry to have to use the word, Jack, but it is the only one that expresses my meaning.'

'Don't apologise, dear. Under present circumstances all words are allowable.'

'Glad to hear you say that, because it makes conversation so much easier. Now let me take hold of your prick, and frig it a little, so that I may judge what size it attains in full erection. So! he's a fine boy, and I think he will fit my cunt to a turn. I must kiss his pretty head, it looks so tempting. Ah! delicious! See here Jack, I will lie back with my head on the pillow, and you shall just come and kneel over me and have me in the mouth. Push away gaily, just as if you were fucking me, and when you are going to spend, slip one hand under my neck and drive your prick down my throat, and do not *dare* to withdraw it until I have received all you have to give me.

195

Sit upon my chest first for a minute and let me tickle your prick with the nipples of my breasts. Is that nice? Ah! I knew you would like it! *Now* kneel up to my face, and I will suck you.'

With eagerly pouting lips and clutching fingers, she seized upon my straining hard, and pressed it into her soft mouth. Arrived there, it was saluted by the velvet tongue which twined itself about the nut in a thousand lascivious motions.

Mindful of Eva's instructions, I began to work the instrument as if it was in another place. At once she laid her hands upon my buttocks and regulated the time of my movements, assisting them by a corresponding action of her head. Once, owing to carelessness on my part, her lips lost their hold altogether; with a little cry, she caught my prick in her fingers and in an instant, it was again between her lips and revelling in the adorable pleasure of their sucking.

A moment later and my hands were under her neck, for the signal, and my very soul seemed to be exhaled from me in response to the clinging of her mouth as she felt my prick throb with the passage of love's torrent.

After a minute's rest, and a word of gratitude for the transcendent pleasure she had given me, I began a tour of kisses over the enchanting regions which lay between her neck and her knees, ending with a protracted sojourn in the last, she said:

'Please to begin by passing your tongue slowly round the edges of the lips, then thrust it into the lower part at full length and keep it there working it in and out for a little. Then move it gradually up to the top and when there, press your tongue firmly against my clitoris a minute or so. Next take the clitoris between your lips and suck it *furiously*, bite it gently, and slip the point of your tongue underneath it. When I have spent twice, which I am sure to do in the first three minutes, get up and lie between my legs, drive the whole of your tongue into my mouth and the whole of your prick into my cunt, and fuck me with all your might and main!'

I could not resist a smile at the naiveté of these circumstantial directions. My amusement was not lost upon Eva, who hastened to explain, by reminding me again that it was 'ages' since she had been touched by a man. 'In gamahuching,' she said, 'the *details* are everything. In copulation they are not so important, since the principal things that increase one's enjoyment—such as the quickening of the stroke towards the end by the man, and the knowing exactly how and when to applying the *nipping* action of the cunt by the woman—come more or less naturally, especially with practice. But now, Jack, I want to be gamahuched, please.'

'And I'm longing to be at you, dear. Come and kneel astride of me, and let me kiss your cunt without any more delay.'

Eva was pleased to approve of this position and in another moment, I was slipping my tongue into the delicious cavity which opened wider and wider to receive its caresses, and to enable it to plunge further and further into the perfumed depths. My attentions were next turned to the finely developed clitoris which I found to be extraordinarily sensitive. In fact, Eva's own time limit of three minutes had not been reached, when the second effusion escaped her, and a third was easily obtained by a very few more strokes of the tongue. After this, she laid herself upon her back, drew me towards her and, taking hold of my prick, placed it tenderly between her breasts, and pressing them together with her hands, urged me to enjoy myself in this enchanting position. The length and stiffness imported to my member by the warmth and softness of her breasts delighted her beyond measure, and she implored me to fuck her without any further delay. I was never more ready or better furnished than at that moment, and after she had once more taken my prick into her mouth for a moment, I slipped down to the desired position between her thighs which she had already parted to their uttermost to receive me. In an instant she had guided the staff of love to the exact spot, and with a heave of her bottom, aided by an answering thrust from me, had buried it to the root within the soft down of its natural covering.

Eva's description of herself as an erotic bedfellow had hardly prepared me for the joys I was to experience in her arms. From the moment the nut of my yard touched her womb, she became as one possessed. Her eyes were turned heavenwards, her tongue twined round my own in rapture, her hands played about my body, now clasping my neck, now working feverishly up and down my back, and ever and again, creeping down to her lower parts where her first and second finger would rest compass-shaped upon the two edges of her cunt, pressing themselves upon my prick as it glided in and out and adding still further to the maddening pleasure I was undergoing. Her breath came in short quick gasps, the calves of her legs sometimes lay upon my own but more often were locked over my loins or buttocks, thus enabling her to time to a nicety the strokes of my body, and to respond with accurately judged thrusts from her own splendid bottom. At last a low musical cry came from her parted lips, she strained me to her naked body with redoubled fury and driving the whole length of her tongue into my mouth, she spent long and deliciously, whilst I flooded her clinging cunt with a torrent of unparalleled volume and duration.

'Jack,' she whispered, 'I have never enjoyed anything half so much in my life before. I hope you liked it too?'

'I don't think you can expect anyone to say

that he "liked" fucking *you*, Eva! One might "like" kissing your hand, or helping you on with an opera cloak or some minor pleasure of that sort. But to lie between a pair of legs like yours, cushioned on a pair of breasts like yours, with a tongue like yours down one's throat, and one's price held in the soft grip of a cunt like yours, is to undergo a series of sensations such as don't come twice in a lifetime.'

Eva's eyes flashed as she gathered me closer in her naked arms and said:

'*Don't* they, though! In this particular instance I am going to see that they come twice *within half an hour!*'

'Well, I've come twice in less than half an hour and—'

'Oh! I know what you are going to say, but we'll soon put that all right.'

A careful examination of the state of affairs was then made by Eva who bent her pretty head for the purpose, kneeling on the bed in a position which enabled me to gaze at my leisure upon all her secret charms.

Her operations meanwhile were causing me exquisite delight. With an indescribable tenderness of action, soft and caressing as that of a young mother tending her sick child, she slipped the fingers of her left hand under my balls while the other hand wandered luxuriously over the surrounding country and finally came to an anchor upon my prick, which not unnaturally began to show signs of returning vigour. Pleased at the patient's improved state of health, she passed her delicious velvet tongue up and down and round and into a standing position! This sudden and satisfactory result of her ministrations so excited her that, without letting go of her prisoner, she cleverly passed one leg over me as I lay, and behold us in the traditional attitude of the *gamahuche a deux*! I now, for the first time, looked upon Eva's cunt in its full beauty, and I gladly devoted a moment to the inspection before plunging my tongue between the rich red lips which seemed to kiss my mouth as it clung in ecstasy in their luscious folds. I may say here that in point of colour, proportion and beauty of outline, Eva Letchford's cunt was the most perfect I had ever seen or gamahuched, though in after years my darling little Flossie's displayed equal faultlessness, and, as being the cunt of my beloved little sweetheart, whom I adored, it was entitled to and received from me a degree of homage never accorded to any other before or since.

The particular part of my person to which Eva was paying attention soon attained in her mouth a size and hardness which did the highest credit to her skill. With my tongue revelling in its enchanted resting-place, and my prick occupying what a house-agent might truthfully describe as 'this most desirable site,' I was personally content to remain as we were, whilst Eva, entirely abandoning herself to her charming occupation, had apparently forgotten the object with which she had originally undertaken it. Fearing therefore lest the clinging mouth and delicately twining tongue should bring about the crisis which Eva had designed should take place elsewhere, I reluctantly took my lips from the clitoris they were enclosing at the moment, and called to its owner to stop.

'But Jack, you're just going to spend!' was the plaintive reply.

'Exactly, dear! And how about the "twice in half an hour".'

'Oh! of course. You were going to fuck me again, weren't you! Well, you'll find Massa Johnson in pretty good trim for the fray,' and she laughingly held up my prick, which was really of enormous dimensions, and plunging it downwards let it rebound with a loud report against my belly.

This appeared to delight her, for she repeated it several times. Each time the elasticity seemed to increase and the force of the recoil to become greater.

'The darling!' she cried, as she kissed the coral head. 'He is going to his own chosen abiding place. Come! Come! Come! blessed, *blessed* prick. Bury yourself in this loving cunt which longs for you; frig yourself deliciously against the lips which wait to kiss you; plunge into the womb which yearns to receive your life-giving seed; pause as you go by to press the clitoris that loves you. Come, divine, adorable prick! fuck me, fuck me, fuck me! fuck me long and hard: fuck and spare not!—Jack, you are into me, my cunt clings to your prick, do you feel how it nips you? Push, Jack, further; now your balls are kissing my bottom. That's lovely! Crush my breasts with your chest, *cr-r-r-r-ush* them, Jack. Now go slowly a moment, and let your prick gently rub my clitoris. So . . . o . . . o . . . Now faster and harder . . . faster still—now your tongue in my mouth, and dig your nails into my bottom. I'm going to spend: fuck, Jack, fuck me, fuck me, fu-u-u-uck me! Heavens! what bliss it is! Ah you're spending too. Bo . . . o . . . o . . . oth together, both toge . . . e . . . e . . . ther. Pour it into me, Jack! Flood me, drown me, fill my womb. God! What rapture. Don't stop. Your prick is still hard and long. Drive it into me—touch my navel. Let me get my hand down to frig you as you go in and out. The sweet prick! He's stiffer than ever. How splendid of him! Fuck me again, Jack, Ah! fuck me till tomorrow, fuck me till I die.'

I fear that this language in the cold form of print may seem more than a little crude. Yet those who have experience of a beautiful and refined woman, abandoning herself in moments of passion to similar freedom of speech, will own the stimulus thus given to the sexual powers. In the present instance its affect, joined to the lascivious touches and never ceasing efforts to arouse and increase desire of this deliciously lustful girl, was to impart an unprecedented stiffness to my member which throbbed almost to bursting within the enclosing cunt and pursued its triumphant career to such lengths, that even the resources of the insatiable Eva gave out at last, and she lay panting in my arms, where soon afterwards she passed into a quiet sleep. Drawing a silken coverlet over her, I rose with great caution, slipped on my clothes, and in five minutes was on my way home.

CHAPTER FOUR

More of Flossie's school-life; and other matters

'Good morning, Captain Archer, I trust that you have slept well?' said Flossie on my presenting myself at the flat early the next day. 'My friend Miss Letchford,' she went on, in a prim middle-aged tone of voice, 'has not yet left her apartment. She complains of having passed a somewhat disturbed night owing to—ahem!'

'Rats in the wainscot?' I suggested.

'No, my friend attributes her sleepless condition to a severe irritation in the—forgive the immodesty of my words—lower part of her person, followed by a prolonged pricking in the same region. She is still feeling the effects, and I found her violently clasping a pillow between her—ahem!—legs, with which she was apparently endeavouring to soothe her feelings.'

'Dear me! Miss Eversley, do you think I could be of any assistance?' (*stepping towards Eva's door.*)

'You are *most* kind, Captain Archer, but I have already done what I could in the way of friction and—other little attentions, which left the poor sufferer somewhat calmer. Now, Jack, you wretch! you haven't kissed me yet . . . That's better! You will not be surprised to hear that Eva has given me a full and detailed description of her sleepless night, in her own language, which I have no doubt you have discovered, is just a bit *graphic* at times.'

'Well, my litte darling, I did my best, as I knew you would wish me to do. It wasn't difficult with such a bed-fellow as Eva. But charming and amorous as she is, I couldn't help feeling all the time "if it were only my little Flossie lying under me now!" By the way how utterly lovely you are this morning, Floss.'

She was dressed in a short sprigged cotton frock, falling very little below her knees, shot pink and black stockings, and low patent leather shoes with silver buckles. Her long waving brown hair gleamed gold in the morning light, and the deep blue eyes glowed with health and love, and now and again flashed with merriment. I gazed upon her in rapture at her beauty.

'Do you like my frock, Jack? I'm glad. It's the first time I've had it on. It's part of my trousseau.'

'Your *what*, Flossie?' I shouted.

'I said my trousseau,' she repeated quietly, but with sparks of fun dancing in her sweet eyes.

'The fact is, Jack, Eva declared the other day that though I am not married to you, you and I are really on a sort of honeymoon. So, as I have just had a good lot of money from the lawyers, she made me go with her and buy everything new. Look here,' (*unfastening her bodice*) 'new stays, new chemise, new stockings and oh! Jack, *look!* such *lovely* new drawers—none of your horrid vulgar knickerbockers, trimmings and lovely little tucks all the way up, and quite wide open in front for . . . ventilation I suppose! Feel what soft stuff they are made of! Eva was awfully particular about these drawers. She is always so practical, you know.'

'Practical!' I interrupted.

'Yes. What she said was that you would often be wanting to kiss me between my legs when there wasn't time to undress and be naked together, so that I must have drawers made of the finest and most delicate stuff to please you, and with the opening cut extra wide so as not to get in the way of your tongue! Now don't you call that practical?'

'I do indeed! Blessed Eva, that's another good turn I owe her!'

'Well, for instance, there isn't time to undress *now*, Jack and—'

She threw herself back in her chair and in an instant, I had plunged under the short rose-scented petticoats and had my mouth glued to the beloved cunt once more. In the midst of the

delicious operation, I fancied I heard a slight
sound from the direction of Eva's door and just
then, Flossie locked her hands behind my head
and pressed me to her with even more than her
usual ardour; a moment later deluging my throat
with the perfumed essence of her being.

'You darling old boy, how you *did* make me
spend that time! I really think your tongue is
longer than it was. Perhaps the warmth of Eva's
interior has made it grow! Now I must be off to
the dressmaker's for an hour or so. By the way,
she wants to make my frocks longer. She declares
people can see my drawers when I run upstairs.

'Don't you let her do it, Floss.'

'*Rather not!* What's the use of buying
expensive drawers like mine if you can't show
them to a pal! *Good* morning, Captain! Sorry I
can't stop. While I'm gone you might just step in
and see how my lydy friend's gettin' on. Fust
door on the right. *Good* morning!'

For a minute or two, I lay back in my chair
and wondered whether I would not take my hat
and go. But a moment's further reflection told
me that I must do as Flossie directed me. To this
decision, I must own, the memory of last night's
pleasure and the present demands of a most
surprising erection contributed in no small
degree. Accordingly, I tapped at Eva's bedroom
door.

She had just come from her bath and wore
only a peignoir and her stockings. On seeing me,

she at once let fall her garment and stood before me in radiant nakedness.

'Look at this,' she said, holding out a half-sheet of notepaper. 'I found it on my pillow when I woke an hour ago:

'If Jack comes this morning I shall send him in to see you while I go to Virginie's. Let him—*anything beginning with "f" or "s" that rhymes with* luck—you. "A hair of the dog" etc., will do you both good. My time will come. Ha! Ha!

Floss.'

'Now I ask you, Jack, was there ever such an adorable little darling?'

My answer need not be recorded.

Eva came close to me and thrust her hand inside my clothes.

'Ah! I see you are of the same way of thinking as myself,' she said taking hold of my fingers and carrying them on her cunt, which pouted hungrily. 'So let us have one good royal fuck and then you can stay here with me while I dress, and I'll tell you anything that Flossie may have left out about her school-life in Paris. Will that meet your views?'

'Exactly,' I replied.

'Very well then. As we are going to limit ourselves to *one*, would you mind fucking me *en levrette*?'

'Any way you like, most puissant and fucksome of ladies!'

I stripped off my clothes in a twinkling and Eva placed herself in position, standing on the rug and bending forwards with her elbows on the bed. I reverently saluted the charms thus presented to my lips, omitting none, and then rising from my knees, advanced, weapon in hand, to storm the breach. As I approached, Eva opened her legs to their widest extent, and I drove my straining prick into the mellow cunt, fucking it with unprecedented vigour and delight, as the lips alternately parted and contracted, nipping me with an extraordinary force in response to the pressure of my right forefinger upon the clitoris and of my left upon the nipples of the heaving breasts. Keen as was the enjoyment we were both experiencing, the fuck—as invariably the case with a morning performance—was of very protracted duration, and several minutes had elapsed before I dropped my arms to Eva's thighs and, with my belly glued against her bottom and my face nestling bnetween her shoulder blades, felt the rapturous throbbing of my prick as it discharged an avalanche into the innermost recesses of her womb.

'Don't move, Jack, for Heaven's sake,' she cried.

'Don't want to, Eva, I'm quite happy where I am, thank you!'

210

Moving an inch or two further out from the bed so as to give herself more 'play', she started an incredibly provoking motion of her bottom, so skilfully executed that it produced the impression of being almost *spiral*. The action is difficult to describe, but her bottom rose and fell, moved backward and forward, and from side to side in quick alternation, the result being that my member was constantly in contact with, as it were, some fresh portion of the embracing cunt, the soft folds of which seemed by their varied and tender caresses to be pleading to him to emerge from his present state of partial apathy and resume the proud condition he had displayed before.

'Will he come up this way, Jack, or shall I take the dear little man in my mouth and suck him into an erection?'

'I think he'll be all right as he is, dear. Just keep on nipping him with your cunt and push your bottom a little closer to me so that I may feel your naked flesh against mine . . . *that's* it'

'Ah! the darling prick, he's beginning to swell! He's going to fuck me directly, I know he is! Your finger on my cunt in front, please Jack, and the other hand on my nipples. So! *that's* nice. Oh dear! How I *do* want your tongue in my mouth, but that can't be. Now begin and fuck me slowly at first. Your *second* finger on my clitoris, please, and frig me in time to the motion of your body. Now fuck faster a little, and deeper into me. Push, dear, push like a demon. Pinch my nipple; a little faster on the clitoris. I'm spending! I'm dying of delight! Fuck me, Jack, keep on fucking me. Don't be afraid. Strike against my bottom with all your strength, harder still, harder! Now put your hands down to my thighs and *drag* me on to you. Lovely! grip the flesh of my thighs with your fingers and fuck me to the very womb.'

'Eva, look out! I'm going to spend!'

'So am I, Jack. Ah! how your prick throbs against my cunt! Fuck me, Jack, to the last moment, spend your last drop, as I'm doing. One last push up to the hilt—there, keep him in like that and let me have a deluge from you. How exquisite! how adorable to spend together! *One* moment more before you take him out, and let me kiss him with my cunt before I say goodbye.'

'What a nip that was, Eva, it felt more like a hand on me than a—'

'Yes,' she interrupted, turning round and facing me with her eyes languorous and velvety with lust, 'that is my only accomplishment, and I must say I think it's a valuable one! In Paris I had a friend—but no matter I'm not going to talk about myself, but about Flossie. Sit down in that chair, and have a cigarette while I talk to you. I'm going to stay naked if you don't mind. It's so hot. Now if you're quite comfy, I'll begin.'

She seated herself opposite to me, her splendid

212

naked body full in the light from the window near her.

'There is a part of Flossie's school story,' began Eva, 'which she has rather shrunk from telling you, and so I propose to relate the incident, in which I am sure you will be sufficiently interested. For the first twelve months of her school days in Paris, nothing very special occurred beyond the cementing of her friendship with Ylette Vespertin. Flossie was a tremendous favourite with the other girls on account of her sweet nature and her extraordinary beauty, and there is no doubt that a great many curly heads were popped under her petticoats at one time and another. All these heads, however, belonged to her own sex, and no great harm was done. But at last there arrived at the convent a certain Camille de Losgrain, who, though by no means averse to the delights of gamahuche, nursed a strong preferance for male, as against female charms. Camille speedily struck up an alliance with a handsome boy of seventeen who lived in the house next door. This youth had often seen Flossie and greatly desired her acquaintance. It seems that his bedroom window was on the same level as that of the room occupied by Flossie, Camille and three other girls, all of whom knew him by sight and had severally expressed a desire to have him between their legs. So it was arranged one night that he was to climb on to a buttress below his room, and the girls would manage to haul him into theirs. All this had to be done in darkness, as of course no light could be shown. The young gentleman duly arrived on the scene in safety—the two eldest girls divested him of his clothes, and then, according to previous agreement, the five damsels sat naked on the edge of the bed in the pitch dark room, and Master Don Juan was to decide, by passing his hands over their bodies, which of the five should be favoured with his attentions. No one was to speak, to touch his person or to make any sign of interest. Twice the youth essayed this novel kind of ordeal by touch, and after a moment's profound silence he said, 'J'ai choisi, c'est la troisieme.' 'La troisieme' was no other than Flossie, the size of whose breasts had at once attracted him as well as given a clue to her identity. And now, Jack, I hope the sequel will not distress you. The other girls accepted the decision most loyally, having no doubt anticipated it. They laid Flossie tenderly on the bed and lavished every kind of caress upon her, gamahuching her with especial tenderness, so as to open the road as far as possible to the invader. It fortunately turned out to be the case that the boy's prick was not by any means of abnormal size, and as the dear little maidenhead had been already subjected to very considerable wear and tear of fingers and tongues the entrance was, as she told me herself, effected with a minimum of pain and discomfort, hardly felt indeed in the midst of the frantic kisses upon mouth, eyes, nipples, breasts and buttocks which the four excited girls rained upon her throughout the operation. As for the boy, his enjoyment knew no bounds, and when his allotted time was up could hardly be persuaded to make the return voyage to his room. This, however, was at last accomplished, and the four virgins hastened to hear from their ravished friend the full true and particular account of her sensations. For several nights after this, the boy made his appearance in the room, where he fucked all the other four in succession, and pined openly for Flossie, who, however, regarded him as belonging to Camille and declined anything beyond the occasional service of his tongue which she greatly relished and which he, of course, as gladly put at her disposal.

'All this happened just before my time and was related to me afterwards by Flossie herself. Then I was engaged to teach English at the convent. Like everyone else who is brought in contact with her, I at once fell in love with Flossie and we quickly became the greatest of friends. Six months ago, came a change of fortune for me, an old bachelor uncle dying suddenly and leaving me a competence. By this time, the attachment between Flossie and myself had become so deep that the child could not bear the thought of parting from me. I too was glad enough of the excuse thus given for writing to Flossie's guardian—

who has never taken more than a casual interest in her—to propose her returning to England with me and the establishment of a joint menage. My 'references' being satisfactory, and Flossie having declared herself to be most anxious for the plan, the guardian made no objection and in short—here we are!'

'Well, that's a very interesting story, Eva. Only—*confound* that French boy and his buttress!'

'Yes, you would naturally feel like that about it, and I don't blame you. Only you must remember that if it hadn't been for the size of Flossie's breasts, and its being done in the dark, and . . .'

'But Eva, you don't mean to tell me the young brute wouldn't have chosen her out of the five if there had been a *light*, do you!'

'No, of course not. What I *do* mean is that it was all a sort of fluke, and that Flossie is really, to all intents and purposes . . .'

'Yes, yes, I know what you would like to say, and I entirely and absolutely agree with you. I *love* Flossie with all my heart and soul and . . . well, that French boy can go to the devil!'

'Miss Eva! Miss Eva!' came a voice outside the door.

'Well, what is it?'

'Oh, if you please, Miss, there's a young man downstairs called for his little account. Says 'e's the coals, Miss. I *towld* him you was engaged, Miss.'

'Did you—and what did he say?'

'"Ow!" 'e sez, "engyged, *is* she," 'e sez—"well, you tell 'er from me confidential-like, as it's 'igh time she was *married*," 'e sez!'

Our shouts of laughter brought Flossie scampering into the room, evidently in the wildest spirits.

'Horful scandal in 'igh life,' she shouted. 'A genl'man dish-covered in a lydy's aportments! 'arrowin' details. Speshul! Pyper! Speshul!—Now then, you two, what have you been doing while I've been gone? Suppose you tell me exactly what you've done and I'll tell you exactly what *I've* done!'—then in a tone of cheap melodrama—'Aha'? 'ave I surproised yer guilty secret? She winceth! Likewise 'e winceth! in fact they both winceth! Thus h'am I avenged upon the pair!' And kneeling down between us, she pushed a dainty finger softly between the lips of Eva's cunt, and with her other hand took hold of my yard and tenderly frigged it, looking up into our faces all the time with inexpressible love and sweetness shining from her eyes.

'You *dears*!' she said. 'It *is* nice to have you two naked together like this!'

A single glance passed between Eva and me, and getting up from our seats we flung ourselves upon the darling and smothered her with kisses. Then Eva, with infinite gentleness and many loving touches, proceeded to undress her, handing the dainty garments to me one by one to be laid on the bed near me. As the fair white breasts came forth from the corset, Eva gave a little cry of delight, and pushing the lace-edged chemise below the swelling globes, took one erect and rosy nipple into her mouth, and putting her hand behind my neck, motioned me to take the other. Shivers of delight coursed up and down the shapely body over which our fingers roamed in all directions. Flossie's remaining garments were soon allowed to fall by a deft touch from Eva, and the beautiful girl stood before us in all her radiant nakedness. We paused a moment to gaze upon the spectacle of loveliness. The fair face flushed with love and desire; the violet eyes shone; the full rounded breasts put forth their coral nipples as if craving to be kissed again; below the smooth satin belly appeared the silken tuft that shaded without concealing the red lips of the adorable cunt; the polished thighs gained added whiteness by contrast with the dark stockings which clung amorously to the finely moulded legs.

'Now, Jack, *both together*,' said Eva, suddenly.

I divined what she meant and arranging a couple of large cushions on the wide divan, I took Flossie in my arms and laid her upon them, her feet upon the floor. Her legs opened instinctively and thrusting my head between her thighs, I plunged my tongue into the lower part of the cunt, whilst Eva, kneeling over her, upon the divan, attacked the developed clitoris. Our mouths thus met upon the exchanted spot and our tongues filled every corner and crevice of it. My own, I must admit, occasionally wandered downwards to the adjacent regions, and explored the valley of delight in that direction. But wherever we went and whatever we did, the lithe young body beneath continued to quiver from head to foot with excess of pleasure, shedding its treasures now in Eva's mouth, now in mine and sometimes in both at once! But vivid as were the delights she was experiencing, they were of a passive kind only, and Flossie was already artist enough to know that the keenest enjoyment is only obtained when giving and receiving are equally shared. Accordingly I was not surprised to hear her say:

'Jack, could you come up here to me now, please?'

Signalling to me to kneel astride her face, she seized my yard, guided it to her lips and then locking her hands over my loins, she alternately tightened and relaxed her grasp, signifying that I was to use the delicious mouth freely as a substitute for the interdicted opening below. The peculiar sucking action of her lips, of which I have spoken before, bore a pleasant resemblance to the nipping of an accomplished cunt, whilst the never-resting tongue, against whose soft folds M Jacques frigged himself luxuriously in his passage between the lips and throat, added a provocation to the lascivious sport not to be enjoyed in the ordinary act of coition. Meanwhile Eva had taken my place between Flossie's legs and was gamahuching the beloved cunt with incredible ardour. A sloping mirror on the wall above enabled me to survey the charming scene at my leisure, and to observe the spasms of delight which, from time to time, shook both the lovely naked forms below me. At last my own time arrived, and Flossie, alert as usual for the signs of approaching crisis, clutched my bottom with convulsive fingers and held me close pressed against her face, whilst I flooded her mouth with the stream of love that she adored. At the same moment the glass told me that Eva's lips were pushing far into the vulva to receive the result of their amorous labours, the passage of which from cunt to mouth was accompanied by every token of intense enjoyment from both the excited girls.

Rest and refreshment were needed by all three after the strain of our morning revels, and so the party broke up for the day after Flossie had mysteriously announced that she was designing something 'extra special', for the morrow.

CHAPTER FIVE

Birthday Festivities

The next morning there was a note from Flossie asking me to come as soon as possible after receiving it.

I hurried to the flat and found Flossie awaiting me, and in one of her most enchanting moods. It was Eva's birthday, as I was now informed for the first time, and to do honour to the occasion, Flossie had put on a costume in which she was to sell flowers at a fancy bazaar a few days later. It consisted of a white tam-o'-shanter cap with a straight upstanding feather—a shirt of the thinnest and gauziest white silk falling open at the throat and having a wide sailor collar—a broad lemon-coloured sash, a very short muslin skirt, lemon-coloured silk stockings and high-heeled brown shoes. At the opening of the shirt, a bunch of flame-coloured roses nestled between the glorious breasts, to the outlines of which all possible prominence was given by the softly clinging material. As she stood waiting to her my verdict, her red lips slightly parted, a rosy flush upon her cheeks, and love and laughter beaming from the radiant eyes, the magic of her youth and beauty seemed to weave a fresh spell around my heart, and a torrent of passionate words burst from my lips as I strained the lithe young form to my breast and rained kisses upon her hair, her eyes, her cheeks and mouth.

She took my hand in her hand and quietly led me to my favourite chair, and then seating herself on my knee, nestled her face against my cheek and said:

'Oh, Jack, Jack, my darling boy, how can you possibly love me like that!' The sweet voice trembled and a tear or two dropped softly from the violet eyes whilst an arm stole round my neck and red lips were pressed in a long intoxicating kiss upon my mouth.

We sat thus for some time when Flossie jumped from my knee, and said:

'We are forgetting all about Eva. Come in to her room and see what I have done.'

We went hand in hand into the bedroom and found Eva still asleep. On the chairs were laid her dainty garments, to which Flossie silently drew my attention. All along the upper edge of the chemise and corset, round the frills of the drawers and the hem of the petticoat, Flossie had sewn a narrow chain of tiny pink and white rosebuds, as a birthday surprise for her friend. I

222

laughed noiselessly, and kissed her hand in token
of my appreciation of the charming fancy.

'Now for Eva's birthday treat,' whispered
Flossie in my ear. 'Go over into that corner and
undress yourself as quietly as you can. I will help
you.'

Flossie's 'help' consisted chiefly in the use of
sundry wiles to induce an erection. As these
included the slow frigging in which she was such
an adept, as well as the application of her rosy
mouth and active tongue to every part of my
prick, the desired result was rapidly obtained.

'Now, Jack, you are going to have Eva whilst I
look on. Some day, my turn will come, and I
want to see exactly how to give you the greatest
possible amount of pleasure. Come and stand
here by me, and we'll wake her up.'

We passed round the bed and stood in front of
Eva, who still slept on unconscious.

'Ahem!' from Flossie.

The sleeping figure turned lazily. The eyes
unclosed and fell upon the picture of Flossie in
her flower-girl's dress, standing a little behind
me and, with her right hand passed in front of
me, vigorously frigging my erected yard, whilst
the fingers of the other glided with a softly
caressing motion over and under the attendant
balls.

Eva jumped up, flung off her nightdress and
crying to Flossie, *Don't leave go!* fell on her
knees, seized my prick in her mouth and thrust

her hand under Flossie's petticoats. The latter, obeying Eva's cry, continued to frig me deliciously from behind, whilst Eva furiously sucked the nut and upper part, and passing her disengaged hand round my bottom, caused me a new and exquisite enjoyment by inserting a dainty finger into the aperture thus brought within her reach. Flossie now drew close up to me and I could feel the swelling breasts in their thin silken covering pressed against my naked back, whilst her hand quickened its maddeningly provoking motion upon my prick and Eva's tongue pursued its enchanted course with increasing ardour and many luscious convolutions. Feeling I was about to spend, Flossie slipped her hand further down towards the root so as to give room for Eva's mouth to engulf almost the whole yard, a hint which the latter was quick to take, for her lips at once pressed close down to Flossie's fingers and with my hands behind my fair gamahucher's neck, I poured my very soul into her waiting and willing throat.

During the interval which followed, I offered my congratulations to Eva and told her how sorry I was not to have known of her birthday before, so that I might have presented a humble gift of some sort. She hastened to assure me that nothing in the world, that I could have brought, would be more welcome than what I had just given her!

Eva had not yet seen her decorated under-clothes and these were now displayed by Flossie with countless merry jokes and quaint remarks. The pretty thought was highly appreciated and nothing would do but our dressing Eva in the flowery garments. When this was done, Flossie suggested a can-can, and the three of us danced a wild *pas-de-trois* until the breath was almost out of our bodies. As we lay panting in various unstudied attitudes of exhaustion, a ring was heard at the door and Flossie, who was the only presentable one of the party went out to answer the summons. She came back in a minute with an enormous basket of Neopolitan violets. Upon our exclaiming at this extravagance Flossie gravely delivered herself of the following statement:

'Though not in a position for the moment to furnish chapter and verse, I am able to state with conviction that in periods from which we are only separated by some twenty centuries or so, it was customary for ladies and gentlemen of the time to meet and discuss the business of pleasure of the hour without the encumberance of clothes upon their bodies. The absence of *arrière-pensée* shown by this commendable practice might lead the superficial to conclude that these discussions led to no practical results. Nothing could be further from the truth. The interviews were invariably held upon a Bank of Violets (so the old writers tell us), and at a certain point in the proceedings, the lady would fall back upon this bank with her legs spread open at the then equivalent to an angle of forty-five. The gentleman would thereupon take in his right (or dexter) hand the instrument which our modern brevity of speech has taught us to call his prick. This, with some trifling assistance on her part, he would introduced into what the same latter-day rage for conciseness of expression leaves us powerless to describe otherwise than as her cunt. On my right we have the modern type of the lady, on my left, that of the gentleman. In the middle, the next best thing to a bank of violets. Ha! you take me at last! Now I'm going to put them all over the bed, and when I'm ready, you, Eva, will kindly oblige by depositing your snowy bottom in the middle, opening your legs and admitting Mr Jack to the proper position between them.'

While delivering this amazing oration, Flossie had gradually stripped herself entirely naked. We both watched her movements in silent admiration as she strewed the bed from end to end with the fragrant blossoms, which filled the room with their delightful perfume. When all was ready, she beckoned to Eva to lay herself on the bed, whispering to her, though not so low but that I could hear.

'Imagine you are Danae. I'll trouble you for the size of Jupiter's prick! Just look at it!'—then much lower, but still audibly—'You're going to be fucked, Eva darling, jolly well fucked! And I'm going to *see* you—*Lovely!*'

The rose-edged chemise and drawers were once more laid aside and the heroine of the day stretched herself voluptuously on the heaped-up flowers, which sent forth fresh streams of fragrance in response to the pressure of the girl's naked body.

'Ah, a happy thought!' cried Flossie. 'If you would lie *across* the bed with your legs hanging down, and Jack wouldn't mind standing up to his work, I think I could be of some assistance to you both.'

The change was quickly made, a couple of pillows were slipped under Eva's head, and Flossie, kneeling across the other's face, submitted her cunt to be gamahuched by her friend's tongue which at once darted amorously to its place within the vulva. Flossie returned the salutation for a moment and then resting her chin upon the point just above Eva's clitoris, called me to 'come on'. I placed myself in position and was about to storm the breach when Flossie found the near proximity of my yard to be too much for her feelings and begged to be allowed to gamahuche me for a minute.

'After that, I'll be quite good,' she added to Eva, 'and will only *watch*.'

Needless to say I made no objection. The result, as was the case with most of Flossie's actions, was increased pleasure to everybody concerned and to Eva as much as anyone inasmuch as the divine sucking of Flossie's rosy lips and lustful tongue produced a sensible hardening and lengthening of my excited member.

After performing this delightful service, she was for moving away, but sounds of dissent were heard from Eva, who flung her arms round Flossie's thighs and drew her cunt down in closer contact with the caressing mouth.

From my exalted position, I could see all that was going on and this added enormously to the sensations I began to experience when Flossie, handling my yard with deft fingers, dropped a final kiss upon the nut, and then guided it to the now impatient goal. With eyes lit up with interest and delight, she watched it disappear within the soft red lips whose movements she was near enough to follow closely. Under these conditions, I found myself fucking Eva with unusual vigour and penetration, whilst she, on her part, returned my strokes with powerful thrusts of her bottom and exquisitely pleasurable contractions of her cunt upon my prick.

Flossie, taking in all this with eager eyes, became madly excited, and at last sprang from her kneeling position on the bed, and taking advantage of an *outward* motion of my body, bent down between us, and pushing the point of her tongue under Eva's clitoris, insisted on my finishing the performance with this charming incentive added. Its effect upon both Eva and myself was electric, and as her clitoris and my prick shared equally in the contact of the tongue, we were not long in bringing the entertainment to an eminently satisfactory conclusion.

The next item in the birthday programme was the exhibition of half a dozen cleverly executed pen and ink sketches—Flossie's gift to Eva—showing the three of us in attitudes not to be found in the illustrations of the 'Young Ladies Journal'. A discussion arose as to whether Flossie had not been somewhat flattering to the longitudinal dimensions of the present writer's member. She declared that the proportions were 'according to *Cocker*'—obviously, as she wittily said, the highest authority on the question.

'Anyhow, I'm going to take measurements and then you'll see I'm right! In the picture the length of Jack's prick is exactly one-third of the distance from his chin to his navel. Now measuring the real article—Hello! I *say*, Evie, what *have* you done to him!'

In point of fact, the object under discussion was feeling the effects of his recent exercise and had dropped to a partially recumbent attitude.

Eva, who was watching the proceedings with an air of intense amusement called out:

'Take it between your breasts, Flossie; you will see the difference then!'

The mere prospect of such a lodging imparted a certain amount of vigour to Monsieur Jacques, who were thereupon introduced into the delicious cleft of Flossie's adorable bosom, and in rapture at the touch of the soft flesh on either side of him, at once began to assume more satisfactory proporations.

'But he's not up to his full height yet,' said Flossie. 'Come and help me, Evie dear; stand behind Jack and frig him whilst I gamahuche him in front. *That's* the way to get him up to concert pitch! When I feel him long and stiff enough in my mouth, I'll get up and take his measure.'

The success of Flossie's plan was immediate and complete, and when the measurements were made, the proportions were found to be exactly twenty-one and seven inches respectively, whilst in the drawing they were three inches to one inch. Flossie proceeded to execute a wild war-dance of triumph over this signal vindication of her accuracy, winding up by insisting on my carrying her pick-a-back round the flat. Her enjoyment of this ride was unbounded, as also was mine, for besides the pleasure arising from the close contact of her charming body, she contrived to administer a delicious friction to my member with the calves of her naked legs.

On our return to the bedroom, Eva was sitting on the edge of the low divan.

'Bring her to me here,' she cried.

I easily divined what was wanted, and carrying my precious burden across the room, I faced round with my back to Eva. In the sloping glass to the left, I could see her face disappear between the white rounded buttocks, at the same moment that her right hand moved in front of me and grasped my yard which it frigged with incomparable tenderness and skill. This operation was eagerly watched by Flossie over my shoulder, while she clung to me with arms and legs and rubbed herself against my loins with soft undulating motions like an amorous kitten, the parting lips of her cunt kissing my back and her every action testifying to the delight with which she was receiving the attentions of Eva's tongue upon the neighbouring spot.

My feelings were now rapidly passing beyond my control, and I had to implore Eva to remove her hand, whereupon Flossie, realising the state of affairs, jumped down from her perch, and burying my prick in her sweet mouth, sucked and frigged me in such a frenzy of desire that she had very soon drawn from me the last drop I had to give her.

A short period of calm ensued after this last ebullition, but Flossie was in too mad a mood today to remain long quiescent.

'Eva,' she suddenly cried, 'I believe I am as tall as you nowadays, and I am *quite sure* my breasts are as large as yours. I'm going to measure and see!'

After Eva's height had been found to be only a short inch above Flossie's, the latter proceeded to take the most careful and scientific measurements of the breasts. First came the circumference, then the diameter *over* the nipples, then the diameter omitting the nipples, then the distance from the nipple to the upper and lower edges of the hemispheres, and so on. No dry as dust old savant, staking his reputation upon an absolutely accurate calculation of the earth's surface, could have carried out his task with more ineffable solemnity than did this merry child who, one knew, was all the time secretly bubbling over with the fun of her quaint conceit.

The result was admitted to be what Flossie called it—'a moral victory' for herself, inasmuch as half a square inch, or as Flossie declared, 'fifteen thirty-*two-ths*', was all the superiority of area that Eva could boast.

'There's one other measurement I *should* like to have taken,' said Eva, 'because in spite of my ten years '*de plus* and the fact that my cunt is not altogether a stranger to the joys of being fucked, I believe that Flossie would win *that* race, and I should like her to have one out of three!'

'*Lovely!*' cried Flossie. 'But Jack must be the judge. Here's the tape, Jack: fire away. Now, Evie, come and lie beside me on the edge of the bed, open your legs, and swear to abide by the verdict!'

After a few minutes fumbling with the tape and close inspection of the parts in dispute, I retired to

232

a table and wrote down the following, which I pinned against the window curtain.

'Letchford v. Eversley

Mesdames,

In compliance with your instructions I have this day surveyed the private premises belonging to the above parties, and have now the honour to submit the following report, plan, and measurements.

As will be seen from the plan, Miss Letchford's cunt is exactly $3^1/16$ inches from the underside of clitoris to he base of vulva. Miss Eversley's cunt, adopting the same line of measurement, gives $3\frac{5}{8}$ inches.

I may add that the premises appear to me to be thoroughly desirable in both cases, and to a good, upright and painstaking tenant would afford equally pleasant accommodation in spring, summer, autumn or winter.

A small but well-wooded covert is attached to each, whilst an admirable dairy is in convenient proximity.

With reference to the Eversley property, I am informed that it has not yet been occupied, but in view of its size and beauty, and the undoubted charms of the surrounding country, I confidently anticipated that a permanent and satisfactory tenant (such as I have ventured to describe above), will very shortly be found for it. My opinion of its advantages as a place of residence may, indeed, be gathered from the fact that I am greatly disposed to make an offer in my own person.

Yours faithfully,
J Archer.'

As the two girls stood with their hands behind their backs reading my ultimatum, Flossie laughed uproariously, but I noticed that Eva looked grave and thoughtful.

Had I written anything that annoyed her? I could hardly think so, but while I was meditating on the possibility, half resolved to put it to the test by a simple question, Eva took Flossie and myself by the hand, led us to the sofa and sitting down between us, said:

'Listen to me, you two dears! You, Flossie, are my chosen darling, and most beloved little friend. You, Jack, are Flossie's lover, and for her sake as well as for your own, I have the greatest affection for you. You both know all this. Well, I have not the heart to keep you from one another any longer. Flossie, dear, I hereby absolve you from your promise to me. Jack, you have behaved like a brick, as you are. Come here tomorrow at your usual time and I think we shall be able to agree upon *"a tenant for the Eversley property."'*

This is not a novel of sentiment, and a description of what followed would therefore be out of place. Enough to say that after one wild irrepressible shriek of joy and gratitude from Flossie, the conversation took a sober and serious turn, and soon afterwards we parted for the day.

CHAPTER SIX

The tenant in possession

The next morning's post brought me letters from both Eva and Flossie.

'My dear Jack,' (wrote the former)
'Tomorrow will be a red letter day for you two! And I want you both to get the utmost of delight from it. So let no sort of scruple or compunction spoil your pleasure. Flossie is, in point of physical development, a woman. As such, she longs to be fucked by the man she loves. Fuck her therefore with all and more than all the same skill and determination you displayed in fucking me. She can think and talk of nothing else. Come early tomorrow and bring your admirable prick in its highest state of efficiency and stiffness!

Yours,
Eva.'

Flossie wrote:

'I cannot sleep a wink for thinking of what is coming to me tomorrow. All the time I keep turning over in my mind how best to make it nice for you. I am practising Evas "nip". I *feel* as if I could do it, but nipping *nothing* is not really practice, is it, Jack? My beloved, I kiss your prick, in imagination. Tomorrow I will do it in the flesh, for I warn you that nothing will ever induce me to give up *that*, nor will even the seven inches which I yearn to have in my cunt ever bring me to consent to being deprived of the sensation of your dear tongue when it curls between the lips and pays polite attentions to my clitoris! But you shall have me as you like tomorrow, and all days to follow. I am to be in the future.

Yours body and soul,
Flossie.

When I arrived at the flat I found Flossie had put on the costume in which I had seen her the first day of our acquaintance. The lovely little face wore an expression of gravity, as though to show me she was not forgetting the importance of the occasion. I am not above confessing that, for my part, I was profoundly moved.

We sat beside one another, hardly exchanging a word. Presently Flossie said:

'Whenever you are *ready*, Jack, I'll go to my room and undress.'

The characteristic naiveté of this remark

somewhat broke the spell that was upon us, and I kissed her with effusion.

'Shall it be . . . *quite* naked, Jack?'

'Yes, darling, if *you* don't mind.'

'All right. When I am ready I'll call to you.'

Five minutes later, I heard the welcome summons.

From the moment I found myself in her room, all sense of restraint vanished at a breath. She flew at me in a perfect fury of desire, pushed me by sheer force upon my back on the bed, and lying at full length upon me with her face close to mine, she said:

'Because I was a girl and not a woman, Jack, you have never fucked me. But you are going to fuck me now, and I shall be a women. But first, I want to be a girl to you still for a few minutes only. I want to have your dear prick in my mouth again; I want you to kiss my cunt in the old delicious way; I want to lock my naked arms round your naked body; and hold you to my face, whilst I wind my tongue round your prick until you spend. Let me do all this, Jack, and then you shall fuck me till the skies fall.'

Without giving me time to reply to this frenzied little oration, Flossie had whisked round and was in position for the double gamahuche she desired. Parting her legs to their widest extent on each side of my face, she sank gently down until her cunt came full upon my open mouth. At the same moment I felt my prick seized and plunged deep

239

into her mouth with which she at once commenced the delicious sucking action I knew so well. I responded by driving my tongue to the root into the rosy depths of her perfumed cunt, which I sucked with ever increasing zest and enjoyment, drawing fresh treasures from its inner recesses at every third or fourth stroke of my tongue. Words fail me to describe the unparalleled vigour of her sustained attack upon my erected prick, which she sucked, licked, tongued and frigged with such a furious *abandon* and at the same time with such a subtle skill and knowledge of the sublime art of gamahuching, that the end came with unusual rapidity, and wave after wave of the sea of love broke in ecstasy upon the 'coral strand' of her adorable mouth. For a minute or two more, her lips retained their hold and then, leaving her position, she came and lay down beside me, nestling her naked body against mine, and softly chafing the lower portion of my prick whilst she said:

'Now Jack darling, I am going to talk to you about the different ways of fucking, because of course you will want to fuck me, and I shall want to be fucked, in every possible position, and in every single part of my body where a respectable young woman may reasonably *ask* to be fucked.'

The conversation which followed agreeably filled the intervening time before the delicate touches which Flossie kept constantly applying to my prick caused it to raise its head to a considerable altitude, exhibiting a hardness and rigidity which gave high promise for the success of the coming encounter.

'Good gracious!' cried Flossie. 'Do you think I shall ever find room for all that, Jack?'

'For that, and more also, sweetheart,' I replied.

'*More!* Why, *what* more are you going to put into me?'

'This is the only article I propose to introduce at present, Floss. But I mean that when Monsieur Jacques finds himself for the first time with his head buried between the delicious cushions in *there*' (*touching her belly*) 'he will most likely beat his own record in the matter of length and stiffness.'

'Do you mean, Jack, that he will be bigger with me than he was with Eva?' said Flossie with a merry twinkle.

'Certainly I mean it,' was my reply. 'To fuck a beautiful girl like Eva must always be immensely enjoyable, but to fuck a young Venus of sixteen, who besides being the perfection of mortal loveliness, is also one's own chosen and adorable little sweetheart—*that* belongs to a different order of pleasure altogether.

'And I suppose, Jack, that when the sixteen-year-old is simply dying to be fucked by her lover, as I am at this moment, the chances are that she may be able to make it rather nice for him, as well as absolutely heavenly for herself. Now I can wait no longer. 'First position' at once, please, Jack. Give me your prick in my hand and I will direct his wandering footsteps.'

'He's at the door, Flossie; shall he enter?'

'Yes. Push him in slowly and fuck gently at first, so that I may find out by degrees how much he's going to hurt me. A little further, Jack. Why, he's more than halfway in already! Now you keep still and I'll thrust a little with my bottom.'

'Why, Floss, you darling, you're nipping me deliciously!'

'Can you feel me, Jack? How lovely! Fuck me a little more, Jack, and get in deeper, that's it! Now faster and harder. What glorious pleasure it is!'

'And no pain, darling?'

'Not a scrap. One more good push and he'll be in up to the hilt, won't he? Eva told me to put my legs over your back. Is that right?'

'Quite right, and if you're sure I'm not hurting you, Floss, I'll really begin now and fuck you in earnest.'

'That's what I'm here for, Sir,' she replied with a touch of her never-absent fun even in this supreme moment.

'Here goes, then!' I answered. Having once made up her mind that she had nothing to dread, Flossie abandoned herself with enthusiasm to the pleasures of the moment. Locking her arms round my neck and her legs round my buttocks, she cried to me to fuck her with all my might.

'Drive your prick into me again and again, Jack. Let me feel your belly against mine. Did you feel my cunt nip you then? Ah! how you are fucking me now!—fucking me, fu . . . u . . . ucking me!'

Her lovely eyes turned to heaven, her breath came in quick short gasps, her fingers wandered feverishly about my body. At last, with a cry, she plunged her tongue into my mouth and, with convulsive undulations of the little body, let loose the floods of her being to join the deluge which, with sensations of exquisite delight, I poured into her burning cunt.

The wild joy of this our first act of coition was followed by a slight reaction and, with a deep sigh of contentment Flossie fell asleep in my arms, leaving my prick still buried in its natural resting place. Before long, my own eyelids closed and, for an hour or more, we lay thus gaining from blessed sleep fresh strength to enter upon new transports of pleasure.

Flossie was the first to awake, stirred no doubt by the unaccustomed sensations of a swelling prick within her. I awoke to find her dear eyes resting upon my face, her naked arms round my neck and her cunt enfolding my yard with a soft and clinging embrace.

Her bottom heaved gently, and accepting the invitation thus tacitly given, I turned my little sweetheart on her back and, lying luxuriously between her widely parted legs, once more drove my prick deep into her cunt and fucked her with slow lingering strokes, directed upwards so as to bring all possible contact to bear upon the clitoris.

This particular motion afforded her evident delight and the answering thrusts of her bottom were delivered with ever increasing vigour and precision, each of us relishing to the full the efforts of the other to augment the pleasure of the encounter. With sighs and gasps and little cries of rapture, Flossie strained me to her naked breasts, and twisting her legs tightly round my own, cried out that she was spending and implored me to let her feel my emission mix with hers. By dint of clutching her bottom with my hands, driving the whole length of my tongue into her mouth I was just able to manage the simultaneous discharge she coveted, and once more I lay upon her in a speechless ecstasy of consummated passion.

Any one of my readers who has had the supreme good fortune to fuck the girl of his heart will bear me out in saying that the lassitude following upon such a meeting is greater and more lasting than the mere weariness resulting from an ordinary act of copulation 'where love is not'.

Being well aware of this fact, I resolved that my beloved little Flossie's powers should not be taxed any further for the moment, and told her so.

'But Jack,' she cried, almost in tears, 'we've only done it *one* way, and Eva says there are at least *six*! And oh, I do *love* it so!'

'And so do I, little darling. But also, I love *you*, and I'm not going to begin by giving you and that delicious little caressing cunt of yours more work than is good for you both.'

'Oh, dear! I suppose you're right, Jack.'

'Of course I'm right, darling. Tomorrow I shall come and fuck you again, and the next day, and the next, and many days after that. It will be odd if we don't find ourselves in Eva's six different positions before we've done!'

At this moment Eva herself entered the room.

'Well, Flossie . . .?' she said.

'Ask Jack!' replied Flossie.

'Well Jack, then . . . ? said Eva.

'Ask Flossie!' I retorted, and fled from the room.

The adventures I have, with many conscious imperfections, related in the foregoing pages, were full of interest to me, and were, I am disposed to think, not without their moments of attraction for my fellow actors in the scenes depicted.

It by no means necessarily follows that they will produce a corresponding effect upon the reading public who, in my descriptions of Floss and her ways, may find only an ineffectual attempt to set forth the charms of what appears to me an absolutely unique temperament. If haply it should prove to be otherwise, I should be glad to have the opportunity of continuing a veritable labour of love by recounting certain further experiences of Eva, Floss and

Yours faithfully
Jack.

Maudie

Revelations of Life in London

Characters

Maudie Stevens ('Maudie'), an amateur of the beautiful, and an exponent of the same in her own face and figure. She loves love and luxury, and all her whims and desires and her great house at Staines are provided for by the wealth of,

Bertie Evans-James ('Tubby'), the cheery fat son of a Lancashire millionaire.

Charles Vernon St. Just Osmond, a very charming 'younger son'.

Phil Learoyd, a young Cambridge undergraduate with a sense of humour.

General Fitzhugh, V.C., a distinguished veteran with a taste for the gay side of life.

Claude Lestrange, a romantic poet, sodomitically inclined.

Lady Lavinia McCree, 'Charlie's' Aunt, a mid-Victorian lady.

Madame Rade, a retired Parisian actress.

Toinette Rade, her 'flapper' niece.

Jeannie, a Newcastle hinny.

Elsie,
May, } Maids at Maudie's mansion.

To The Reader

I think you'll like 'Maudie'; she's fanciful and frivolous. I should hardly call her 'fast', though she does the most dreadful things, but she does them so very nicely that probably the most strait-laced of people will have to forgive her, when they read her in the privacy of their own or other people's bedrooms – not only forgive, but love her and her bad ways and her worse friends.

Maudie deals frankly with the wicked senses, ordinary and bizarre, of a number of charming people, who refuse to be trammelled by the usual conventions of Society. We meet them in London, and we meet them in their delightful riverside palace, where full rein is given to all their loves and lusts, until there comes a very unexpected *dénouement*.

Our ancestors used to have a thing called the 'Horn Book'. What it exactly was I'm not quite sure, *but* touching the horn question, if *Maudie* doesn't give it you, you're past your job.

Settle down in bed with a cigarette, and a drink and the evening paper, and give your lady companion *Maudie* to read – well, you won't get much evening paper. *Maudie* is a 'horn book'.

One

The Mansion of Maudie

An awakening in a whore's bedroom is, as a rule, cheerless.

One is vague as to one's whereabouts, as a rule sore on the John Thomas, and a general feeling of having made a bloody fool of oneself is most often mixed with a wonder whose pyjamas you've got on, and whether you've got the clap – or possibly worse.

Charles Vernon St. Just Osmond, fifth off the succession to the Earldom of Osmond, a very much 'younger son', with a good deal less money even than most younger sons, turned over twice, flicked his eyes at the sunlight dribbling through the blinds, bit a tongue which felt like leather, sniffed a distinct aroma of whisky, and wondered where the hell he was, why he had done it, and who he had done it on.

He raised himself on one elbow, and *looked*. Then he was pleased. He had obviously not made a very drunken error. The good lady who lay by his side, in a charming silk pyjama suit with a deep Venetian lace collar, was not only pretty, but interesting. Her chestnut hair flowed over her shoulders. Her arms, bare from just above the elbows, were deliciously rounded, and her very delicate little hands were heavily be-ringed. This, Osmond (or, as we shall call him, Charlie) concluded, was no ordinary tart, and the question of finance smote him suddenly. He had a vague recollection of friends and the Empire and the Continental, and he knew that he couldn't have much on him. He was just slipping out of bed to look through his pockets when she woke up, and put a soft arm round his neck.

'Remember what you came here for last night, and which you *didn't* do, darling,' she cooed.

Charlie had forgotten that. He *must* have been very drunk, he thought to himself, and as he sat up in bed his head whirled in confirmation. The girl pulled him gently down, and kissed him softly and lovingly.

'Naughty boy to have been so drunk last night,' she purred. 'Think of me, full of lust, ready to do *anything*, and you went to sleep like a log. I suppose you don't remember how you got undressed?'

Charlie admitted that he didn't.

'Well, I didn't take your clothes off, but my maid did, and put you into your pyjamas. She's out of the common pretty, yet with two women by you, you couldn't summon up a flicker of a stand. You've *got* to make up for it now, my lazy darling.'

Her little hand slipped over his stomach, undid the knot of his pyjama trousers, and played delicately with a very limp and lethargic phallus. Her other hand reached up behind her, and touched a bell. Charlie sank back, dreamily anticipating some further surprise.

Almost immediately a very smart and pretty girl, dressed in a sort of comic-opera maid's costume, came in without knocking.

'This gentleman isn't well,' said Charlie's hostess; 'bring the usual remedies.'

'The usual remedies' arrived very swiftly, and a tired and dejected Charlie noted, with a relieved glance, tea, coffee, tiny caviare sandwiches, delicately cut toast, almost smokingly hot little rolls, and more severe comforts in the shape of half bottles of champagne, and several brands of liqueurs and brandy. On a separate tray were all sorts of fruit.

'If you are *very* hungry, darling,' said the little fairy of the bed, 'you can have anything you like in the way of a serious breakfast, but my advice is, play about with these little things now, and when we are up and bathed, and things, we'll have a proper meal in the garden by the river; it's a beautiful morning, and the lilies are lovely.'

'River, garden, lilies' – every evidence of wealth – Charlie began to wonder what he *had* struck, and to think more nervously than ever of his waistcoat pockets.

The pretty maid slipped a soft, rounded arm under Charlie's back, and raised him gently. She sat on the bed by his knee, the trays by her side on a table, and began to feed him like a baby. Charlie's delightful bedfellow lay back in an amorous abandon.

'Nothing for me just yet, Elsie,' she said, smiling.

Charlie didn't quite know which way to look – both girls were so delicious. The maid's left hand lay, whether by accident or design, right on his cock, as she handed him drinks and sandwiches with her right. She had crossed her knees as she sat, and her lovely calves showed right up to the garter.

She wouldn't let him help himself, but he couldn't keep his hands idle. One toyed with her breasts; his fingers within her bodice dwelling lustfully on the swelling globes. The other hand his bedfellow had captured, and it was not idle. She had thrown the bedclothes aside, pulled her pyjama trousers a little down, and had Charlie's hand pressed gently on her clitoris.

Charlie ate and drank, and in a moment or two all lassitude had left him. His cock was rampant and erect, and his eyes wandered lasciviously and eagerly from one wickedly-smiling face to another.

The pretty maid gave him a long, hard-breathed kiss, which nearly set him on fire before she left.

As the door closed behind the maid, the other girl kissed him savagely on the neck.

'Take my things off,' she said, jerkily, to Charlie.

It was the work of a moment, and she was exposed in all her naked loveliness.

To his surprise, Charlie noticed that her *mons Veneris* carried no hair whatever; it was perfectly shaved, and as his fingers strayed downwards, he felt no trace of any stubble – even as he inclined his head and kissed it, he felt conscious that his chin, though he had had a late shave overnight, was far the roughest.

Charlie knew a bit; he hadn't knocked about town for nothing, and he was accustomed to pictures of the female form divine in which the hair was as conspicuously absent as the clothing, but he had never run across it in real life, and, curiously, it opened up a new vista of thought to him.

He kissed the shorn vagina and tasted some strangely sweet effluvia, which contrasted attractively with the caviare and the Georges Goulet.

Charlie, hardly able to contain himself, was just turning to fuck her in the old sweet Adam and Eve way, but her little hand, strong with passion, pushed him back.

'Lie quiet, darling,' she said; 'I'm going to be jockey,' and delicately she knelt astride him. 'Do you want it very much, sweetheart?' she cooed, as her fingers toyed with the luxuriant hairs of his bush.

'Want it, my God! I can't hold it – *be quick*.'

She parted the dainty red lips of her cunt with her diamond-flashing fingers, with just a movement of her wrist guided Charlie's member in, and sank softly down on him till her bare breasts caressed his, and their lips became as one reciprocating engine of love and lust.

It was a convulsive grapple of two naked bodies; a passionate mingling of flesh, a communion of kisses, and a good deal more communion of souls than those two young people quite realised at that time. Charlie really thought it was the best fuck he had *ever* had, and yet he didn't even know the girl's name, nor anything at all about her.

Somehow, though, he felt he had met an affinity. As her legs twined over his bottom, and her strong, young arms grappled him to her with loving vigour, he felt somehow that he had never known the time when that red, hot, little tongue had not darted over his.

He did not quite know when he actually finished.

257

He had half fainted; the girl's grip was loosened too; he seemed to be swimming in mid-air in a red mist. The most delicious fatigue possessed him. When he came to, she was still on top of him, but wide-awake and alert.

'Where are we?' he hesitated. 'I expect I owe all sorts of apologies.'

'You don't remember the motor drive?'

'No.'

'Well, you're near Staines, and you'll learn all about things when you feel a bit better. Try a little more caviare; it's extra, straight from a grand duke friend of mine. You couldn't buy it in a shop.'

'Grand dukes – oh, Lord!' thought Charlie, 'what will she expect?'

She jumped up and went to a curtained door.

'The bath-room's here, dear,' she said; 'you can have it in a moment,' and she was gone.

Charlie Osmond finished a glass of champagne, got hastily out of bed, and examined his pockets.

One pound, fourteen and seven was the net – obviously useless.

He had done these sorts of things before, and subsequently paid, but there was something about this girl that made him uneasy. She was very much out of the ordinary.

He had some more champagne, and listened apprehensively to the splashing in the bath-room.

We have to go through this book with Charlie Osmond, so our readers may just as well know a little about him.

A gentleman by birth, he had most of the right

instincts and perversions. He had left Eton for the usual reason, and he regretted it. He did *not* want to bugger other boys, but some did, and he somehow hated to be out of the fashion. Unfortunately, he was found out.

At Oxford his career had been meteoric. He could not go to a very good college, owing to his school troubles, and his good allowance made him a star at —(we will suppress the name). He did many things he should not have, and his final exploit of sowing the word 'CUNT' in mustard and cress in the front quad grass, which came up under the astonished eyes of the dean's daughter, led to his final exit. His defence – that he had meant the word as a moral admonition to those of the Varsity who had leaned to malpractices in the sodomitical line – was not accepted, and he went.

The home-coming was as usual – nobody to meet him at the station but the chauffeur, and father in the gun-room.

Your son's devotion to landscape gardening [ran the dean's note] is undoubtedly commendable, but we must remind you that the grass in the front quadrangle at—has for 500 years preserved its virginity, and the word inscribed makes not only a blemish on the grass, but conveys a reflection on the locality. We are only pleased that no word has found its way to the American papers. – We are, etc.,

HY. CHARTERIS (*Dean*).

Charlie Osmond came to town with £300 a year, and a paternal kick on the arse.

He could *not* live on £300 a year, and he didn't try

259

to. It cost him that in clothes and drink.

Well, it had gone on somehow for some time, but the end, and Canada – or something worse – was near.

Yet he realised that he was really a very nice young man; everyone liked him, and he liked most people, but he hadn't got a *carrière*, and he wanted it.

The divinity came back, and sat down on the bottom of the bed, lighting a cigarette.

We have got to know about her.

She was *not* a clergyman's daughter.

Her father had prospered in the nitrate market, and, until the inevitable end, had prospered exceedingly, so his children were well brought up. Maudie Stevens went to school at Eltham, in Kent, and was 'finished' – well 'finished' – at a convent near Rouen.

She had her baby in a suburb of Paris, and her family gave her money and her *congé*. The money was luckily tied up, so that her father's sensational end at the Old Bailey did not affect her financially.

She had a few hundreds a year, a detestation of suburbia, and no morals.

She took the inevitable end quite calmly, and became a tart, *pure et simple*.

She was very popular, and – but we shall see.

Charlie Osmond started bluntly.

'I don't quite know,' he blundered, '*what* you think of me?'

She laughed, and twisted her hair into a

bewitching knot over her forehead.

'Where I am, I don't know,' he went on. 'Who you are, I don't know; and I've no money to speak of. I feel a pig.'

'I know you well enough, Charlie Osmond. I shouldn't have picked you up, and brought you down here if I hadn't wanted you – but I *did*. Now make yourself at home; get into the bath-room. You'll find clean collars, and a new tooth-brush and things, and we'll have breakfast and talk. I haven't exactly brought you here for nothing.'

Charlie felt considerably relieved when he found himself alone in the dainty bath-room.

Every imaginable sort of comfort was ready to hand, and he enjoyed a most elaborate scented bath. After the final cold shower douche, he put down a stiff ice-cold brandy and soda, and was ready for *anything* the world might bring forth.

Maudie was dressed when he came back into the bedroom, dressed in a simple summer muslin, which made him remember with a shock that he had been in evening clothes the night before.

Maudie obviously divined his thought.

'I expect you'll find flannels to do you in the wardrobe,' she said laughingly. 'I keep several sizes.'

In a few minutes Charlie was a smart young man, in immaculate boating flannels, and as he followed his hostess through the pretty hall and across the lawn to where a breakfast table flashed its silver, glass and napery temptingly under the trees, he felt he'd like to stop here forever.

Another pretty maid, in white, and a page-boy, in white ducks, waited.

Charlie frankly made a pig of himself. A cool

breeze flickering over the Thames had given him a raving appetite, and everything was so *very* nicely done, and the pretty eyes opposite his were so twinklingly alluring.

Two

Maudie's Garden and Studio

On a little slope, very green and fresh-looking, and completely shut off from the house by the trees, a number of really sensible-sized cushions were spread. Thither, after breakfast, Maudie led the way, and flopped, making no bones about showing her lovely legs right up to the knee. Openwork stockings are distracting enough at the best of times, but when it comes to the very finest of red silk, and the tiniest of little, red, morocco shoes at the end of them, matching exactly the scarlet sash which encircled Maudie's tapering waist, it takes a strong man to think of anything but the worst. Charlie flopped by her side, and took a kiss, which was only stopped by the page-boy's judicious cough. He had the daily papers and cigarettes.

'I'll ring if I want anything,' she said. 'Now see that we're not disturbed.'

There was an electric bell fixed to one of the trees, likewise a telephone extension.

'My word, you *do* do yourself well,' said Charlie, nestling down very comfortably, and toying idly with the little dear's knees, 'telephone and all.'

'Oh, it's very convenient. I've a lot of journalist friends who like to lie about here in the summer, and telephone lies to their offices. It's wonderful what nice things you can phone when you've got a nice girl all over you, and a feeling of delicious laziness. These cushions could tell a bit.

'Now, you put your hand up higher, *right* up; nobody can possibly see us unless they go past on a boat. I want to talk a little business to you.

'First of all, you'll want some clothes. I'm sending my car up to town. My chauffeur can take my message to Half Moon Street – you see I know where you live – and get what you want. Are you on the phone?'

'Yes.'

'Well, ring your man up; have you got a man?'

'Yes; it runs to owing for that.'

'Well, get on now; I want the man to go soon. I'm going to keep you here to-night, unless you've got anything very important on.'

'No; and if I had I'd miss it.'

'You won't be able to sleep with me. My really best financial boy is coming, and I've got to go through it. I think you know him, Bertie Evans-James.'

'Bertie – Tubby Bertie; oh, Lord, yes! I wonder I haven't met you.'

'I don't come up to town much. I love this place and Paris. Now you ring up and tell your man that a chauffeur called Gerstein will call with your card.'

264

Charlie reached up to the receiver, which was hung conveniently low.

'One minute, dear,' whispered Maudie. 'I've a wicked little fad. When any of my men pals are telephoning, I like to get on top, and just ride on it; it's ripping.'

Charlie was only too pleased, and lay back as she knelt over him and unloosened his trousers.

Lord knows what came out was stiff enough. Eight good inches of it, hard as steel, and panting with hot lust.

She bent and kissed it, first running her tongue lightly round the glans; then, with a quick movement slipped her leg over, and seemed to flick the great member into her boiling little volcano of a cunt.

It hurt Charlie a little as she thrust herself right down, and began to slip slowly up and down, but it was delightful pain.

His man's voice seemed strangely odd, and Charlie wondered what on earth that staid personage would think if he knew exactly where his master was getting on the phone from.

Suits he asked for, collars, shirts, etc., boots and ties, and at the hats he spent violently. He felt a savage bite on the neck, and collapsed with his man's voice in his ear, saying, 'Yes, sir, and your aunt's here, sir, and would like to speak to you, sir.'

Charlie gasped, but there was no way out of it; Aunt Lavinia must *not* be offended.

'Oh, Charlie, is that really you? What wonderful inventions these are. I feel I can almost *see* you –'

Charlie shuddered.

'– and I hear you're having your things sent down by motor. How nice. Do you know, I've never been in one. I shall take the chance of running down to see you; I can get back by train. See you later – bye-bye' – and he was rung off.

Charlie explained the situation to the girl, as she leisurely buttoned him.

'Oh, let the old lady come,' she said. 'I can behave like a lady; don't you worry. I was brought up as one. I'll put on my very best party airs, and she won't complain of her dinner, I give you my word. Does she know Bertie, by the way?'

'Oh, certain to.'

'Very well; I'll be a foreign widow, met Bertie at Homburg or somewhere. I speak perfect French and German.'

Charlie weakly acquiesced.

'I'm afraid you don't quite know Aunt Lavinia,' he said; 'she's very, very mid-Victorian!'

'Never mind, I can be *early* Victorian. I'll be her friend for life before she's been here two hours. Now come along into the house, and I'll tell you what I really want you to do for me – or – it is a lovely morning, and I don't know whether you like swimming or not, but I do, and I've a lovely little private bathing place near by here.'

Charlie was very much ready, and after the page-boy had been sent to give the chauffeur his instructions, they wandered off, hand in hand, down a little lane, to a highly palisaded backwater.

There were two big and comfortable dressing-rooms, for men and for women.

'Sometimes we are very respectable and wear bathing costumes and things,' Maudie explained; 'but sometimes, like this morning, for instance, we don't do anything of the sort, and you are just going to undress me, mother naked, and we'll swim about like Adam and Eve.'

It was not the first time Charlie had got into a bath with a cockstand, but it was the first time he had dived in to swim like that. When he turned over to float, the little syren Maudie swam up to him and laughingly tied a dainty handkerchief on to his rampant mast.

'*Now* you can show your colours,' she said. 'You look like a submarine with the periscope stuck out of the water.'

She swam like a sea-nymph, and her figure, all naked and glistening with the water, as she poised herself for her dives, made Charlie forget all about Aunt Lavinia, tailors' bills, or any worries in this world. He made an ineffective attempt to get into her while they were both floating – he had heard of such things being done – but the result was nearly a watery death for both. However, they managed to toss each other off, then Maudie called a halt, and they clambered out and on to the landing stage.

The mattresses, covered with thick towelling, were beautifully soft, and their wet bodies sank luxuriously into their embrace.

'There's a very pretty little grass slope over there,' said Maudie, 'if you prefer nature. For my part, I agree with the late lamented Oscar Wilde: Nature may be very nice to look at, but it was not intended to sit on. Let's lie here, and let the sun dry us. There are lots of little towels lying about if you want one.'

Charlie's only reply was a passionate kiss.

His hand strayed to where it shouldn't, but the girl put it gently away.

'Not just now, dear,' she said; 'we've had a good

bit. Lie quiet in the sun. You can smoke if you like. You'll find cigarettes in the cupboard in the dressing-room, and all sorts of drink if you want it. Personally, I should like a little champagne cup. Yes, I should: my butler makes it extra. I'll phone up to the house.'

'But – he mustn't see us like this.'

'Oh, he won't; there's a sliding door opens into the cupboard.'

She went to the telephone. How lovely she looked standing there in a naked grace, quite like a Grecian goddess – and *what* a contrast to the very modern apparatus in her hand. Charlie longed to take a photograph of her, and the girl seemed to divine his thoughts.

'Like to take a picture of me? There's a camera in the shed. I know you photograph.'

Charlie took six. He was an ardent and expert photographer, and he had taken many pictures in the nude, but he had never had such a model as this. He realised now the beauty of the shaven Mount of Venus; she was shaved under the arms too.

The cup came in a beautiful old china bowl, also two Venetian glasses with long silver stems, like magnified punch ladles.

They squatted with the bowl between them, and sipped. It was very heavenly.

'Does old – er – Tubby come to do stunts like this?' asked Charlie.

'Oh, Lord, yes; he flops about like a porpoise.'

'Lucky beggar!'

'Well, I suppose he *is* lucky. He spends a great deal on me, of course; you can see this house isn't run on air, but he is lucky in getting a girl a little out of the common to arrange amusements for him; you've no idea yet what we *can* do for you.'

'I should die.'

'Oh, no, you wouldn't. If you take lust delicately and scientifically, it hurts no one; only people who fornicate like animals, and have no thought above the actual parts of their bodies which are in contact, upset their constitutions. This is a pretty little swimming place, isn't it?'

'Ripping.'

'And the mixed bathing very much *au naturel* is jolly, isn't it?'

'Rather.'

'My own idea. They used to do it, I believe, in Medmenham Abbey days. Now we'll dress and get in; I want to show you the house. Bring the camera, and we'll develop those. Take some more of me in various stages of my getting dressed, and use up the whole spool.'

Charlie, nothing loth, did. First with just her stockings and shoes on, then with a hat added to that, next with drawers, and so through the stages till the complete, idyllic, muslin-clad river girl used up the last film.

They got back to the house by another route, through a somewhat severely classical garden, peopled with very excellent statues of heathen gods and goddesses.

'Tubby doesn't like this,' she said; 'he calls it the *Lemprierium*. I caught him one day trying to shoot the fig leaf off that Apollo with an air-gun. I punished him by making him strip, gumming a great fig leaf on him, and making him walk about here for two hours: each time he passed the Apollo he had to apologise to it and kiss its behind. The others did laugh; you know what Tubby's figure *is*.'

Charlie was prepared to be surprised at the house, but he was more than surprised. Very large, an old Elizabethan mansion, slightly built on to and modernised; without it was the embodiment of stately grace, within of the most up to date comfort. Charlie remembered that Tubby's father owned many factories in Lancashire, but they must do pretty well to keep up this, and the old man himself had a bit of a reputation for chorus girls.

They went cursorily through the house. It was not furnished much like a tart's house, but rather like that of a great lady of fashion. The servants were certainly rather comic opera, and a prettier lot Charlie thought he had never seen. The men servants he encountered were French, bar the very staid old butler.

They came at last to a little boudoir overlooking garden and river.

'Now we'll talk,' said Maudie. 'First of all, give me that camera; I'll have them developed.'

The white-clad page-boy took the machine.

'Firstly, Charlie Osmond, I know all about your skill as a photographer. Well, I'm mad on it myself, and I'm pretty good, you shall see directly.

'Now, what I want you to do is this. I know you're not too well off – pardon my being blunt. I want you to look after my photography, and incidentally see after getting models for me. You'll have to use a lot of tact, but you'll have a thundering good time.

'Why I want you is that I must have a gentleman; I can't have an ordinary professional photographer. I couldn't stick working with him, and Tubby

270

wouldn't like it. My great hobby is pictures of girls, in the nude, of course, and that's why I have my own pussy shaved: they have to have it done too. They are shy at first, but soon get used to it. We have quite lively parties. But come along, you shall see the studio first before you decide.'

Maudie unlocked a curtained door.

'This room I *do* keep under lock and key,' she said.

It was a huge octagonal room, glass roofed, with an admirable north light. One end of the octagon was a complete small theatre, 'With,' said Maudie, 'a large plant of scenery and every facility for producing all classes of stage plays.

'Wait till you see *some* of 'em: home made,' said Maudie. 'We've got some pretty wits among our members – we call it a club. It's supposed to exist for the practice of the higher photographic art, and the exhibition of *real* life on the stage.

'It is damned real, too, I can tell you.

'Our finest bit of realism was a play which lasted, on and off, for nearly a year.

'It started with a courtship, rivalry, seduction – dark man, dark night, and that sort of thing, you know – of course in full view of the audience. Then he marries her, and we ran through the first nine months of their life together, their lusts and their quarrels. How they both were untrue, and how she gets gradually larger in condition till she gets her belly bang right up, and she finally pups in full view of the audience.

'Of course we were lucky in having a girl who was not only a very good actress, but happened to be like

271

that, and was strong enough to play right through. It was Miss –,' naming a very well-known player.

Charlie started.

'Yes; that's how she spent her time when the papers said she was touring in Italy. Oh, she *is* a brazen bitch.'

But to the photography. Bar a number of photos lying on a big table on the carpeted daïs at the other end of the room, there was not much evidence of photography at all. No cameras, no pictures on the walls, which were entirely covered with what seemed to be a patchwork of little curtains.

'*Voilà*: hey, presto!' exclaimed Maudie, pressing a button at the side of the proscenium.

The walls altered as if at the touch of a fairy's wand, and a most gorgeous vista of photographic voluptuosity met Charlie's astonished and delighted eyes. Photos of every size were there, very many of them coloured, and most beautifully coloured.

There were no paintings except a life-sized oil of Maudie herself as Diana. That had been hung on the line at the academy. Charlie remembered it well now: it was signed by a well-known French portrait painter, in fact the greatest of them all, and the discoverer of genius in many an Englishman.

But this picture, magnificent though it was, was quite dwarfed by the variety and beauty of the photos.

First in numbers came the nudes. They were none of them of the blatantly crude, erotic, fucking, all-ends-up type, but they were – well – not the sort that Aunt Lavinia ought to see.

There were many single nudes, very nearly always the model being Maudie herself. For this she apologised.

'You see, Charlie,' she said, 'I have a paucity of models. This GREAT IDEA is only in its infancy yet; *that's* where I'm looking to you for help. Tubby's no good. If I left him to get me models he'd bring women like cart horses. Tubby has strange ideas of female beauty – why he is so infatuated with me, I *can't* think.

'No; I want more girl models for the *single* figures. It doesn't matter so much for the groups, as long as we have good principals.'

The single figures were very beautiful. There was a complete set of Maudie's life – Maudie in her bath – Maudie drying herself under the trees – Maudie in varying stages of dressing – Maudie riding, cycling, rowing, and in various gowns. The nearest approach to being very suggestive was Maudie with only her stockings and shoes on, but every strip of jewellery she possessed.

There were a number of pretty girl pictures, but nearly all the same models again.

'We *must* have more flappers,' said Maudie, vehemently.

The groups, however, were of the more surpassing interest, very many depicted great – and small, but interesting – events in the world's history. Biblical subjects were quite prevalent there; for instance, we had Susanna and the Elders. A lovely Susanna, mother naked, admiring herself in the well water, and the most lascivious-looking Elders admiring; in the middle distance, a pretty girl and boy, quite naked, were playing prettily with each other. The scenic effects were splendid. Maudie confessed that she had the help in that line of a very well-known

273

French actor manager, and that an English actor manager had put his scenic stock at her disposal.

Potiphar's wife was well treated. A naked Mrs. Potiphar had just rent the garment from the fleeing Joseph, who, with one hand attempting to conceal his parts, was rushing from the room.

Mrs. Potiphar, who blazed with jewels, was of a pronouncedly Egyptian type, sinuous and wicked-eyed. In Joseph, Charlie had not the slightest difficulty in recognising a prominent young stock-jobber.

'Where had he been in London all this time, and never heard of this place and their goings-on?' he wondered.

Samson and Delilah – God bless my soul – it was the famous wrestler, and *very* little clothes on, and *what* a Delilah – Maudie herself this time.

In Samson Agonistes, Samson was unencumbered with clothing. In the fight between David and Goliath, the giant had been, by some ingenious photographic trick, made to look a very real giant, and his John Thomas was a thing like a quarter-staff, his balls like melons.

A sweetly-pretty little David stood boldly forth in the foreground, aiming the sling.

There were some pictures of the historic intimacy between David and Jonathan, which left little to the imagination.

We have missed the earlier episode of the Garden of Eden. Adam and Eve were very frankly naked and unashamed in several positions, and there were the dearest possible Cain and Abel.

The scene where, after the fall (which, by the way, was realistically treated), the man and woman get themselves clothed was admirably arranged.

The strange behaviour of Lot's daughters, when they sat in turn on their poor old father's prick and got themselves in the family way, was reproduced in detail, as also was Onan's strange behaviour to his sister, when he foolishly spilt it on the floor.

King David and Bathsheba on the roof, and later the same pair in bed, were fully illustrated.

Of other historical pictures ancient Greece and Rome were mostly represented, especially the mythology of the former. A swan ('One of the King's from the Thames', giggled Maudie) was on top of Leda, this time Maudie again, and Jupiter enveloped Danäe in a most cunningly-contrived shower of gold. Venus, Anadyomene, and all the other chances to show the gods and goddesses naked, were fully utilised, but perhaps the best was Vulcan's revenge on the guilty lovers. Tubby figured always as a very tipsy Silenus.

In fact, everything in history of a picturesquely indelicate tendency was utilised.

Charlie was loud in his expressions of praise.

'This must be very valuable,' he said.

'Tubby's papa offered me a good deal above a bit; said he wanted to present it to the Manchester Watch Committee.'

Apart from the historical groups, which, of course, included Lady Godiva, there were some very charming allegorical pictures. A humorous one was 'Fecundity', in which Tubby and a portly dame were surrounded by sons and grandsons, daughters and grand-daughters, all dressed like Adam and Eve.

There were pretty modern pictures also, of life behind the scenes, river pleasure parties, and many clever snapshots.

'Well, that'll do for the present,' said Maudie; 'come and lunch. I'm rippingly hungry, and after lunch we'll have to get ready for Tubby and Aunt Lavinia.'

'I don't want any lunch, or Tubby, *or* Aunt Lavinia,' grumbled Charlie. 'I want to go to bed with you for the rest of the day.'

'Oh, you'll see lots of me in the future. I think you see the possibilities of our GREAT IDEA. This is only a penny peep-show at present. I, with your help and Tubby's money, am going to make it world-famous.'

Lunch was simple, but very delicate. After the salmon cutlets there was just a duck and salad, and a light savoury. Only hock cup and Grand Marnier with the coffee.

Two new maids, whom Charlie had no difficulty in recognising as originals of some of the photos, and in the page he recognised at once the boy David.

'Now,' – Maudie lifted an admonitory finger – 'this is the lie.

'Firstly, regarding your presence here. I knocked you down in Kensington last night. You were unconscious, but not bad enough for the hospital, so I brought you here.

'To Aunt Lavinia, I am the widow of a Polish count, and I knew Tubby abroad. That's all. Ah, I think I hear the car.'

The hum of the motor drew nearer, like a fury flying on the wind. Charlie fidgeted uneasily, and mechanically turned face downwards one or two very *outré* photographs. Aunt Lavinia mattered financially very much indeed, and *could* his

276

charming hostess be trusted?

Maudie was perfectly calm. As the scrunch of the wheels on the gravel denoted the arrival, she gave a little final twirl to a kiss-curl, and said to Charlie:

'Kiss me for luck.'

It was Aunt Lavinia.

The door swung open, and before the footman had time to announce them Lady Lavinia and Tubby were in the room.

Three

With the Nature Worshippers at Maudie's Mansion

Charlie's aunt, the dowager Lady Lavinia McCree, was not a woman who 'came' into rooms, nor could she be said to 'enter' them, or even 'rush' or 'burst' or 'sweep' in. She was there all of a sudden, before you had any idea of her arrival. Charlie was kissed, and Maudie warmly shaken hands with.

'How are you, Charlie? How foolish of you to be knocked down: I'm sure it was very good of this lady to knock you down. Of course you were drunk, so like your poor father. If there'd have been motorists about to knock him down and look after him, he'd have never got into the Thames at Westminster Bridge, thinking it was his bath, and caught his death –

'– And so my dear, you are Countess Orloffsky. Of course you must be sister-in-law or something of poor Paul Orloffsky; I knew him well. He married his cook, and she poisoned him with "rough on rats" in a paté, or something, and married the butler, and they took a hotel in Switzerland and had so many children. I fear he was a sad lot, my dear, your brother-in-law, I mean, not the butler, just like Charlie's father, and Charlie – but now that he has found a friend in you, I *know* you will have an *immensely* good influence. *And* that dear, good Mr. Evans-James, too, I do wish Charlie could see more of him – *such* a good influence.'

Tubby, who had been stifling a silly giggle, now almost exploded.

'So good of you, my dear, to let me use your car, such nice things, and so convenient, especially for people like Mr. Evans-James, being so fat, and unable to get about for his good works. His dear mother tells me how often he has to be away from town seeing after his camp missions.'

The old lady, having rattled this out at express speed, shut up as suddenly as she had begun, and sat down.

When she had been borne away to tidy up, Tubby took Charlie into the smoking-room.

Tubby was a very fat little man, with an exceptionally solemn cast of countenance, except when drunk, which was not infrequent. He had more money than he knew what to do with, and he welcomed anyone who would help him spend it as a benefactor.

'I say, old chap,' he said, 'this *is* a go.'

'Oh, I think your lady friend'll carry it off – auntie won't stop long.'

'I'm not so sure about that; she's after me and those damned camps that I've talked so much about.

279

The place at home is full of photos of 'em. Maudie faked 'em here. There's a wonderful studio here y'know – perhaps she's shown it you?'

'She *has*.'

'Oh, I say, you mustn't be upset or anything – but this *is* a hot shop, y'know. Well, I thought it too hot even to ask you. Oh, I say, did you *really* get knocked down by Maudie and the car. I could have *sworn* I saw you coming out of the Empire, boozed as a cock-bird. You didn't go and pick her up anywhere, did you?'

'Of course not; she wouldn't. She's been talking of nothing but you.'

'Bless her little heart! Well, we must make the most of it, Maudie says. You're staying the night. All the maids block, y'know,' he giggled fatuously. 'Try little Jessie.'

'Oh, I don't think so, old chap. I don't do much of that sort of thing.'

'More do I; not 'cos I don't like it, y'know, but I'm so fat, and it's such a dashed sweat. Like seeing other chaps do it much better. Lots of that here: oh, it *is* a hot shop. Pa's been here, he! he! Gad, if your old aunt tells him. I must put Maudie up to the settlement-camps business. Well, I must go and wash. You'll have the green room – artichoke, I call it – next to ours tonight. I'll wake you to-morrow morning.'

Charlie had fully determined to take this job on. He foresaw but little trouble over the Tubby business. He would make himself so useful that he knew he would be forgiven anything.

After dinner that night he begged to be excused. Sitting alone in the little smoking-room, he began to

280

think out his plans.

It *was* a *great* idea. With that wealth he could ransack Europe for girls. Wasn't it better than £300 a year and the secretaryship of a club – and if, in duty bound to Tubby, he mustn't go wrong with Maudie, for whom he already felt an almost ungovernable lust, there certainly would be no lack of others.

At that moment one of the pretty maids came in without knocking.

'Oh, mistress's compliments, sir, and she'd forgotten to give you the key of the wine and spirit cupboards; there they are. I'll open them.'

She brought out the necessaries, also a pile of books.

'Mistress says you might like these, too,' she giggled. 'Let me show you the best,' and she flicked over the pages of an obviously very erotic book, full of coloured plates of lust in every form. 'Saucy, aren't they? Look at this.'

It protrayed three couples, hopelessly mixed up, tongues, lips, cocks and cunts in helpless and joyful confusion.

She put her hand on Charlie's shoulder, playfully flicking his ear, and bending over kissed his forehead, pressing her breasts against the back of his head.

'I'm glad you've come,' she cooed; 'so are all the girls. We like you. I'm going to bring your hot water up to-night; mind you're awake.'

Charlie couldn't help it. He pulled her round on to his knee. She put his hand under her clothes herself, and wriggled.

'It's all right,' she said; 'no one will come in. This is what I'm best at,' and she slipped between his legs and undid the fly buttons with her teeth.

'You little devil!' was all Charlie could say.

A confused, gurgling noise was the only answer – his prick seemed to be half way down her throat.

He nervously fingered her head – she had deliciously soft hair – and gave himself to an abandon of lust.

She gently tickled his balls till his cock seemed to throb like a motor bicycle engine, and, well, it couldn't last for ever; he spent like Niagara.

The pretty girl threw back her head and gulped it down.

'I say, old chap,' came Tubby's voice from behind, 'you're beginning soon, y'know, and you've got the nicest, by God, y'have, and, I say, your aunt's looking for you, and she's going to stay the night, and what the devil are we going to do, what, what!'

The pretty maid stood up, blushing, and hung her head.

'You'd better be off, my dear,' said Tubby; 'and, for heavens sake, be careful what you do or say when that old lady's in the house.'

When they were alone, Charlie apologised.

'Oh, don't worry about *that*, old chap. You can do what you like to the girls, but it's your aunt – quick, for God's sake put those books away: I hear a rustle.'

Charlie was just in time. Lady Lavinia was in the room just as the cupboard door slammed.

She sniffed at the collection of liquors.

'As I thought, drinking, and *solitary* drinking. Why couldn't you be like your friend and come in the drawing-room for a little music?

'And what's this?' She picked up a maid's cap from the floor. 'One of the *servant's* caps! What's it doing

282

here?'

'Oh, I suppose she must have dropped it,' answered Charlie, pettishly. 'I'll come down to the drawing-room now. It'll be bed-time in a few minutes.'

In the servants' quarters of the house, discussion as to the identity and *raison d'être* of the new guests ran rife.

Young men of the world like Charlie were no new thing, but Aunt Lavinia – in such a house – well!

'Such particular instructions I've had to clear her room of anything saucy,' said the old housekeeper, gossiping in her room with the butler and the chauffeur; 'and I'm to take 'er tea myself: let none of them 'ussies go near.

'It makes me fair nervous, it do. Not that I altogether 'old with these games 'ere, but we're all in it, with our eyes open – oh, dear, *if* she should see some of them pictures.'

''Twould be a to-do, and no error,' said the butler.

'And the good lady she tink Mr. Bertie so good young man vos – ha! ha!' and the chauffeur laughed viciously. 'She into what you call a 'ornet's nest got, is it not?'

In the greater servants' hall speculation was also rife: guests seldom arrived at that house except in very large parties, in motor loads at a time, as a rule. And as for mistress bringing home a single young man, she hadn't done such a thing for years.

No one had seen his condition when he arrived except the chauffeur, who had maintained a dogged silence. He had been told to do so, and his job was too good to lose.

They were a free and easy lot in the upper servants' hall at Maudie's, with a very large preponderance of women, mere girls, many of them, and all pretty. In fact, the house was ridiculously over-stocked with females. There was nothing for them to do save when the very big parties were on, and then they were more required for the photography than anything else.

There were only two men, both deft-handed servants, and both French, and a French-American cook, who was rather a wet blanket on the general irresponsibility of the girls. There remained the page-boy, and several other young boys and girls who helped in the scullery.

The girls did not care much for the two Frenchmen, and the cook thought of nothing at all but inventing new dishes; hence the joy with which Charlie was received.

It was an appetising scene. Everything in the house was done, and the girls sprawled in varied alluring *déshabillés* – it was a hot night, and drawers and chemise, or chemise only, or drawers and vest, and one or two, vest only. Two were quite naked. The room was very comfortable to lounge in, and Maudie didn't care what happened so long as she was waited on quickly. Two girls remained dressed, ready to see their mistress and Lady Lavinia to bed when rung for.

The page-boy was in general request, fetching coffee and cigarettes, and came in for a good deal more petting than was good for him. In fact, he was quite *blasé*. The warm caress of a semi-naked divinity had *no* effect on him.

284

They disappeared to bed by degrees, till only Elsie and May were left.

'Are you going to take the new gentleman any hot water?' queried May.

'Yes,' answered Elsie.

It was she who had come into the smoking-room.

'May I follow you?'

'A good half-hour after me. I tell you, dear, I need something badly; I haven't had my legs opened for a week, and it's just about time. You come in later, and we'll see what the two of us can't make him do: he's got a rare big 'un.'

'Right' – and they sealed the compact with a kiss.

There are few things prettier than the sight of two pretty women who are both lustful, and who really care for each other, kissing as if they meant it.

Upstairs, after two whiskies and sodas, which she was not accustomed to, Aunt Lavinia became first garrulous, then sleepy. After her departure, the three culprits first looked serious, then giggled.

Maudie spoke first.

'Look here, Tubby,' she said, 'the Lord blew Charlie against my carburettor: I recognised him, and brought him here, *for a purpose*.

'That purpose I have explained to him, and will to you. I want him to entirely supervise our photographic and theatrical séances. What do you think?'

'Oh, I think he'd do admirably,' said Tubby, a little doubtfully; 'but what does Charlie think?'

'Oh, I'm game enough.'

'Then let's call it a deal right off,' said Maudie. 'I know you two boys will get on ripping. We'll just have a nightcap, and so, like Mr. Pepys, to bed.'

Tubby rolled over in bed, and grunted, then he kissed his bedfellow, and was immediately asleep. Maudie sighed. She had had a great deal too much of this of late. She thought over the events of the day, and longed for Charlie. For one wild moment she recollected how firmly Tubby slept, and contemplated making a dash for Charlie's room – but prudence prevailed. She mustn't jeopardise the future. She took up a book, *Nadia*, a lustful romance, and tried to read herself to sleep, but in vain. Her blood boiled, and at last she woke up Tubby roughly.

'Tubby, dear, I *must* and *will* be fucked,' she said. 'You hardly ever touch me, and yet you expect me to be true to you. Come on.'

Tubby acquiesced sadly. His extreme stoutness made it quite impossible for him to attack in the old Adam and Eve fashion. He had to do it as the beast of the field. He got out of bed and turned Maudie over its edge. Then, without seeming in the slightest enraptured by the sight of her snowy white buttocks, he deliberately plunged his sausage-like machine into that gap which should only have been reserved for connoisseurs.

Of course he liked it: he was very healthy, and full of good food and wine, and his penis swelled enormously as his strokes increased in vigour. Maudie lay on her stomach, her pretty little face buried in the lace-edged pillow, and her brain, behind her closed eyes, just a blissful vision of Charlie.

Oh! if it had only been Charlie!

The fact is known that sometimes women who, when madly lustful for particular men, are forced to be carnal elsewhere, derive really more pleasure from the beatific dream of their fancied darling, who in a vision is responsible for the flesh spasms which the unseen operator manipulates, than they do when the real darling is in the saddle, so to speak.

Maudie certainly loved it, and she was only just conscious enough of what had happened to bite her tongue to stop crying 'Charlie' as the last violent stroke from her fat lover sent a hard-shot torrent right up to the doors of her womb.

'My God,' she thought, 'I really believe Tubby has copped me this time.'

She hastened to syringe, a precaution she seldom took with her fat lover.

Tubby, on his part, sank exhausted into an armchair.

'You've fair whacked me this time, petlet,' he gasped. 'I've never had a fuck like this with you before. What's come over you?'

The dream was still in Maudie's brain as she answered vaguely, 'How – how can you help it, when you love so much?'

When Tubby did turn off to sleep he dreamed rapturously. Maudie, too, slept well: she was thoroughly tired at last. These physical and mental fucks combined are pretty fairly damaging to the vitality.

Lady Lavinia, when the pretty maid had helped her out of her clothes and given her a nightdress, the decorations of which ill coincided with the elderly widow, removed her wig, put her teeth in a glass, and sniffed round the room.

She could not but approve of the comfort. No detail necessary to coax comfort to the weary or lazy bed-goer was missing.

Maudie had put it to her very delicately that if she had neuralgia – or anything – there was 'something' in the cupboard.

She had a look, and found, in addition to the 'something', a pile of books, one of which she picked out at random.

It was prettily bound, and called *Nemesis Hunt*. She took it back to bed with her, had a very hearty drop of the 'something', and opened it.

A good many readers of this book may have read *Nemesis Hunt*. They will remember that that charming and loquacious lady somewhat lets the tail go with the hide in her confessions. A fuck is called a fuck, and there is *more* than fucking in the naïve three volumes.

Lady Lavinia's eyes dilated as she read. Once before, in the very early days of her married life, she had been shown a book like this by her husband, and she remembered now, with a sigh, *what* a night they had subsequently had.

Her first impulse was to throw down the book in anger, the consciousness of her position, her reputation, flashed through her brain, but – curiosity prevailed, and Lady Lavinia, firmly adjusting her glasses, took another strong sip of the 'something', and started seriously in to read the first volume of *The Confessions of Nemesis Hunt*.

When young, she had been very pretty, and had been much courted. She had loved admiration, and had flirted above a bit.

Her short married life with the late earl had been a long round of love and lust, and frank sexual enjoyment, but his sudden death had brought about an equally sudden revulsion of feeling.

Lady Lavinia had turned suddenly very good, mid-Victorian good. She had mourned her husband, and put a great deal of mournfulness into other people's lives by doing so – as have other illustrious widows.

Now there came back a rush of something – it must have been Georgian – and she let down the drawbridge.

At the end of the fifteenth page of Nemesis Hunt's pleasant confessions, she decided to leave on the morrow, *but* return.

Nemesis was put under the pillow, and in that very ultra-modern house there slept what may be described as a memory of Cremorne.

Charlie Osmond went to bed with mixed feelings. He had had a very good time: he had a prospect of future life in view, which he rather welcomed – *but*, he wanted to be with Maudie – not to be immoral, but to talk. It flatly bored him to go to bed.

Outside, the Thames valley looked very peaceful. The dogs, the chickens, everything slept, except Charlie, *and* Elsie and May, who, after seeing to the little wants of Lady Lavinia and Maudie, bided their time for an invasion into Charlie's room.

That worthy had his suspicions of impending events. He did not lock the door, but sat by the window in his pyjamas, and gazed peacefully out over the moonlit garden and river.

It was altogether rather too nice, too idyllic, and – well – the door opened, and Elsie came in without knocking.

She was fully dressed, and carried a tray with hot water and glasses.

Charlie laughed.

'I somehow expected you,' he said; 'but do you know it's very wrong. You don't know what I am, whether I'm married or not, or *what* trouble this might get me into.'

Elsie laughed.

'Well, I've done it,' she said. 'I meant to from the first moment I saw you. Give me a cigarette and a drink, and let me come and sit in the window, and you won't be bored for the next half hour, I can promise you.'

Elsie curled up on the corner of the window-seat, the moon full on her delicate little features, lit the proffered Albany cigarette, sipped a little of the whisky and Rosbach, and grinned, frankly grinned.

'I suppose you think it frightful cheek,' she suggested.

'Well, I can't say I don't like your cheek,' and he kissed it.

Elsie kissed him back on the lips, and took off her bodice. She had very pretty arms, and a gold bangle with a purple enamel medallion, worn just above the left elbow, did not make them less attractive.

She had a little more of the Three Star Bushmills, stood up and slid her skirt off: then her chemise – she wore no petticoats – and to cut a long story short, her next sitting-place was on Charlie's knee, and the next kiss had nothing to do with cheeks.

Charlie lifted her on to the bed. Even then, though

she was exasperatingly pretty, he could not help thinking of Maudie.

She curled over him, slowly, deliberately and maliciously taking both his hands in hers, and rubbing her soft cheeks against his.

There must be something in telepathy, for at the moment, the precise moment that Charlie reconciled himself to a connection which he *knew* would be nice, but which he really did not want, save for the exquisite pleasure in thinking that Elsie's arms were Maudie's, that latter lady saw in a blue mist of ecstacy the image of a very loving Charlie – poor Tubby being merely the engine-driver who drove the imagination of her recklessly lustful brain.

Charlie let himself frankly go. There was no light in the room at all bar the shafts of the moon, filtering through the swaying trees. The silhouetted skyline and the delightfully placid atmosphere made Charlie lazy.

He had some recollection of little tickling fingers swiftly undoing the strings of his pyjamas, little tickling fingers also playing with an already erect member, naked arms twisted round his neck, firm, plump legs twisted round his thighs, and – well – he was in – well in – and those soft cheeks were most lustfully pressed to his.

Maudie had been very loving, *but* – all said and done – as he felt all his love juice being sucked out of him, *this*, Charlie couldn't help admitting, was better still.

He came in a long rhapsody: the girl jerked the eiderdown over them, and snuggled up. He didn't know whether she meant to stay the night, or not, or what the morals of this peculiar house permitted, but it was *very* comfortable.

He was just going to sleep when the door opened very quietly, and *another* girl came into the moonlight.

Charlie gave up. He remembered where he was, and determined to die game. The 'other girl' apologised laughingly, and the original giggled in the sheets.

'You don't mind May, do you?' she said.

'No,' was Charlie's answer; 'but it's got to stop at May, you and May. If I've got to go through the whole *personnel* of the establishment, I give up.'

May did not answer – but just, just seemed to *slide* – just as Elsie had done – out of her clothes, and into bed.

Poor, but happy Charlie – he realised quite what a squeezed lemon must feel like – but he valiantly did his duty.

May was more placid than Elsie, more tender, more caressing, perhaps, but Charlie's cock was just as stiff as he felt his balls right against the soft buttocks of his new love.

It was a long fuck and a delightful one. Elsie, wicked little devil, gave every help in her power.

She flung back the clothes, and there they lay, three naked bodies in the moonlight. There was no artificial light save the glow of Elsie's cigarette end.

Elsie slipped the pillow down so that her little friend's bottom was just correctly raised, and, as Charlie knelt between May's legs, guided his penis dexterously in.

May, of course, was shaved, in the fashion of everyone in Maudie's mansion, and Charlie began more and more to appreciate the added charm of the hairless cunt, as he thrust his fingers between their bodies and felt the soft, warm, smooth flesh.

Elsie crept right on top of them, her head between Charlie's legs, so that her tongue swept over and over his swelling balls. As his cock slipped in and out of May, her fingers played with it. May had a large cunt, and Elsie's little finger could slip in beside Charlie's cock.

Her cunt was on his backbone, and on that she frigged herself – he felt the warm love moisture much about the same time as he spent himself in May.

He didn't recollect the actual end, didn't recollect anything till a stream of daylight dazzled him into being, and he found himself alone – with a little note pinned on each side of his broad pillow.

Each read the same: 'Thanks *so* much.'

Only the handwriting and the signature were different. One 'Elsie' – the other 'May'. He was thoroughly wakened up by the arrival of the page-boy with tea and a note.

The note simply ran: 'Get down to breakfast as quick as you can – in the garden – Tubby's going – so's Aunt Lavinia, and we've *got* to talk business.'

Aunt Lavinia was 'deadly' at breakfast, but she made it plain, in no uncertain terms, that she was coming back.

Tubby, rather a weary Tubby, shovelled her into the car, and they disappeared with a toot and a cloud of dust.

'Well,' said Maudie, coughing the petrol fumes out of her throat, 'I shan't ask you what you've done with your night. I want to get to business at once. Tubby *quite* sees the business side of the affair.'

Four

Near the *Barbican* is a London street of which one would *not* expect great possibilities. All the busy city traffic roars by at the street end, but in itself it is very unobtrusive.

There, in a large, rambling, old-fashioned house Charlie Osmond had established what he liked to call his 'office'.

Ugly enough to look at from the outside, the 'office' was not without attractions within.

Photographs, not so elaborate as in Maudie's own studio, were conspicuous, and the furniture, especially the two lazy divans, very comfortable, and suggestive.

Here Tubby paid the rent, and here Charlie presided, when he was not travelling in search of his models.

Maudie had a tiny suite of rooms on the top floor,

with a staircase leading on to a flat roof.

She sat there one evening, waiting for Charlie, who was due home, with, she hoped, further prey.

The hum of a motor made her look over the low parapet. It *was* Charlie, and the closed car likewise disgorged four cloaked little figures, and Elsie.

Maudie went down, just pausing on the way to telephone Tubby's club the one mystic word 'Tenuc', which, as all our readers possibly know, is back slang for cunt.

Charlie came into her room.

'I've got four little peaches, all from the north. The last is a hot'un, and no mistake. She had to sit on my knee as the car was so crowded, and, oh, Lord, I have had a horn: I thought my poor John Thomas would burst.'

Maudie laid her hand lovingly on it: it sprang into being again.

'I'm sorry, dear, I can't oblige,' she said, 'but I'm unwell, and very badly unwell. I *daren't* when I'm like that. Shall I suck you off, or will you have Elsie?'

'Well, don't think me a beast, darling, you know how I love you. I'm so damned randy that I feel I *must* have a good square fuck. Oh, God, take your hand off, or I shall come in my trousers.'

Maudie rang, and a neat little, semi-flapper maid was sent to fetch the fuck to be.

'Another thing, I'm expecting Tubby, and he still thinks I'm true to him, bless him.'

'On the sofa, Elsie, and quick, the poor boy's randy.'

The pretty girl put her tongue out saucily, got quickly on the broad sofa, and pulled up her clothes to the waist.

'My word, you *have* got pretty legs,' said Maudie; 'I believe they're more perfect than mine. Let's measure.'

She pulled up *her* clothes.

'Oh, for God's sake, come off it,' said Charlie. 'I haven't had a blow through for a week. Neither of your legs is as fine as this,' and he produced his throbbing member.

It certainly was a very fine one, and it had been admired all over Europe. They've got a model in clay of it in Suzette de Vries place in the Rue Colbert. On his birthday it is hung with ribbons.

'No time for taking down trousers,' he said, and in a twinkling his arms were clasped round her shoulders, and her shapely calves were twisted round his thighs.

Maudie slipped her hand between them to see how close they were.

They might have been a single being. There was not the usual commingling of hair, for Charlie was now shaved, in deference to Maudie's wishes, and Elsie, of course, was.

They hardly moved. Most of Maudie's friends were adepts at what she called 'thrill fucking'. That barred the rough piston-like 'in and out' thrust, and the consummation was reached after a delicate succession of clasps and pressures and limb thrills. Elsie, her hands beneath Charlie's coat, tickled his spine. His hands massaged her back. Their eyelashes met in gentle titillation, and their tongues played softly with each other's. Maudie, sitting alongside – the couch was very broad – gently smoothed Charlie's head.

'Oh, I say, y'know, Maudie, you *ought* to lock the

door. It's damned indecent, y'know, Maudie. I've got some fellers with me, and they might have come in, dashed awkward, y'know.'

Tubby's voice seemed quite concerned.

'Don't be jealous, fat head, *you're* going to have a genial afternoon.'

'Good, oh! I say, who's the artist on top in the fuck?'

'Only me, old son,' grunted Charlie.

'Then buck up, laddie,' said the fat man, and gave his bottom a sturdy smack. 'I want to hear what's going to happen. Fuck on, Macduff, and get it over.'

Charlie finished with a deep sigh, and uncoupled.

'Now then,' said Tubby, 'I've got fellers waitin'. There's old General Fitzhugh, randy as a bull, and young Phil Neville, just down from Cambridge, and that poet chap with the long hair, Claude Lestrange: he's been making poetry all the way down.'

'I'll just run down and see the kids,' said Maudie. 'Charlie'll explain.'

'Buck up, old sport, then,' said Tubby; 'shove your cock in, and tell us all about it. Elsie, run along and syringe: we don't want you with your belly up.'

Charlie explained briefly that he had got some girls for more photography.

'They're all north country, Newcastle hinnies – the eldest knows above a bit, I think. I've had some new shaped razors made for you in Sheffield. They couldn't think what the devil I wanted them for.'

Maudie met the girls in the little waiting-room near the studio. They were examining the pictures with interest.

Charlie certainly had done well. Four sweetly pretty faces met Maudie's pleased gaze.

The eldest and tallest, a brunette, had an almost Spanish face, rich, ripe red lips, and a haughty poise. She was the relic, perhaps, of some Spanish Armada prisoner who had dropped his love-stick in a Northumberland wench.

The other three were about the same height. One had a mass of Titian red hair, and the extreme pallor of skin that goes with it.

The other two were blondes, obviously with Danish and Norse blood in them, and with clear blue eyes.

They were all daintily clad. Charlie had stopped at Manchester and seen to that. The eldest had her skirts just below the knee, but the others showed the knee-cap, and a fringe of pretty *frou-frou* under-clothes.

They were all consciously proud of their obviously unaccustomed finery.

Maudie kissed them, found out their names, made a fuss of them generally, and gave them tea.

She was alone for a moment with the eldest girl.

'Say, mum,' said the latter, 'I'm no kid, and I can see that we weren't brought here only to be pretty artist's models. Now, *I'm* game for anything, and I expect the others will be. They can't read or write, so I'll do the writing home to their mammas; that'll be best, won't it?'

It certainly was sensible, and Maudie was very glad. There had been times when she *had* been a bit nervous.

Likewise, which was very awkward, there was a little disaffection in the camp. May had fallen frankly and openly in love with Charlie, and was obviously jealous. Charlie did not return it, but

298

Maudie could not afford to have a split, and had almost to *beg* of him to afford her occasional embraces.

If May chose to give things away in the outside world, it might be very unpleasant. They were always prepared for flight, motors in readiness, and a big steam yacht, but they did not *want* to have to fly.

Charlie and Tubby went down to the 'office' or studio. General Fitzhugh was tramping round the room, fiercely twisting his moustache, and ejaculating. 'Ha!' at intervals, as he spotted anything particularly tasty in the photographs.

Tubby's undergraduate friend sat meekly, rather uneasily, on a divan, and the poet wandered soulfully about, humming faintly.

'Ah, General,' said the poet to the old officer, who was very closely examining the life-size portrait of a fascinating young lady, and which particularly emphasised her vagina, 'ah, General, a tempting subject:

'How sweeter than the horrid clash of arms,
The contemplation of those naked charms.'

The General sniffed: he did not like poetry, or poets.

'A dashed fine young woman, sir,' he snorted.

The poet persisted:

'Dost thou not yearn, oh, son of Mars, to thrust
The vibrant signal of a lusting man
Into yon fragrant arbour, there to place

299

In form of sperm ambrosial, a fair child?
Dost thou not –'

But the General turned on him.

'I don't know what the hell you mean, sir, by all that tomfool nonsense, but if you've the accursed effrontery to call my cock a "vibrant signal", I'd have you know that the word cock has been good enough for the Fitzhughs for generations, sir. "Vibrant signal", indeed, you'll be calling my arse-hole a railway tunnel next.'

'Oh, sir,' protested the poet, ''tis but poetic licence.'

'Then you ought to dashed well have your licence taken away – and, look here, if by "fragrant arbour" you mean that young person's cunt, I'd have you to know that the Fitzhughs call it cunt, sir, and always have. My father called it cunt, my mother had a cunt, I came out of a cunt, and many a cunt have I stuck my good cock into.

'"Fragrant arbour"! there's a damned good stink attached to some of them, and I *like* it.

'And don't you refer to my good spunk as ambrosial sperm, or I'll toss myself off in your eye, and let you know whether it smells ambrosial or not.'

Tubby, overhearing, laughed loud.

Directly afterwards, Maudie, followed by her flapper recruits, entered.

The girls stared about them in amazement, all save the eldest, who frankly grinned, and returned the old General's ogle with interest.

Elsie entered with a friend of Maudie's, a middle-aged, Anglo-French woman, whom we have not met before in this narrative.

She was a Madame Rade, and had been an actress. Still the amount of money she had made, *not* at acting, had enabled her to consult her growing corpulency, and retire.

She was a jolly woman, very sexy, and there was very little wickedness she was not up to, and expert at. It was she who had taught Maudie the art of the 'thrill fuck'.

With her came her adopted niece, a very typical French flapper.

Her skirts were short and plaid, her boots, on her slight, delicate legs, were very high and elegant, and her rather long hair fell in two plaits down her back.

Madame was educating her for the stage, equally for a life of smart prostitution, and she was having her taught all languages.

'I have seen *so* much money lost by charming tarts,' she said, 'just because they could *not* talk any language but their own. After all, fucking is very nice indeed, but a man *does* like a little love chat, and a student of nature *does* like to be interested. There's one new brothel in Berlin, where the girls have regular lessons every day.

'Those girls *do* score over the lassies whose conversation is limited to phrases such as, "You fuck my cat: oh, just such nice cat, ten franc."'

Madame Rade had not let the girl go wrong yet; she wanted a big price for that precious virginity, but there was nothing the little darling didn't know. Her greeting kiss to Charlie was by no manner of means virginal.

Maudie had explained to the girls that the studies would be in the nude, and that they mustn't mind being inspected by quite a number of artists.

The assembled men were introduced as artists, and then one of the girls was told to undress. She rather timidly asked if she was to do it there, or was there a screen.

'Here, of course, darling,' said Maudie; 'you'll soon get used to that. Never mind your shoes and stockings this time. We only want to see the upper part of your figure now, so that we can tell *what* sort of picture you'll do for.'

Charlie had bought very pretty underlinen indeed, and as the upper garments slid away the little darling was a scrumptious sight. The poet sighed voluptuously. He was about to burst into song, when he caught the General's eye.

'Oh, one thing,' said Maudie, 'I forgot, dearie; have you any hair on your body?'

'Yes, a little, mum,' she replied.

'I'm afraid, then, dear, that you must let that be shaved off. You see, all our pictures here have no hair on. It won't hurt you: don't be frightened, and this gentleman,' pointing to Tubby, 'is quite an expert, aren't you, Tub-Tub?'

Tubby grinned: he had been examining the ingenious razors which Charlie had brought from Sheffield: no wonder the good Messrs. Rogers had been surprised. They were in several shapes, and no steady hand could do possible harm.

'Oh, yes, you have, it must be done,' said Gladys, as the girl stood naked, a sea of *frou-frou* undies round her ankles. The poet could not resist it:

'Child Venus rising from the sea,
No crested waves could fairer be

302

Than those sweet frills:
Oh, daintier than –'

'Young man,' said the General, very severely,
'during the Mutiny I had men blown from the
cannon's mouth for *less* than that.'

Maudie patted the blushing girl on her naked
shoulder, and led her to a big chair, with a front
extension, something like a dentist's.

She lay back, her bottom raised on a cushion, her
legs wide apart.

Tubby approached with his tray of instruments.
The poor girl shuddered, and involuntarily closed
her legs.

This was too much for the poet. Waving his hand
first towards the girl, and then the General, he
declaimed:

'Back, ruthless youth, oh, spare, oh, spare, I crave,
That down ethereal. Can'st thou dare to shave
The rippling foliage of the Venus Hill?
Turn rather HERE, and thy vandal will
On *this* brave warrior, used to clash of steel,
HIS manly forest clip –'

'Bu God, damme, sir,' roared the General, 'if any
one dares to lay one finger on my bush, I'll cut off his
cock and balls, and make him eat 'em, damme, I
will.'

Before the poet could answer, a small voice
chirped up:

'There once was a General brave
Who refused his cock whiskers to shave,

303

Till the crabs that he got
 Made him clip off the lot,
 And *didn't* that General rave.'

It was the young Cambridge undergraduate: the first words he had spoken.

The General did rave.

'Crabs, sir, crabs, you insolent puppy! Look here, sir,' and he ripped open his trousers, showing a flabby penis, fringed with grey-white hair; 'crabs, sir, I'll give you a thousand pounds if you can find *one*.'

'Oh, la! la!' ejaculated Madame Rade.

'I apologise: I apologise, ladies,' said the General hastily. 'I had forgotten your presence.'

He put back his penis.

The young man said he had meant no offence, and giggled feebly.

The patient, consoled by Maudie, opened wide her legs once more, and Tubby operated.

First he ran lightly over the slight downy bush with a clipper, then lathered it with some sweet-scented soap.

Quickly, with a small razor, he slid off the top part of the bush – the girl had very little. Then, with rounded razors, he removed the soft, glossy down just beginning to show between her legs.

She was quite bare-shaved. Maudie and Elsie brought a basin of sweet-smelling liquid with which Tubby anointed the girl.

Maudie and Elsie withdrew a little, and Tubby was left gazing at his work.

An added pink tint to the shaved parts of the flesh seemed to accentuate the roseate beauty of her cunt itself.

A little demure *débutante* of a flower-bud it seemed, half shy to open, half conscious of the beauty that should spread to give its honey to the expectant bees of mankind.

The little audience was very silent: Tubby seemed to hold the key to the situation: *something* was expected of Tubby.

He went 'bafil' all in a second, tore off his clothes, pirouetted nakedly in front of the nymph, like a porpoise on heat, and threw his head between her thighs.

The dainty little legs curled instinctively over his neck: the watchers could see his tongue dart into the moss-bare orifice – and the watchers could also see Tubby's by no means inconsiderable penis distend itself alarmingly.

It throbbed in time to the darts of his tongue: it was like a conductor's baton guiding the strokes of that first violin of lust – his tongue – and his buttocks heaved with it, suggestive of an accompaniment of brass and drums.

Suddenly the girl's legs tightened, a happy cry escaped her, and her fingers tattooed on Tubby's head.

For a moment he was *quite* quiescent, muscles flaccid, penis even semi-rigidly dependent.

Then he sprang up, gave a loud cry, and fell upon his penis with his own hands.

Two convulsive grips, and he shot a stream of semen amongst his audience.

Then he blushed all over, tomato red from forehead to toe and, forgetting his clothing, fled from the girl's side.

'The Paean of Silenus,' murmured the poet.

Quickly Elsie sponged the nymph's cunt, wiped dry the rosy lips of love's portal, all humid with the juice of rapture, kissed her on the forehead, playfully slapped her bottom, slipped a Japanese kimono on to her, and beckoned another.

Meanwhile Tubby had hidden portions of his shame with a towel, and was endeavouring to hide his confusion amidst a whisky and soda and Charlie's loud laughter.

'Damme,' he expostulated, 'I couldn't help it, damme if I could. Those sort of things come on a fellow so damned sudden like, y'know.'

'Oh, Onan, Onan,' it was the poet's voice, 'turn'st thou in thy grave, to see thy foul example impulsed by a shave, of dainty flappers' cunts –'

But Maudie shut him up.

'Quiet, now: here's another flapper for Tubby – come on, Tubby.'

Tubby went forward to the attack: his hand a little shaky perhaps, but with a determined glint in his eye.

It was the red-haired girl.

And the Titian glory that covered her head scarcely eclipsed the flaming beauty of the curls at the pit of her stomach. Her absolutely dead ivory white skin seemed literally to have burst into flame between her thighs and arm-pits.

She sat back in the chair, more confidently than the first one.

'No, no, damn it, no,' cried the General, 'it's a wicked cruel shame to cut that off.'

'I agree,' said the poet, 'let, Madame, let, that flame torch of love remain.'

The general opinion seemed to be the same.

'She shall be the *one* exception to the rule then,' said Maudie.

The pretty girl got up, seemingly a little annoyed that she had been bereft of Tubby's affections.

The north country girl, Jeannie Taylor, came next. She was more mature, and her figure was almost a woman's. With frankly lascivious eyes she smiled on the onlookers, and lay back on the chair with a tempting wriggle.

Her skin was olive in tint, a pretty contrast to the scarlet of her nipples, scarlet which rivalled her lips. The hair on her body curled jet black, rich and luxuriant, almost covering the red lips of her cunt.

Tubby saw, as he brushed back the hair, that the moisture came trickling to the lips. As he looked into her eyes he read lust incarnate, and he could feel a throb of desire as he touched the skin.

Once more his member asserted its manhood, as he knelt, delicately razing away the hairs; it flung up its head, casting aside the guardian towel, and when, the shave completed, the hairs and the lather washed away, and he looked at the now fully-viewed cunt lips, pouting and swelling, almost seeming to talk to him, he promised himself more than a mere kiss this time.

He did kiss it, and had gone so far as to get one knee on the chair between hers when he was interrupted. Maudie didn't want her own particular, jewelled-in-every-hole Tubby to get *too* fond of this sort of thing – with *others*. 'We haven't much time, my Tubby,' she cooed, 'so *that'll* keep for the present. Next lady forward please.'

The young undergraduate from Cambridge gave a heavy sigh of relief. *That* he intended to be his own bit, if possible.

'Next,' repeated Maudie.

'First lady forward, *second* lady pass, *third* lady's finger up the *fourth* lady's arse,' hummed the young undergrad, Phil Learoyd, in remembrance of some alleged ballet instructions.

Tubby smilingly obeyed, and Charlie lifted the pretty girl from the couch, and left her to wander among the others, mother naked as she was.

There was no question of the fact that the absence of hair was as becoming to her olive skin as the presence of it was to the fiery-haired beauty. Charlie couldn't help thinking what a lovely sight it would be to see *soixante-neuf* between the two – and mentally decided that he would see it.

Tubby, his frustrated cockstand erectly grinning at his fat stomach, sulkily refused to shave any more, and Maudie took the last girl in hand herself.

This last had perhaps the daintiest figure of the quartette, and she was the subject of the first photograph.

The magnesium flashed and the naked loveliness was transferred to the film.

Once more the flash, and Charlie felt sure he had a beauty, the red-haired girl and the dark one clasped in amorous embrace, arms and legs intertwined, bodies pressed tight together, and the glorious Titian red tresses mingling with the equally voluptuous raven hair. It was only a suggestion of wild eroticism – Charlie meant to keep his *soixante-neuf* tit-bit till later.

The party broke up, and the word was given out to set forth for Staines and the joys of 'Rosedale'.

308

Five

'Phil's Fuck'

The journey was to be made by motor, but there was
not quite enough room, and young Phil, Tubby's
undergraduate friend, developed a stroke of genius.
He volunteered to take Jeannie in a taxi.

They all thought him too young to be harmful,
and taxi it was for Jeannie and him.

London, and such things as taxis, were revelations
to Jeannie. Of course she had seen plenty of motors
up north, but she had never been in one. She hadn't
much idea where she was going. Phil Learoyd, her
young companion, explained that it was a long way,
but she felt deliciously comfortable.

He wasn't quite certain what to do. There was
time to do a good bit before Staines.

'Had any dinner?' he said.

'Not yet,' the lady said, 'we should when we get
there; where *is* "there", by the way?'

'Oh, it's a jolly place. You'll love it: every sort of comfort, but it's a bit hot, you know.'

'I guessed that: I'm not quite silly, though I haven't been to Lunnon before.'

He took her to Frascati's, expecting her to be open-eyed.

'Marvellous, isn't it?' he queried.

'It isn't the Midland at Manchester,' she answered. 'Mr. Osmond took us there, and we had a lovely time, such lovely bedrooms.'

'So Charlie had done his little charges pretty well,' Phil thought.

'Did you sleep alone?'

'Ah, that's telling.'

But the second glass of champagne loosened her tongue. When he repeated the question, she admitted, with a good many blushes, that she 'hadn't *exactly*'.

'He was an actor,' she said, 'awfully good-looking, and he sat opposite us at dinner, and Mr. Osmond took us to the theatre, and he was *just lovely*, and I saw him again in the winter garden, and I heard him ask the waiter who we were, and I saw him give the waiter something, so I suppose he got the number of my room. At any rate, about one I heard a tapping – and – well, I didn't know whether it mightn't be Mr. Osmond, but I opened the door – and he shut it behind me, and locked it, and put the key in his pyjama pocket before I knew what he was doing.'

'What infernal cheek!'

'He was *awfully* nice about it.'

'Did he –?'

'Of course he did – four times.'

'You little devil!'

'Yes, and he gave me a fiver, and told me he'd take me on, *at once*, in his company, if I'd go. Of course I'd promised Mr. Osmond, but I should have liked it. That wasn't my first time, you know.'

'What!'

'No – the first was the timekeeper at the works. He forced me, and then got me the sack because I told father. He was a beast. Then there was an old man who used to deal with father – father's a dog-stealer – I mean a dog-dealer. He took me to Blythe for the night. I think father knew – he seemed to have more money than usual just after that. I only got a new frock. He was a nasty old man, used to make me run round the room, naked, and smack my bottom.

'He was good to us, though; when father got into trouble over the prize bull-dog he st – that got lost, he kept all of us.

'Then there was a Japanese sailor officer, over for building a ship.'

'And the actor of Manchester was the next and last.'

'Yes.'

'And who's going to be the next?'

The girl sipped her champagne, looked Phil straight in the eyes, and grinned.

The taxi swung through the West End, and into the Hammersmith road.

Jeannie was on his knees, a little excitedly intoxicated, and very loving.

She was commenting on the way the twopences jumped up, when Phil had an idea.

He put his hand right up her clothes, and met with

311

no opposition.

'Am I to be the next?'

'Of course, you silly.'

'Well, I've got an idea. You sit on it, and watch the taxi-dial. You sit *absolutely* still, with your arms round me, and every time it changes you jump up and down once, and every time you do that you get five bob – it ought to take me about five miles to fuck you at that rate, or more. That's £1 a mile: is that a bet?'

'Of course, dear; it's a lovely idea.'

He put her on, she had to sit with her back to him, and every quarter-of-a-mile till Hounslow Heath she bobbed deliciously. It worked out at about £7.

Phil came rapturously. He had never enjoyed a fuck so much before – the flashing lights that passed them – it was getting dusk – the whole novelty of the thing, and the obvious enjoyment of the girl, coupled with her extreme prettiness, made it a thing to be always remembered.

Thus was originated 'Phil's Fuck', which subsequently became almost world famous.

Throughout the big cities of the continent of Europe, of America, and even of Asia, young men and old patronised the taxi, and ran bumping races with nature. With some it came very expensive. London to Brighton costs a bit, when the prices per quarter mile are not so moderate as Phil's.

They pulled up in the swelling moonlight at the little village of Bedfont – for drink, and to repair disorders – Phil's trousers were drenched.

The charm of the tiny hamlet, its old church and oddly-cut, bird-shaped trees made them both absurdly romantic – Phil especially – and he nearly

312

threw his heart, hand, very considerable fortune and chance of an earldom at the feet of a dissolute little Newcastle 'hinny'.

Jeannie, to digress a little, had in the time to come a very interesting career. After we're done with her in this story she became a sort of second Otero, the toast of Europe, and married – well, you'll have to wait for subsequent volumes of *Nemesis Hunt* and *Pleasure Bound* for that. It first amazed, then scandalised, and ended up by delighting the civilised world.

But to go back. Phil kept himself under; he thought of his mother and father, *and* the family solicitor.

Maudie's house, 'Rosedale' – had I forgotten to mention the name before? – was ablaze with light when the taxi swept up the drive.

Phil felt, somehow, as he paid the fare, that the jumped-up twopences were dear in comparison to Jeannie's five bob jerks. He lied glibly to Maudie, and they found they were in time for dinner after all.

Jeannie was hurried upstairs to find a flapper evening dress; the other girls were already dressed.

The dinner company were oddly assorted. All our friends, of course. Maudie in a sumptuously dazzling evening gown, her friend Madame Rade very *décolletée* and Parisienne – but Elsie and May had returned to being servants.

The poet and the General had stopped *en route* in town to get evening clothes – Phil was excused.

Charlie looked very distinguished and handsome, and wore an order of barbaric design. It had been conferred by an Asiatic potentate for swopping a Scotch girl he had acquired for a flower of the

Sultan's harem. Madame Rade's niece wore a quaintly babyish frock, and talked to the poet in outrageously indelicate Parisian *argot*.

Maudie's beautiful dining-room was softly, delicately and eccentrically lighted. Apart from a great cluster of electric globes dependent from the carved ceiling, and very heavily shaded, little electric lights appeared from the most unexpected places. In one corner a tall statue of Venus showed pin pricks of light from the nipples. A large bronze of the 'Mannikin Pis' diffused some sweet-smelling scent into a crystal basin before him.

The waiting was very deft and quick, nor was the dinner elaborate, so that its course was quick.

Short though dinner was, Maudie had not forgotten to see that the viands served a lust-compelling purpose, and the wines were chosen to heat the blood, leading carefully up to the idea-forming champagne.

Madame Rade was the wit of the table: Maudie didn't talk much, she was thinking too much of her new charges, also of Charlie whom, she began to fear, she had rather too sneaking a regard for.

After dinner the big studio-cum-theatre was sought. The blinds rolled back from the great skylights showed the star-fretted sky, and a bright half moon competed with the green-shaded lamps of the great room. Here all was green, in contrast to the rose of the dining-room.

The guests sat about on divans, or reposed on cushions and rugs on the floor, and there was music, very soft and suggestive. Maudie did not intend to-night to go in for any very elaborate entertainment. There was to be a little dance of Charlie's, a semi-proper one, later – meanwhile the guests could get to know each other better, and enjoy themselves.

The old General paired off with one of the pretty servants, who seemed to enjoy a joint personality of servant and convive. She lit his cigar for him, brought his coffee and liqueur, and reclined on the great divan by his side, boldly showing her leg well up to the frill of the drawers.

She did not stir an inch when the General passed his old hand lustfully right up her leg, and on to her cunt. She promised softly to come to his room late that night, where he might do *whatever* he liked.

Young Phil had been undone in his competition for Jeannie by the poet, but found consolation in the red-haired girl.

They wandered from the house to the moonlit garden, and by the riverside he first kissed her, and then felt her. She told him she was a virgin, but had been sick of her quiet life in the north, and had been tempted. She didn't quite know what was going to happen to her, but could guess.

Phil found her very loving, and with luck they found the private bathing shed, with luck also the electric-light switch.

She looked very lovely, and Phil, though he had been earlier romantic with Jeannie, felt he had full room enough in his heart for two.

The night was so very warm that even in this semi-out-of-doors it was pleasant to undress. Phil made her do it, made her stand in her naked beauty in the moonlight, then lifted her back on to the cushions in the shed – and she *was* really a virgin.

Poor Phil, a little weary after his taxi-fuck, had a painful struggle, and the girl cried for pain, but –

when the fatal barrier was passed, the last twisting ecstacy of painful pleasure – it was all joy.

Phil rummaged about the shed, and found that hot water was actually laid on from the house, and that every washing convenience conceivable was available: it was indeed a beautifully complete *maison de la chair*. He bathed her hot little cunt – it had bled very little – and had a short swim himself. They walked back to the house happily, hand in hand.

More people were in the studio when they returned. A motor had brought a little party from London, two very smart girls and two irreproachable young men about town.

The blinds were drawn, and the lights turned on full. The company were obviously expecting something.

It came in the shape of a 'semi-proper' dance.

It was called 'The Dance of Emancipation'.

First the dainty little *trottin* of the Boulevards – band-box on arm, tripping rather than dancing, gaily, irresponsible, round the stage, all in pantomime, the pursuit of the elderly admirer – *La Débâcle*.

Scene II. The smart *horizontale* in all her glory, dancing, semi-naked, to her own reflection in the cheval glass.

Scene III. The dance of the end – beginning, as you would expect, by impending death. She is in bed. The room is not so smart.

To her come dancing grinningly, the clown, Arlequin, Pantaloon and the doctor, and Columbine.

She raises herself: she fears, she stumbles from

bed, her hair is awry, she dances awkwardly: Columbine pirouettes mockingly – one expects always the end – but Arlequin waves a smack of his wand across the doctor's chest. The doctor starts: he gives to the girl the phial – in a moment all in her is life again. She flicks her fingers, and she is still dancing as her old self as the lights fade gradually away – till in utter and absolute darkness, you hear the gay flutes. That was all.

The audience woke from its hush, and took very resolutely to supper.

Six

Madame Rade's Idea

Supper over, a cheery, chatty little supper, there
came the necessary sorting out of the visitors for
bed.

Maudie did not mean to thrust couples upon each
other, so she gave each man a separate room. She
herself slept, of course, with Tubby, but she put
Charlie alone. Jeannie alone of the flappers she put
in a room by herself, delicately insinuating to Phil
that his room was adjoining, and had a communi-
cating door. The other three flappers were together
next to the General. Next to him was the little head
page-boy. The rest of the *personnel* of the house
were in a separate wing, and among them the poet,
who had begged to be nearest the sky – so he went up
to a daintily-furnished garret, facing four ways to
the skies.

Thither he was shown by a plump semi-flapper

servant, of whom he had hopes, but who banged the door and did him in.

Sorrowfully he undressed, regretfully surveyed his slim, naked form in the long cheval glass, and mournfully stared out at and over the moon-swept Thames valley. It was very beautiful, but the poet was *not* inspired, he was carnally mundane. His penis stood up in mockery; he gazed at the lights of the windows of the opposite wing, and distinctly saw the silhouettes of two figures in close and rapt embrace. He could stand it no longer; firmly grasping his staff of love, he gazed wistfully at the moon, and brazenly tossed himself off on the lawn below.

Then with a sigh he got into his very elaborate, flowered silk pyjamas, sprayed himself elaborately with some perfume which smelt like honey, and sank back into the luxurious bed.

It was very comfortable. The lights were all that could be wished for night reading. Drinks were at his hand, and Maudie had given him a little key which she said opened a cupboard of erotic books.

He found a full selection. He felt that as a poet – and *several* society weekly papers had said so – he ought to have chosen Catullus or Verlaine, but he didn't. His fingers lingered for a while over a little brochure called *Fucksome Frolics*, but they ended up with that dear, delightful work, *The Confessions of Nemesis Hunt*. With a violently wicked scene between 'Nemmy' and her foreign prince lover we will leave him, the scented breath of a cigarette mingled pleasantly with the fumes of whisky and a solid determination on his part not to stay another night alone in this house.

Madame Rade undressed her niece, unplaited the pretty hair, and looked at her for a moment or so. The naked form was very sweet.

'*Eh bien, Tanta, que penses tu?*' said the child.

'*Les bêtises,*' answered the elder woman, '*Toinette, chérie, il t'en faut un homme, et un homme riche, riche à millions. Attends, petite chatte. Ce sont ici des hommes très comme il faut, richismes, galants et généreux au bout des ongles. Faut choisir, ma mie, avec beaucoup de soin.*' Then, breaking into English, 'You must promise, child, not to let a man absolutely *have* you unless I give my consent. Let him do anything else if you like, lead him on, fondle him, let him kiss you, but he must *not* put it in.'

Toinette, smiling roguishly, intimated that she understood.

'In this house,' went on Madame Rade, meditatively, 'there are, firstly, the little fat man, Tubby: he is the richest, *but* he belongs to Madame, our hostess.

'There are then Monsieur the poet: he is also rich, but more fond of himself than women. Also too, M. le General Fitzhugh, very rich, but old, "very old".'

'And M. Charlie?' queried the child, interestedly.

'Charlie, oh yes, very charming, but poor, poor, very poor is Charlie – you must not look there.'

'Two nice men motored down to-night.'

'They I do not know, but each have their madame.'

'One is Mr. Flowers, of Flowers and Grapes' – Madame gasped – 'and the other is Lord Saxeholme. One of the girls told me.'

'My child,' murmured Madame maternally, 'they are *both* millionaires. Now go to bed' – and she bundled the little darling into her bed by the window and sat down to think.

She had not been to Maudie's house before, and had no idea quite what wealth it represented.

It was now or never, she decided, with Toinette. The child was now sixteen. She herself, though fairly well off, could not give her a big *dot*. Besides she wanted her *kept*, not married.

The pretty girl lay peacefully asleep in a little bed by the window. Madame decided to consult Maudie.

She had been told she could ring all night. She did. A maid was immediately on the spot, and very shortly a message came that Maudie would see her.

Madame Rade hurried down the corridor: she was a little nervous, and she narrowly escaped the General, who was lying in wait.

'Maudie,' she said, when the latter had explained that it didn't matter about Tubby, that nothing short of physical violence woke him up, 'Maudie, I want to talk to you about Toinette. If she stops here much she'll get raped somehow, but I don't intend to have it done for nothing. What am I to do?

'Now, dear, you know I need money. What about a race with the girl's maidenhead as a prize? These rich men would go in, and then, if the one who wins it, wants to keep her – well and good. Make it a running handicap, and put the girl on a pedestal as a prize, eh?'

Maudie agreed readily.

'I'm going to have the sports after the photography, the day after to-morrow,' she said. 'I'll guarantee there's a rattling good entrance fee. We women will frame the handicap. I envy the man who gets that little bit of love for the first go.'

Madame Rade went back quite satisfied. The General was no longer waiting to pounce. He *had*.

He had rung the bell without thinking, and a pretty girl came. It was a simple, business-like proceeding, but the old gentleman did better than he expected, and enjoyed the best sleep he had had for some time.

Seven

The 'Kangaroo' Fuck

Notes were sent round in the morning that guests could lunch and breakfast when they liked, but that everyone was requested to be in the big studio at 1:30. The earliness of the hour was because of the light.

The séance to come was to consist of the proper shaving of the other flappers, and the subsequent photographing of them. There were also a few boys, mostly Italian, who had also to go through the ordeal.

Charlie, as soon as he had disposed of his aunt, had sent for Jeannie. He decided she would be invaluable as a leader of the flapper lot.

He was sitting rather moodily in his room, vaguely annoyed about May, and about his Aunt Lavinia, when Jeannie came. He had scarcely noticed before how really very pretty the girl was.

She came up to him, and bent down her face to be kissed, in the most natural manner. The kiss ended with the girl on his knee, and his hand up her clothes. He could feel that there was a little bristle already, even after only one day's shaving.

'There's going to be some fun to-day, ain't there?' she queried.

'Yes, dear, very funny fun.'

'Oh, I do hope so.'

She wriggled her cunt right over his finger. He had never had that done to him before.

'Where did you learn that, you little monkey, where *did* you learn *that*?' as her cunt contracted in a vice-like grip.

'Oh, I had a Japanese lover.'

She told him the story we have heard before, and then he asked for more Japanese tricks.

'Clothes'll be in the way; come on, I'll undress you.'

She had his shirt and flannel trousers and slippers – he was still in his bathing rig – off in a jiffy, and playfully smacked his great rigid tool.

She wouldn't let Charlie help her, but slid out of her light summer frock like a practised quick-change artist.

'Have you ever tried a kangaroo fuck?'

'No.'

'Well, it is rather difficult, but very nice, and as *I'm* very light, and *you're* so big and strong, we ought to manage.

'I take a little run, and jump for your neck, throwing my legs open to go right round your waist. If you're clever you catch me just under the armpits, and my cunt fits perfectly over your cock. If you don't catch me properly, I get a nasty blow in the stomach with that stiff ramrod of yours. Are you game?'

Charlie was game, *and* at once. He stood waiting for the spring like a wrestler waiting for his adversary. His muscles stood up under his white skin, and his penis seemed almost bursting, so tense were the veins.

Jeannie kissed him lightly once, her tongue just brushing his lips, gave him one sounding smack on the buttocks, and retired about seven feet.

She clapped her hands, gave what seemed to Charlie a few kangaroo-like bounds, and was in his arms – *and* not only in his arms, but he had judged her spring to perfection, and the soft pulsating walls of her cunt were throbbing round his staff of very much life.

He was almost brutal to the girl– something made him forget his great strength – like 'Gurt Jan Ridd,' and he almost crushed the little dear.

'Carry me round the room, dear,' she whispered hotly in his ear, 'and get very, very slowly on your back on the sofa, *but* for heaven's sake, *don't* jerk it out, and keep it right so that there isn't a bit of an inch to show between us, and then I'll show you how to finish a fuck.'

He got down, very gently indeed.

'Lie quiet, now,' she said, and sat up, *'quite* quiet,' for Charlie was wriggling.

She smacked his face to emphasise her words.

'Now, I don't suppose you've had it this way, you fucking sod,' she muttered – she was mad with lust now – 'and if you come before I want you to, or let your cock get just one little bit loose – I'm going to use it as a lever – you'll never fuck me again.'

Very slowly she lifted up her legs till they were almost parallel with the flanks of her soft, vibrating body, clasped them round with her arms, and twisted her little fingers behind her curly-haired head.

Then she began to sway – it was a wonderful rythmic movement, and it appeared almost marvellous that the girl could keep her balance.

Once or twice Charlie lifted his hands, fearful she would fall, but with a clench of the lips and a flash of the eyes, she bade him put them down.

'*Now* – now!' she said, dreamily, 'as I put my legs *very* slowly down, just let your – your spunk drift down till my knees are on the bed, and we'll just come wonderfully together. Stare *straight* into my eyes, darling, and by our eyes we can gauge the final spasm to the absolute tick of a second – now watch me.'

There was something snake-like in the fascination of her stare, as she gradually brought her legs down. It seemed to Charlie at first almost a superhuman effort to keep from madly clutching her and crushing her on to his stomach.

But gradually he came under the magnetism of her devilish eyes – he could almost feel that she was pumping the semen up his cock – a cock that to him now seemed almost a detached thing – he was fucking with his brain, not his penis – with a power from her eyes acting back on her brain.

At last her knees touched the bed. She threw her arms straight above her head, clapped her hands, screamed some strange Japanese-sounding jargon – and – Charlie shut his eyes, while a mist of wondrous

326

colours floated across the cinematograph sheet of his brain – a mist illumined with – well, when the present writer asked Charlie to describe it, Charlie frankly admitted that he could not. It was a dream of lovely women, and always eyes, eyes, eyes of lust, he was being fucked by *eyes*.

Jeannie's voice brought him to his senses. She was standing by his side, her hands on her hips, looking down quizzically.

'Well?' she queried.

'God Almighty,' groaned Charlie, 'if there are any more at home like you in Newcastle, that's where I die.'

'You're to thank Tokyo, *and* a little innate impulse for that, darling,' she said; 'but it's mainly Jap – *and* your cock: very few men could have kept me up like that – and now I've gone and fallen in love with you.'

Charlie didn't dare answer except by a shower of kisses all over her body, which she returned with interest. She kissed what remained of the semen from his glans, and he greedily fed on the white stream which slipped down her thighs.

Charlie might have forgotten everything but for the whistle of the speaking tube, and the admonition from his employer, Maudie, that the time had come for the beginning of the séance.

'Get the other girls together, dear,' he whispered. 'May'll look after you all, but I'm relying a lot on you. We're going to take 'em in batches.'

They were to begin with the boys, and Charlie, somewhat foolishly from the *really* erotic stand-point, had produced his *bonne bouche* first.

The drawn curtain presented a young Sicilian,

about sixteen, and almost matured. He was very beautiful, in a girlish way, as far as his face was concerned, for his figure was that of an athlete, upright as a dart. His black hair curled crisply over his temples: his eyes were very large and passionate: his lips like a cleft rose.

He was quite naked, save for sandals, and a cloth round his loins. A hum of appreciation went round the spectators.

No word was spoken, but a concealed band was heard playing soft, dreamy music.

Tubby came forward with his little tray of razors, and bowed, first to the audience, then to Charlie, and then to the boy. Charlie removed the cloth, and it was seen at once that Tubby had a fine subject to work on.

The boy's tool, semi-erect, was surrounded by a forest of luxuriantly curling bush. It seemed a shame to cleave the 'love-mane' from the young Narcissus – but *yet* – is not the human form, male or female, more perfect in its entire nudity of hirsute growth. *I* think so, my readers, and so did the 'clean-shave' devotees of Rosedale house.

There was a chair, similar to that in the London studio, and gently Charlie placed the boy, who was half laughing, half shyly blushing, in position.

Tubby, looking ridiculously modern in his lounge suit, faultlessly cut, beside this young naked god, stepped up and laid his hand on the quivering penis.

Instantly it shot into life – the poet bit his thumb – lustful glances filled the eyes of the women.

Quickly Tubby lathered the rolling curls with some soap which drifted a delicious aroma into the nostrils of all. As he followed the action of the brush by a rub of his fingers, the boy's eyes became dreamy, his phallus was stiffly erect, a mighty one for a youth, and his arms hung listlessly over the edges of the chair.

One of the girls, dressed in a black skin-tight *maillot*, with red sleeves, a female Mephisto *en effet*, handed Tubby a razor. Deftly the fat young man played round that staff of eager love. One curiously shaped instrument after another he called for, till the last curl had fallen.

He bowed in reply to the plaudits of the audience.

A girl, one of the smallest, not quite naked, but very suggestively half-dressed, came forth with a tray of unguents and powders. A boy, fully dressed in Lord Fauntleroy style, held a basin, a third girl, quite naked, gave a cut-glass bottle of scent.

Tubby, his work completed, stepped back, and Maudie, pouring the scent into the silver bowl of water till a dense, but delicate, aroma filled the room, softly sponged the remaining lather from the boy.

That done, she rubbed the virgin skin with an unguent, and followed with powder.

It was a pretty sight, a contrast again of the old world and the new – for Maudie was still in her light summer frock, just the 'River Girl' *in excelsis*, and this young Narcissus made a beautiful foil. *But* all the time his ramrod was stiffly rigid.

During these precedings the poet had behaved in a very odd manner. Being conveniently distant from the General, he had ventured to hum one or two 'little unconsidered trifles,' such as :

329

'See how the ruthless scythesman reaps
His cruel harvest with relentless sweeps
      Of Sheffield steel
Oh! lovely youth, oh! sweetly formed Apollo,
Thy forest falls to Roger's best ground hollow.'

He paused. *But*, when the final act of desecration
had been performed, and Charlie had raised the lad,
still soulful-eyed, still prick erect, to his sandalled
feet, the poet displayed his true nature.

Bounding to his feet, he rushed upon the boy, and
flung his arms round him, raining kisses on his lips.

Charlie was at first disposed to interfere, but
Maudie restrained him.

'This is delightfully unexpected,' she said.

The poet awoke to lights, faces, subdued music, a
general *tohu bohu* of clatter, laughter and applause.

The naked youth turned over to him and kissed
him.

The poet got up, and, with as much bravado as
he could muster, swaggered back among the
spectators.

He passed the General, humming, 'A wandering
minstrel I – a thing of –'

'Wandering minstrel, my arse, sir,' thundered the
General. 'You're a bugger, sir, a God-damned
bugger, and you ought to have an umbrella stuck up
your arse, and opened inside, sir. Isn't a *cunt* good
enough for you?'

Very brilliant limes focused a large patch of the
stage, and on to that were hurried the four latest
virgins, 'Jeannie's little lot,' as Charlie announced,

330

and prominent amongst them the red-haired flapper whose bush had been spared because of its flamboyant beauty. 'The burning bush,' as the poet had termed it.

After that little interlude, done because Charlie wanted Jeannie's turn over so that she could help him, the boys were proceeded with.

None were so beautiful as the first Sicilian, but they were very pretty lads. No English, but a brace of young Highlanders whose parents had sold them for the Sassenach's gold, and a red-headed Irish youngster, rather on the plump side, who thoroughly enjoyed the proceedings.

Each of the youths in his turn was quickly operated on, but the poet made no spring. It was an enthralling rather than an 'erotic' exhibition – that is, 'erotic' from the lust-compelling point of view of the word. Minds, however sensual, were compelled more to a rapt admiration of the beauty of the naked human form, than a passionate longing to do anything to it.

Charlie's choice had been very admirable. North, south, east and west had he gone; *and* were there to be no question whatever of immorality – *in persona* –there was opportunity, and enough, and more than enough, for the most eclectic photographic panoramas of the nude.

With the girls, Maudie – now no more the Maudie of the demure 'summer girl' costume, but Maudie radiant in her glorious, flaunting nakedness, took up the razors.

She was quick, almost brutally quick, with them all, and as each nymph was clean cunted, brushed her aside, till, as she rose from the task with a pant, she had a flock of little naked loves giggling and blushing around her.

'Now,' said Maudie, as she stood up, triumphant, 'we have decided not to have the sports till tomorrow; there is so much to arrange. In the meantime, remember, all of you, that this is absolutely Liberty Hall. You can do *anything* you like.'

The poet began to think.

A maid brought her a peignoir elaborately designed with flowers. She left the great room with her graceful, lissom walk, followed by hungrily lustful eyes.

Tubby announced that he was going for a motor drive, and Charlie said he would go too. They collected Madame Rade and her niece and went.

The old General, when he heard the hum of the departing car, began to think. Even at his age, he was very lustful, and he *did* want Maudie. He was safe now, with both her young men out of the way, and he knew her room.

He risked it, found the door unlocked, and walked straight in. He found Maudie lying quite naked on the bed, the sun-rays glorifying the ivory whiteness of her flesh. He made a cheap excuse about 'Wrong room, my mistake,' etc., and paused.

'Oh, don't go, General,' said Maudie, pleasantly. 'Stop and chat; I'm all alone.'

He sat on the edge of the bed, and caressed her naked knee. She stroked his cheek softly.

The General was a fine-looking old man. Many years of active service had given him a figure upright as a dart. His eyes were clear and bright, and in his trousers there thrilled a lusty cock.

'You must think this place a bit thick, General,' said Maudie.

'Madame,' answered the old soldier, 'I have fought and fucked all over the world, and I have seen most things, though nothing to equal your beauty.'

Maudie was pleased. The General was old, but still he was a distinguished man and a V.C. She had had pretty well every variety of young and middle-aged men, but this old hero, who had listened with the stricken prisoners of Cawnpore to the distant skirl of the coming pipes, was a novelty. She thought she'd like it, but she left it to him to ask.

He tarried. He sat closer to her, toyed with her shapely legs and beautifully-moulded breasts, kissed her ears, her eyes, her lips, but still was a little nervous to ask so much loveliness to give *all* of herself to him.

She made him tell her of his fucks and fights. How after dining with 'the Mate' at Constantinople during the Crimea, he had found a Turkish officer whose life he had saved in the trenches, and how, with an invalided French Zouave they had been invited by the grateful Turk to see his harem, *and* do what they damned pleased.

It appears they 'damned pleased a lot,' and the old warrior described vivaciously.

'I was only a boy then, my dear girl,' he began, 'and by God I loved the girls, bless 'em. I believe I was the only English officer in the war able to get into a really swagger harem, but this chap, Ramuz Pasha, was so grateful that he wouldn't take no for an answer.

'We went into a luxuriously got up set of rooms, with about thirty women, some mere children, lying

333

about, reading, sewing or smoking, or playing with the little tots of children who pottered about the marble floors.

'Well, the Pasha bet Sous Lieutenant D'Alberique and myself £100 English that we wouldn't account for the lot of them between us.'

'My Gad, my dear, we did, and I won another £25 off D'Alberique as a side bet. I was seven ahead. Oh, it was lovely. Those warm, smooth Eastern beauties, their breath smelling of strange spices, their lazy, languorous lust, and the delicate vice of their actions. Lord, they did know how to fuck. When Ramus told 'em I had saved his life they nearly ate me. I never faltered. Between each fuck I jumped in the great bath in the middle of the big room. The water was warmed exactly right, perfumed, and strengthened with some pick-me-up mixture. The slaves brought us coffee, liqueurs, sweets and cigarettes, and it was one triumphant carnival of vice. If there had been any more I could have gone on.

'D'Alberique and myself lay back on couches, and looked at the chorus of our victims, lovely, lustful-eyed Circassians, Greeks, Roumanians, Hertz-govinians and Turks – there were even two English girls. And after that, my dear, when I went back to the hotel I found an English society lady on her way out to the front to see her husband, and what a night I had with her. Yet, when I looked out of the window in the morning over the sparkling waters of the Bosporus I felt like a lion.'

Maudie was interested.

'Were you ever wounded, General?' she asked.

'Only once, Madame, but that badly, I have the

scar still.'

'Oh, *do* show me.'

'It's in rather an awkward place.'

'What odds; do I mind your seeing me naked? Come on. I'm *sure* it wasn't behind.'

'Madame!'

The old soldier quickly took down his trousers, and there, just below his balls, was a long vicious-looking scar. Above it his balls were swollen, and his cock stiff as an iron rod.

'How dreadful,' said Maudie, 'and supposing it had been a little higher, why you might have lost *this*,' and she fingered his cock.

That did it. The General read assent in her eyes, and almost rent his clothes off.

He was a fine naked figure, upright as a dart, muscular and clear of skin, and he gripped Maudie in an embrace which she certainly did not expect from a man of seventy odd.

Their bodies writhed in unison as Maudie gently put the General's cock into her greedy little cunt. It was big and the entrance was difficult at first, and painful, but the pain was the pain which you and I, readers of both sexes, know to be the perfect poetry of pain.

'Oh! oh! General,' Maudie gasped.

'My dear girl,' said the old soldier, 'in one part of South Africa where I was quartered, the maidens were sewn up, damme, just before they were married, and if the man couldn't get in, he was considered no man.'

The struggle was over, the pass passed, and the General was right in, his grey hairs thrust on Maudie's clean-shaved Mount of Venus.

Maudie took it as a 'dream fuck,' possibly the very best form of fuck there is. With tightly closed eyes she imagined the old man who held her in his impassioned embrace, whose finger strokes made her back boil with pleasure, and whose prick seemed to be drawing every atom of strength out of her, as a young soldier of early Victorian days, fucking this tearful girl on the eve of the departure for the Crimea. She imagined him, bearded, begrimed, and half-frozen in the trenches. She could see him carrying the wounded Turk to safety under the fire of the Russian guns. She thought of the harem episode, thought too of the honours of the Mutiny. Of the triumphal return and of the pinning of the V.C. on his breast by the great Queen. Cabul, Burma, Egypt, Majuba, they all rushed like the pictures of a cinematograph across her brain.

In fact she fucked herself through fifty odd years of history – and as the rumble of the returning car warned them, they woke out of their lust dream and spent in unison.

'Dress quick, you old darling,' whispered Maudie. 'Tubby mustn't know.'

He was into his clothes with the speed of the practised old campaigner, and met Tubby at the end of the passage with Madame Rade.

'Rippin' drive,' said the fat young man, 'took Madame Rade's kid too – she's going to arrange about sports now, ta ta.'

Maudie had sponged herself, but was still naked when the two came into her room. She made Tubby be lady's maid, massage her a little, find her clothes, and put her into them.

Then she gave him her keys, and asked for all her

jewels.

It was a large order, for Maudie had not made love for nixes all her young life.

Tray after tray Tubby lifted out of the great jewel chest. Every variety of precious stone glinted there, and Maudie got all on she could, bar the tiaras. Somehow her unexpected act of lust with the veteran of Mars, and the cloud visions of the gorgeous and gory scenes she had pictured, made her want to show off, to be extravagantly over-dressed. She would be Ninon de l'Enclos – in ultramodern clothes.

The result was very dazzling, and as Tubby clicked to the last hook, and stood up to look, he gasped.

So did Madame Rade.

'Chérie,' she said, 'you look like a modiste's and jeweller's window combined, turned into a rainbow.'

Maudie did not answer. She was in the thralls of the full sensual capture of jewels. As she looked in the glass at her fingers, her arms, her breasts, her waist, her throat, she read stories of love and lust, of battle and murder, of every unrestrained crime committed for the sake of a woman's kiss.

With a click of her tongue she rang down the curtain of her dreams. 'Now,' she said, 'for the great handicap race for Toinette. I think I have got it right. It's a hundred yards.

'Charlie, of course, is scratch. Phil I've given five yards, he's a bit of an athlete, and the poet has long enough legs and I think eight is fair mark. Tuberino mio, you get fifteen, and old General Fitzhugh must have thirty-five. He'll hardly last. Now, there's old Rosenberg, an immensely wealthy stock broker, who's coming down to-night. He takes fifteen also, and Sandy McPhail, the Paisley shawl merchant, as a ten pin man. He'll be here to-morrow.'

Tubby rather grudgingly assented. He had set his heart on winning the race. He coveted little Toinette, and he meant to prove his manhood by taking her maidenhead properly.

'It's going to be £250 apiece,' Maudie added – 'you may as well whack up now, Tubby.'

Tubby wrote a cheque. 'But,' he said, 'Charlie may not –'

'That's all right,' Maudie interrupted. 'I owe him a bit for a job he's going to do for me. That'll be £1,750 in all.'

Madame Rade heaved a happy smile. £1,750 – well she didn't care who broke that little wisp of skin which guarded Toinette's womb.

Tubby went, and she stayed with Maudie to smoke and chat.

Eight

Toinette's Trial

Charlie, strolling from his room, came upon Mlle. Rade standing at the door of a bedroom a few yards down the corridor.

He had scarcely even spoken to the fascinating French girl before the motor ride, but he had noted her delicate *petite* airs and graces.

'*Tanta* has gone to Miss Maudie,' she volunteered. 'Everybody's gone out; I'm supposed to stay here learning lessons. I feel *so* lonely.'

Charlie suggested that he *might* keep her company.

'Oh, do,' she answered, 'come in here. It's a bedroom, but it doesn't matter.'

Charlie was nothing loth: she was pretty as a little bit of Dresden china – and he longed for a kiss, just a tiny playful toying with her lips.

He followed her in.

Mlle. Rade – dear, sweet, diminutive Toinette – had not her hair now in plaits, but fluffed out over her forehead, and luxuriantly flowing over the shoulders.

She was still very short frocked, her skirts *well* above her knee. She was not high-booted as we first met her, but the daintiest little shoes gave every chance for effective display to her ankles.

She curled up on the bed, and Charlie, a little nervously, sat down beside her, and, a little more nervously, kissed her ear. He got a sweet, thrilling kiss back, right on the lips, and, without further hesitation, drew her over his lap and ran his hand up her legs.

She let his hand go right to its goal, then slid her fingers after it.

'Listen, you great big darling,' she said, 'you *must* do just as I tell you. Understand, I am little and young, but I mustn't have it *all* – just yet. Tanta says I may do everything except exactly "it" – that is "fuck" – it makes me blush to say it' – it really made Charlie blush to hear it from those *petite* lips – 'and – well – play with me as much as you like – oh, do: I love it so: I know I shall be *terrible* when I grow older and *Tanta* lets me.'

She slid from his lap, and lay with her legs wide open. Her eyes glittered as they twinkled invitingly into his.

'Get all naked, dear,' she said, and ran her fingers over his fly buttons.

He did, and lay by the girl's side – she was still fully dressed. His cock was very stiff, and when her tongue touched its end, and her fingers toyed with his balls, he knew that she could taste a drop of semen. She could hardly get her mouth over the whole glans – Charlie was very largely made – but she licked ecstatically.

Charlie had a curious sensation: he felt he wanted this dainty little darling always, and an almost overmastering lust to disregard her request and rape her came over him! Little by little he undressed her, while she still sucked him, and he had the greatest difficulty to keep from spending. She had just managed to get *all* the tip in now.

Charlie couldn't bear it any more. Gently he pushed the little darling's head from his cock, and lustfully he grasped her to him, smothering her throbbing lips with kisses. As her tiny, red-hot tongue darted in and out of his mouth, he felt a thrill of lust all over him which he never remembered before. Then he took what little clothing was left from her, and buried his head between her legs. It was delicious, divine. His tongue must have touched her maidenhead, for she shuddered a little with pain, and he felt her fingers clutch on his head.

The girl lay back, her eyes closed, in an ecstacy of lust. She too had a mad longing to be really properly fucked, to have this great, strong, handsome young man clasp her to him with all his strength, and thrust that throbbing tool of his up, right up, no matter how it hurt. The tongue was lovely, but oh! the thought of the other, the *real* thing. But she wouldn't disobey her aunt. She knew that her maidenhead was for sale; she knew too that it would probably fall to the lot of some horrid, rich old man, who would pay a fabulous price for it – and oh! *wouldn't* she be untrue to him afterwards. But the first she *did* want with a man she was in love with.

341

She wavered a little – heaven knows what *might* have happened, for Charlie, his lips all wet with the sweet moisture flowing from those red-hot cunt lips was almost mad with lust, had there not been an interruption.

Both were so wholly carried away with the lust tremors which gripped them from head to toe that they had lost consciousness of all else.

Charlie, when he felt a smack on his bottom, thought at first it was Toinette – but – still there were both her hands on his head. She couldn't have three hands.

A voice brought him back to life.

'So Mister Charlie, it is so you play with my little niece. It is so, missie, that you would learn your lesson. Fie, fie!'

Charlie got up – and did feel a fool. Stark naked, with a rampant cockstand, he stood in the presence of this ultra-Parisian lady, who, to his immense relief, seemed to view the situation as a little humourous.

Little naked Toinette sat up, feebly giggling.

Madame Rade was plump, but she was very pretty. In her stage days in Paris she had been a very noted beauty. Even now, tho' she was nearer forty than thirty, she was a tasty dish.

'Well, *ma petite*,' she said, 'have you enjoyed your lesson from Monsieur Charlie?'

'It was divine, *Tanta*,' answered the child, now unabashed and smiling.

'An apt teacher, *hein*?'

Charlie was blushing all over, but regaining his composure, now he saw that he was not blamed.

'One thing, Mister Charlie, I must ask you,'

continued Madame, 'you have not deflowered *la petite*?'

'On my word, no, Madame; your niece said you didn't mind her going just as far as that, but no further. Perhaps it's as well you *did* come in, I was madly randy, and I don't know what *might* have happened.'

'Poor boy,' and she laid her jewelled hand on his great stiff cock. 'Poor boy, would you like it satisfied? I'm not a little girl now, but there are worse, *n'est ce pas*?'

'Oh do, Charlie,' said the girl – 'oh do fuck *Tanta*. I have read a great deal, and I have seen pictures, but I have never seen it really done. Oh *Tanta*, darling, do it quick.'

'Well,' said Madame Rade, '*veux tu*?'

Charlie did not speak, but the kiss that Madame Rade got made her sting with lust.

'Do you know, you dear, delightful bad boy, that I haven't done it for six whole months. Now, *ma mignonne*: *this* is going to be your lesson. Undress me, Charlie darling.'

She wore a pretty shimmery summer frock of forest green, with red roses in her belt, and more roses beneath the great drooping brim of her hat. The skirt was short and fully displayed her very dainty ankle and tiny foot – how often plump women have such deliciously tiny feet and hands, and what an especial charm lies in them.

She was dressed to correspond right through. The rose and the forest leaf dominated everything, but there were two shades in each colour; the soft rose of love, and the scarlet of passion. A gilded thread tied her chemise and her drawers – the note of avarice.

It was the woman's nature in a dress poem.

She stood at last naked, save her scarlet stockings – the upward note in the confection – plump, *piquante, ravissante*.

The girl lay on the bed, wide-eyed, intently curious.

What was to follow, Charlie thought, ought to be done in a deep forest glade. Satyrs ought to be there, grinning their lust, nymphs idly wandering, cupids half ashamed, the great god Pan himself, and Orpheus with his lute, and, and – but it was only a bedroom in an ultramodern riverside house, and he still felt the vibration of the motor wheel in his fingers, and motors and mythology don't quite synchronize.

The bed was roomy, and there was a space for Toinette to lie at the side while Charlie lifted plump, *pimpante* Madame Rade on to the soft mattress.

They were both nervous. Charlie felt that he was expected to give a lesson to the doll-like divinity by his side; Madame felt the same. Before the eyes of this critic both were abashed.

The end was rather vulgar.

Charlie felt a warm hand delicately placing his phallus in its home – and then his brain walked down his spine to his balls. He became an engine; even his unceasingly kissing lips were engines. Madame Rade was the same, and the couple spent simultaneously just as 'Arry and 'Arriet might have done behind a bush on Hampstead Heath.

Madame, as Charlie slid from her, turned to her niece.

'Eh bien, ma mie?'
'J'ai vue chiens en rade,' was the simple reply.

Charlie got back to his own room with thoughts
about the philosophy of Onan.

Nine

The Games – And – Vale

Charlie, wakening a little heavy-eyed, sought solace in the bathing pool. Maudie was there before him, and – well – he couldn't help it; he satisfied his lust on the greensward 'midst the song of the breeze and the birds in the boughs.

When he came back to his room he found Jeannie there, prettily posed on the edge of the bed.

Charlie kissed her, and felt her, and pressed his face languorously against her soft, hot cheeks, but beyond that he dared not go. He had fucked Maudie by the waterside, and it had been lovely – Maudie improved every time, and took more out of him every time, but what this day might bring about, and what might be expected of him he could only conjecture. He knew it would be pretty hot, and he felt he must keep fit.

Little Jeannie shuddered convulsively in his arms,

and finally openly begged him to fuck her. He had only been in his shirt when she came in, and she lifted it right up to his breasts, looking lovingly and longingly at his cock.

'Darling, darling,' she implored, 'do, do fuck me. I shall be ill, horribly ill, if you don't. I know you've been at it already, but can't you spare just a little bit for me, just a very quick one?'

'Dear girl,' answered the perplexed Charlie, wanting it, and yet wanting not to want it, 'I *have* been at it, and I want you again, you know I do' – it was obvious, his cock was gun-barrel stiff – 'but I shall kill myself if I go on like this.'

She dropped on her knees before him, and snatched a kiss on the glans. That settled Charlie. It had to be.

'Very well, you little devil,' he said, 'I give in, but it's got to be a very wicked one. Run quick, and fetch Luigi.'

Luigi came, rather wondering-eyed, and very picturesque in the Sicilian peasant's costume which he always wore now. Charlie banged the door and locked it: this was to be entirely a *séance à trois*

His eyes gleamed in a way which rather frightened Jeannie, and as he took a birch made of dried seaweed from a cupboard, she began to be scared.

'You've got to go through it,' he said, roughly. 'Luigi undress her and beat her.'

It did seem a shame, when that ravishing body was all naked, that scarlet lines must be traced across the pretty brown skin, but Charlie felt like that. He was half genuinely angry that the girl should have tempted him, and half lustfully cruel. It was going to be sadism and blunt, brutal wish to punish combined.

'You, too, Luigi, get yourself stark.'

The boy obeyed.

They made a handsome couple, and Charlie's lust was for a moment overcome by his artistic sense.

He took a hand camera, found a position for it on the top of the commode stand, and posed the two. It was difficult to avoid the boy's very rigid cockstand, but clever draping did this. Running a plain grey screen behind them, they were naked shepherd and shepherdess to the life, and the shutter clicked.

His artistic thoughts had tamed his lust for the moment: his member was no longer rampant, and he was thinking more of breakfast than fucking, till the timid bending of the pretty girl over the bed, her bottom raised shiveringly expectant of the stroke, fired him again.

'Give her five, Luigi, quick,' he cried.

The boy, savage-eyed also now, flicked the stinging twigs with a sharp wrist twist over the girl's flesh. Twice, thrice, he struck, and at the fourth the blood came.

'That'll do,' cried Charlie; 'come here, Luigi, and suck me.'

Poor Jeannie stared aghast – was *she* to have nothing then? This was sadism with a vengeance, and Charlie revelled in it as he saw the girl's pitiful eyes, while he felt the warm embrace of the boy's lips on his penis.

He spent very quickly, but he hardly felt any actual sensual pleasure. His delight was in watching the girl's pain. Her skin must be smarting badly now, he knew, from the after-sting of the blows, but more than that, what must she be suffering from the lust she had, and the sight of it being robbed from her by another.

'Keep it in,' he ordered, and he filled the boy's mouth with the hot juice, 'close your teeth on it. Now, Jeannie, kiss him, and drink my love juice from him.'

The girl did. She kissed the handsome boy with a long tenacious kiss, and she sucked all the sperm from his mouth, her eyes longingly and expectantly fixed on Charlie all the time.

Finished, she threw back her head with a jerk and gulped it.

'There,' she cried, 'my health to you.'

'Well, you've had what you wanted, *my* spunk in you. You can't say I haven't given you my fluid of life. Now you can dress yourself and go. Luigi, stop here and shave me.'

There was an evil glint in the girl's eyes, but she said no word and dressed hastily. Charlie did not even turn his head to look at her as she left the room.

Outside she cursed him deeply and bitterly and long. What should be her revenge she could not quite decide.

The sports were to be early. They didn't want any unexpected visitors from town, and the company was strictly limited to the people we have met already – with one exception.

A strange young man with an engaging manner managed somehow to get into the grounds and recalled himself to Tubby as an old school friend. Tubby had only a hazy recollection, but the man was so nice and seemed such a sport, and seemed to know so many people Tubby knew, and Tubby was flustered, so he hadn't the heart to turn him out.

Maudie's lawn, as we have before met it, ran down to the river, and was fairly visible to passing water traffic, but there was a portion, a long green alley between great trees, which was completely shut off from any possibility of observation. It was admirably suited for the great race.

First came a pretty flapper race. The girls had to run fifty yards, undress fully and race back. It was won very easily by the Titian-haired nymph whose Venusberg had been preserved intact. She led at the turn: her clothes came off her like a split cloud, and she raced back laughing, her red locks floating behind her.

There was a bicycle handicap for the boys and the flappers, all nude – it is surprising how sexy a naked girl looks on the saddle of a bicycle – and a match between May and Elsie. They had to run twenty-five yards, toss off the two men servants – a judge was present to see it properly done – and run back. Elsie won easily.

Then came *the* event: the contest for the flower of Toinette.

It was nicely stage-managed.

In a great china bowl, full of heavy-scented, dried rose petals, sat Toinette, fully dressed, in a dead black costume, relieved only by a silver belt, silver garters below the knees, and a silver collar. In her hand she held a laurel wreath. Her hair was straightly and severely brushed, and for ornament she wore only a silver butterfly, streaked with *crème de menthe* green.

Quite close to her was the young man who had

introduced himself as Tubby's friend. He had a camera in his hand.

One hundred yards away the runners waited. All, even the General, wore proper running clothes – a hasty motor expedition to Windsor had secured those.

From the start the General made the pace hot. He had put half a bottle of Martell Three Star down him, and reckoned that would just carry him through. Tubby panted in his rear; the poet galloped rather than ran; the two strangers were quickly outclassed; and Phil and Charlie were closing with their leaders.

With ten yards to go, Tubby had the General beat, but he could almost feel Charlie's breath on his shoulders. A superhuman effort flung him across the tape, a bare foot ahead of Charlie, the General beating Phil for place money by inches.

Tubby's friend clicked his camera shutter once more, grinned, and went.

Outside the gates he met a friend with a low-hung racing car.

'Well?' said the friend, as the photographer climbed in.

'First stop, Carmelite House, and you can put the Agapemone scoop inside this.'

Whilst the General was being violently ill among the trees, Tubby carried his little black and silver trophy, all vibrant with emotion – she had prayed for Charlie's victory – back to the pavilion.

There was a throne for her there, a black velvet daïs and there she sat while Maudie presented her with £1,750 in a plain oaken casket, with the name *Toinette* set in opals fringed with diamonds.

It was up to Tubby. He had 'doped' himself before the race, and helped himself very considerably to Martell and Mumm afterwards.

Toinette was his. After the ceremony of health-drinking, she slipped her little black-gloved hand through his arm, and smiled up at him. He waggled as he walked back to the house with her. She made no pause, but led him straight to her bedroom.

Tubby walked rather sheepishly and vacuously to the window. He heard the girl click the key in the lock.

She turned on him with a radiant smile -- she was sorrowful at heart that it had not been Charlie, but at any rate she was going to get rid of this tiresome maidenhead at last. She supposed it would hurt, but she was no coward, and she knew that ever afterwards it would be nice.

'Aren't you going to kiss me? I'm *all* yours for the present, you know.'

Tubby kissed her rather awkwardly, he wasn't much used to vice with such a young girl, and this very up-to-date, chic little Parisian flapper rather scared him. Also he was a little drunk, and he was painfully conscious that it was odds on his being impotent.

However, he was as gallant as possible. He played with the little darling's still-stockinged legs, long silk stockings which came very near to the place of joy itself; he fingered her cunt, and he put his head up her clothes and kissed it, before he started to undress

352

her. He tried all he knew to get randy, but he couldn't.

He would have given pounds to have been downstairs in a comfortable smoking-room chair with a brandy and soda.

She was all bubbling with lust, and shook with anticipation as he undressed. The naked beauty of the girl as she lay back eager-eyed on the bed should have roused any man to a state of frenzied lust, but Tubby's cock when he took off his trousers and revealed it, was a pitiable object, and Toinette stared in horrified amazement.

Blushing and ashamed, Tubby sank on the bed beside his victim designate, and tried by kissing and embracing to stimulate some passion. With the deft aid of the girl's fingers something in the nature of a cockstand appeared. Little Toinette gave every help: smoothed his head, his limbs, darted her hot tongue in his mouth, and eventually the end of his cock was guided into a hot, juicy little cunt.

Once in Tubby felt a flicker of sensuality, but soon realised it was hopeless, and resorted to strategy. Attempting some vigorous strokes which didn't get his flaccid battering ram near the expectant gate, he crushed the little darling in his arms, and made belief that he had come, and she was deflowered.

Toinette had her doubts. There had been no pain, and where was the expected blood?

Tubby elaborately sponged her, and told her, what she thought was a lie, but which was really the truth, that she was the first virgin he had ever been into. Then he made a cheap excuse to go, and fled to solace himself in drink.

He was greeted with rounds of applause by the

other contestants. He told a few lies about his prowess, and got rapidly drunk.

Little Toinette, vaguely disappointed, dressed, and wandered out to the garden, where she found Charlie alone, reading *Candide*.

He was delighted to see her and they strolled down to the bathing place.

She told Charlie she didn't think much of being seduced.

'However, it may be better next time, and I can have *anyone* now.'

It was a direct invitation, and Charlie made no bones about it. Like lightning he stripped himself and the child, and the two naked bodies rolled in ecstacy on the soft mattresses.

Charlie's cock was so stiff that it was almost pain. They didn't waste time on preliminaries. Her eyes wild, almost savage, with passion, she guided it in, and Charlie gave a great thrust.

'Oh, oh!' she shrieked, 'you are killing me; it's awful; it wasn't like this with Tubby.'

Charlie took no notice. He thrust brutally on, till at last he felt that the obstacle had vanished. Toinette's maidenhead was fairly and squarely broken.

She had borne the pain bravely, but her eyes were streaming with tears as Charlie withdrew a penis dripping with blood.

'Why, the damned fool never seduced you at all,' he cried. 'I *have* been the first, the very first, my darling.'

He wiped the blood from her torn little cunt – she had bled freely – and got her champagne.

Arriving back they found the house in turmoil.

Servants rushed hither and thither, the old General fussed and fumed, Maudie was hysterical, and Tubby collapsed.

'Whatever's the matter?' cried Charlie.

'Matter, good God, man,' answered young Phil Learoyd, 'that young stranger at the sports was a *Daily Mirror* reporter and photographer. I was motoring up to town and found him broken down. He didn't recognise me in my goggles, and I overheard his talk to his pal. He's got photos of *everything*, and what's worse, he knows what we were racing *for,* and he means to *publish* it.'

'There's only one way out,' said Maudie tearfully. 'Luckily, I've always been prepared. The yacht is in full commission; I've just telephoned to Southampton to get steam up. The motors are all ready, and we've got to bundle into 'em and be off. A few months' cruise for the benefit of our health won't do us any harm. The motors'll carry all the baggage we want, and there are plenty of spare clothes on board.'

It was a hurried flight. The great cars tore down the pleasant road to Southampton, to find Tubby's magnificent steam yacht, the *Lesbia*, with steam full up, everything ready. By dinner time they were well out at sea.

The stockbroker could not possibly leave England, and Maudie had arranged for him to go to Lands End and pick them up on the wireless as to the news in the papers.

At four o'clock on the following day the message came through.

It was worse than expected.

Both the *Daily Mail* and *Mirror* had full accounts,

355

only hinting, of course, at the naked flapper events, but hinting strongly that there *had* been scenes of unmentionable depravity.

But, the race was described in full detail, and the fact that the prize was a young woman's virtue was severely commented on. Each article ended with an impassioned appeal to the powers that be and the British public to rise up and destroy this hell, this monstrosity, this blot upon England.

'The *Mirror*,' ran the message, 'has got two pages of photos, and states that they have others too indecent to print, but which they will gladly supply for purposes of prosecution.'

There was a general chorus of groans.

'I should like to see those photos,' said Charlie.

'So should I,' said Tubby.

'Well,' said Maudie, 'we'll risk it. We'll hang off the Land's End, and Phil can nip into Penzance this evening in the motor launch and get the papers.'

Phil returned that night with a sheaf of papers.

'I kept my goggles on,' he said, 'and my collar up, as I thought my face might be in the pictures, and by God it is. I've bought all I could. Lord, there is a rush for 'em. I popped into one or two bars, still keeping my goggles on, and the place is ringing with it, probably all England is now. The general opinion is that burning is too good for us.'

The papers were eagerly scanned; it *was* awful. The *Mirror* had four photos of the big race, an especially good one of the finish, in which the faces of all the runners were distinct, and an excellent one of Tubby leading off his little prize. There was a picture of the house, 'Hell Castle,' as the writer dubbed it, snapshots of Maudie, Madame Rade, and several other single ones. The groups taken before the race began included nearly everyone.

They had no names, but at the bottom of the page was an appeal to the public to come forward and identify the characters.

'Lord, Lord,' gasped the General, 'this means a long cruise for us.'

'We're very heavily victualled,' said Maudie. 'I vote we make for the islands.'

And Pacific bound it was. But before they had made the Horn, one dark night a large vessel overhauled them and signalled them to stop.

'Full steam ahead,' said Charlie, 'we've got the heels of anything but a destroyer.'

But the strange vessel seemed to steam two to their one, and the message came, 'Stop or we sink you.'

A moment later a shell screamed overhead, followed by two more placed neatly to port and starboard.

After a hurried council they gave up. The strange vessel came close alongside, and dropped a launch. In a few moments several elegant young men and a young girl dressed as a middy were on deck.

'What does this mean?' spluttered Tubby.

'Piracy, my dear sir, piracy, simple, unabashed piracy. *Why*, it's Tubby. Well, Tubby, we can't even spare our friends in this business. Fork out.'

Charlie came forward.

'Look here, St. Ed –'

'No names, please,' snapped the young man.

'Well, I don't know what your game is, but look here, old chap, we're fugitives from justice too, and if you collar all we've got, God knows what'll happen to us.'

The young man was interested.

'Tell me,' he said.

For answer Charlie took him into the chart-room and showed him the papers.

The young man was deeply interested.

'That alters the circumstances altogether,' he said, 'and it's a dashed good job for you you ran against me. I've got an island no one in the world bar ourselves knows of: we can do with some more genial inhabitants. It's obvious you can't go back to England, so you come with me. I'll send you a couple of steersmen on board to give you your course. You pop over and have dinner with me, and we'll talk things over. You know who I am, and why I left England. We're all in the same boat over there, all gentlemen. You'll have a good time.'

Well, it was arranged, to the immense relief of the passengers of the *Lesbia*, and the two yachts set off in company, southward bound.

And now, sweet readers, if you want to know any more about Maudie and her friends, you must look for the forthcoming volume of *Pleasure-Bound Afloat*.

Au revoir.

Publisher's Note

We hope you have enjoyed *Maudie* and will want to read its sequel. To whet your appetite we include the opening chapters of *Pleasure-Bound Afloat* which is also available from Star Books.

Pleasure-Bound Afloat

The Extraordinary Adventures of a Party of Travellers, et Leurs Affaires Galantes.

One

It was a rough spring, and after the *Mesopotamia*
had passed the Statue of Liberty and cleared Sandy
Hook, she stuck her nose into the Atlantic with a
robust determination, which made the purser reflect
genially that he was going to save money on the
meals.

The company on the liner was varied. There was
the usual complement of millionaires, some who
worked, and some who belonged to the 'Father-
made-the-money club'; assorted Anglo-Saxon
nobility; quite a number of widows, grass and
otherwise; and not a few very dainty American
flappers – why is it that Yankee flappers are nicer
than English? – *but they certainly are.*

Silas Ahasuerus P. Q. Silverwood stood near the
stern and, as the night came down with a rush, gazed
at the receding lights of New York, blinking in the

gloom. It was his first visit to 'Yerrup,' and he was a bit nervous. He had his money sewed in the arse of his pants, and when Miss Sylvania Jepps from Jeppville, O., whom he had met casually at the Waldorf Astoria on the preceding evening and, incidentally, not shared sheets with, sidled up to him, he instinctively covered his bum pocket with a horny and capacious hand.

'Say,' chortled Miss J., 'guess did you ever hear the bright bit about the lady on the herring pond trip, *and* her dairy?'

'Naw.'

'Waal – a fren'o'mine found the book. Listen to the contents.

'Jan. 1. Leave N. Y. entrusted to care of captain. Cap. very pleasant and fatherly.

'Jan. 2. Cap. more like a brother.

'Jan. 3. Cap. tries to kiss me.

'Jan. 4. Cap. makes immoral proposals to me. Refuse indignantly.

'Jan. 5. Cap. repeats proposals. Threatens if I refuse to sink the ship and the five hundred passengers. Say that I will take my honour and virginity to the bottom of the vast Atlantic rather than consent.

'Jan. 6. Cap. repeats threat, and displays tools with which to scuttle the ship.

'Jan. 7. *Save* ship, crew and five hundred passengers.

'Now wasn't that real noble?' concluded Miss Jepps, 'and just the strange thing is that I have the life of this ship in my hands – just the same.'

'Well, you?' began Mr. Silverwood, in an agitated manner.

'Do you think I haven't the interests of humanity at heart? Mr. Silverwood, siree, precisely at 9:30 this evening, on my back I go, on the settee in the Cap's stateroom, open my legs, raise my skirts, *and*, precisely *what* he does to the gap nature has left between them is his business, not mine – *and* the interests of humanity.'

Mr. S. began to ponder. He knew a bit about women who were not as pure as supposed, but this *was* a bit brazen.

'I guess I wish *I* was the Cap –' he hazarded.

'Mr. S., they tell you are a millionaire?'

'Waal – I have dollars – some.'

'Mr. S., I wish to buy new costumes in Paree. My stateroom is No. 72, and it's three hours before I meet the Cap. I'll just say, *au revoir*.'

Mr. Silverwood thought hard. He *had* money, and to spare, and Miss Jepps was very, very tempting. Very petite and dainty, she had a seventeen inch waist, a divine ankle, wore probably a two shoe, to the accompaniment of $5\frac{1}{4}$ gloves, and her face, in especial her eyes, was something to dream about.

Half an hour later he was swallowing a Martini cocktail, with a generous drop of absinthe therein, and chatting to the purser. The name of Miss Jepps cropped up.

'Oh, yes, she's a mermaid,' said that worthy.

'A *what?*

'A mermaid: guess you know what that is?'

'You don't tell she's really got a tail, and her legs are false!' Mr. Silverwood's eyes bulged.

The purser laughed, and squeezed a little more lemon into his cocktail.

'No, sir,' he said, 'it's apparent you don't know the Atlantic crossing. A mermaid, a "merm" we call them, is a dear, delightful dot of dimity, who doesn't exactly traverse this boundless waste of wave because she loves it, but because there are gents like you, sir, who have money to spend and want a little occasional diversion. We've had this particular one before. The "old man" knows her well.'

Mr. Silverwood thought a lot, and wetted his thoughts copiously. He was far too wide to want to get let in by an adventuress, but Miss J. *was* nice.

He left the smoking room, walked slowly down the promenade deck, and Satan gripped him.

He had more money on him than he really needed for his European tour, to say nothing of letters of credit available all over the continent.

Stateroom No. 72 tempted him like hell.

He went towards the gangway. The phosphorus glinted on the waves; the great liner sang her way through the Atlantic. Mr. Silverwood was not altogether an ordinary millionaire. He had some romance in his ample frame, and the brain that ticked in the square-jowled head held other thoughts at times than hogs and hams and dividends.

He was an amateur of the beautiful, and his palace by the lake outside the churning turmoil of Chicago held many art treasures. There was a 'Rape of the Sabines' by Morazioff, which people would have paid hundreds to see, and as for the statuettes and bits and things which were kept under lock and key, many an enterprising fellow millionaire had seriously considered a little burglary.

The siren hooted as the *Mesopotamia* cut down her speed through a big fishing fleet. A great white yacht loomed by like a ghost and loosed her siren in return. Silverwood thought of the siren in stateroom 72, hesitated, *and was lost*.

Miss Jepp's door was not locked. She whistled quietly an obvious acquiescence when the millionaire knocked – and Silverwood entered.

Miss J. obviously expected her visitor, for she made no attempt to disguise the fact that she wasn't even in the middle of her toilet for dinner.

The shaded clusters of electric light – Miss Jepps was not travelling cheap – shone down upon a ravishing little vision. She had her stockings and shoes on – scarlet silk, both – her drawers, with scarlet silk insertions, and a chemise.

That was all..

Mr. Silverwood blinked. Little Miss J, was very, very pretty, and the ankles which had made him feverish in the twilight on deck, were now supplemented by deliciously-proportioned calves, which swelled up in graceful curves to delicately moulded knees, not quite covered by the lace frills of the *pantalons garnis des rubans écarlates*. There was a little bare, pink flesh above each garter which made the Chicago multimillionaire delirious.

Miss J. had a very dainty china-shepherdess skin tint, obviously her own, blue, and very bright, eyes, naturally her own, and a mass of bronze hair which was open to doubt – at least, so Mr. S. decided as he noted the gap in the little darling's drawers which disclosed a forest on her Mount of Venus which was quite a different tint.

She caught his eye, and, with a cheeky grin, put

her two bejewelled hands between her thighs.

'Hullo, hullo,' she giggled, 'I know what you're thinking.'

'Well?'

'You're thinking, either my head, or my – what ma's got – is dyed. Well, my hair on my head is tinted a bit. You know the story, don't you, of the girls in the car – two sisters-in-law. They saw two girl friends, with beautiful auburn curls.

'"I'll bet you they dye," said one.

'"How do you know?"

'"I go to the same Turkish bath, Cissie," said the one who knew.'

But Mr. Silverwood didn't care whether Miss Jepp's hair was dyed or not. His whole body flamed with desire; he seemed to swell all over, and the buttons on his trousers strained at their cables. He sank on the floor by the side of Miss Jepps and flung one arm round her knees and the other round her waist, pulling her down on to the soft carpet.

Miss Jepps made no protest. She opened her mouth to let his tongue run in between her ivory teeth and laid her pretty bejewelled hand on the throbbing swelling between his legs. Mr. S. nearly went mad.

He thrust his hand between her thighs, but she pushed it away –

'One minute, dear,' she murmured, softly. 'I want it as badly as you, but – I hate to say it – I make my living out of that little place you're after. Just a hundred dollars and you shall have the fuck of your lifetime.'

Mr. Silverwood did not hesitate a moment.

'Done,' he gurgled, 'open your legs.'

'Take your trousers off then, I hate being scratched by buttons.'

Mr. Silverwood hastened to obey, slipped off his breeches, and exposed a really remarkable member, as stiff as a ramrod and pulsating with lust.

Little Miss Jepps lay back and opened her legs wide, raising her knees.

'Give me the pillow for my head,' she said, and, taking it from him, rested her lovely head on it.

Mr. Silverwood wasted no time. Like a duellist who meant killing his man, he rammed his steel-stiff ramrod into the soft and slippery Abode of Love.

It was all too short: *she* was hot, too, and when she got him with a double nip which nearly broke his shaft in two, Mr. Silverwood let fly a stream which would have done credit to a fountain in his own ornamental garden on Lakeside.

Mr. Silverwood uncoupled with a sigh and a last passionate kiss, in which he nearly choked the little darling.

'Gee, but that *was* bully,' said the millionaire as he rose, panting.

'You know why kisses are like ham sandwiches?' queried the girl.

'No.'

'Because they're both the better for a bit of tongue – see.'

'Guess you're a bright bit all through,' said Mr. Silverwood.

'Well, I've been around some – I'm glad you liked it – I've had more hundreds than I can count, but you didn't find it too large, did you?'

'It was just a dream.'

'Do you know the story of the man who married a

three times widow?'

'No, not that I know.'

'His friend met him the morning after his first, and asked him how he liked it.

'"Man," he said, "it was like opening a window and fucking the wide, wide world!"'

Mr. Silverwood chuckled again. 'Know any more?' he said.

'Lots. I always make it a point to remember 'em. It pleases men. I'm a whore, I admit, but I'm nothing if not *thorough*. Mine is one of the oldest professions in the world, and I'm not ashamed of it. Here's another on the same subject.

'A man married a widow who had had fourteen children. His pal met him and queried solicitously:

'"I hope old man, you haven't put your foot in it!"

'"No: but I *could*!"'

Mr. Silverwood took a wad of dollar bills from his pocket, and settled his little account.

'That's the best spent hundred dollars I ever remember, and its yours again, little lady, whenever you've any spare time, but I guess you're like to be popular this trip.'

'Oh, I can manage a deal of fucking. I'll tell you some more tales next time. Now run along.'

Miss Jepps, left alone, filled a basin from the sea-water tap, and syringed (and I may tell you, gentle, and otherwise, readers, that a salt-water douche is a dead snip preventative).

With a few dexterous touches, she put up her shiny auburn locks, fixed a fillet ribbon round her white forehead, with a single small diamond and ruby star in its midst, slightly rouged her cheeks, drew a red salve stick across her little Cupid's bow of a mouth, and then turned to her dressing.

Simple, but with Paquin stamped all over it, was Miss Jepp's dinner gown. Dead black, a fine contrast to the almost scarlet hair, tiny in the waist, and Miss Jepps went easily into a seventeen corset, and very, very *décolletée*, indeed. In fact the little crimson buttons which were the crowning glory of her snowy breasts narrowly escaped peeping over the rim of her corsage. She wore a spidery net over the décolletage, which, if anything, exaggerated its daring.

With a final twist of the skirt, and a little wriggle of the rounded shoulders she smiled approval of herself in the long cheval glass.

Mr. Silverwood walked very quickly to the smoking room, crossed straight to the bar, and drank three cocktails very quickly. Lord Reggie Cameron, a decadent Scots chieftan, who was also attending to his ante-prandial digestion, stared in amazement.

'What, what, laddie,' he said – he always began his sentences with that – 'you seem in need of spiritual comfort!'

'So would you, lord, if you'd had my little afternoon.'

'So?'

'Yes – you'll see her at dinner – she's *the very last thing* that ever came down the Pike.'

Lord Reggie looked inquisitive.

'Introduce me?' he queried.

'Your cheque book, I guess, will be your best introduction.'

'Das vos right,' interrupted Herr Kunst, a massive German, 'it vos alvays der payments dat mit dese

371

most loveliness womens der affectionations make, ain't it?'

'Right oh,' chipped in Billy Neal, the well-known English actor, 'whenever I stay at a country house, I always tell my man to put my cheque book in my pyjama pocket. It *does* help the sacrifice to Venus.'

'It vos make it less troublessness, ain't it,' assented Herr Kunst, 'but der fucking in dese days of der jewellery der most expensive der great costliness vos, ain't it?'

'Oh, I don't know so much about that,' said a good-looking young man who was drinking as if he wanted to put paid to the ship's whisky stock before the Irish coast hove in sight; 'just listen to this story of a pal of mine.

'I'm naturally a shy chap, you know, and I'll be damned if ever I can find anything to talk about at balls and parties and things. But my pal *isn't*, and I just asked him how he managed about small talk.

'"Oh," he said, "when I'm first left alone with a girl, I just say to her, casual like, y'know – 'Are you fond of fucking?'"

'"Good God, man," I said to the bounder, "surely you get your ears boxed a lot, and get kicked out of a lot of houses?"

'"Well, I do, I admit," he answered, "but I get a hell of a lot of fucking."'

The *raconteur* smiled appreciation, and hastily ordered drinks for the assembled party on credit – his elder brother, the heir, was meeting him at Southampton.

The party then broke up to dress for dinner, all save Herr Kunst, who was so rich that he was excused the conventionalities and whose excuse of a

372

'weak chest' was allowed to keep him in morning dress.

Herr Kunst sat gloomily by the fire, contemplating the ship's dog, which lay placidly asleep, and pondering over the late conversation.

Though *riche à millions* – made out of a successful railway rig – he was not generous, and, though he loved the good things in life, he equally disliked paying for them. He stared long at the dog.

'Ach,' he muttered suddenly, 'you: you vos remind me of the dog of mein neighbour Schmidt in Chicago.

'Mein neighbour Schmidt und meinself, ve 'ad to der bier-halle been, und after ve make a backslidings into a bad house, und, vot mid der vucking mid der Frauleins, und der drinkings mit, ve vos some very much late kom 'ome.

'Schmidt – he vos look at his dog.

'"You," he say, "you vos only a dog, but I vish I vos you. To-night now, it vos time to go to bed. You, *you* vos turn over three times, you vos stretch yourself, and you vos asleep. *Me*: I haf to let der cat out, I haf to lock up der place. I haf to piss in der fire so dat it more safeness vos, I haf to undress meinself, und ven I reach mein room der vife she vos scold because I so lateness vos. Der baby vos squeal und I half to valk mit 'im round der house until by der time it vos time to go to bed it vos time to get up.

'"*I* haf to make der fire, to cook der breakfast, to dress meinself. *You*, you stretch tree times und you vos up. I give you your breakfast, und *I* haf to vork all day.

'"*You*, you play all day, and *you* ven you die, you vos dead; ven *I* die, *I have to go to Hell*: ain't it?"'

Herr Kunst spat venomously into the fire, and the dinner gong sounded.

They were a mixed lot in the first cabin on the *Mesopotamia*. Silverwood, Kunst, Miss Jepps and Lord Reggie Cameron we have already met. In addition there were the usual gang of rich Americans crossing to Europe for the early season, a number of business men of no particular interest, and Lady Felicia Tittle.

Lady Tittle was the relict of a middle-aged peer, who had outrun both his purse and his constitution, but had managed to leave her just a fair income, and she lived solely for pleasure.

She had been an ugly, ill-dressed girl, and knew nothing of the world till she met the late lamented Tittle, who had her forced on him, with a comfortable dowry, by her and his parents.

He had to do his duty as a husband, and he had taught her above a bit.

From the gaucherie of the schoolroom, Lady Felicia Tittle had developed into a really bad middle-aged woman.

The arts of cosmetics and the acquirement of the art of dress had given her a strangely fascinating charm, especially for very young men. She loved lust, and took every opportunity of gratifying that love.

With her was her flapper daughter, Honoria – Hony for short – 'Hony soit qui maule ses pants,' as a nasty young man once said as he was feeling her in the dark.

She was sixteen, deliciously pretty, and her figure, though still in the flapper mould, gave men to think a good deal.

She was still a virgin; that is to say, she hadn't actually had it *in* her, but she had seen a good deal of the human form divine, and only prudential motives had kept the little skin web in her vagina unpierced.

Next to her at dinner sat Moss Hell, the eminent financier. His real name had been Moses Eli. The Moses, of course, became Moss, but in casting about for a second name when he settled down in London, he lost his temper and exclaimed, 'Oh, Hell!'

'Ma tear, you've got it,' said little Hannibal McGregor of Smyrna, McGregor Castle, N.B., and Warne Court, and Hell it remained, and was a pretty good prop to him, as is any eccentricity to a clever stock-jobber.

Moss Hell, profiting by a lurch in the ship – *he knew* some of the tricks of the trade – twined his leg round the unprotected calf of little Honoria, apologised effusively, and was rewarded by a genial wink.

Moss Hell loved flappers, and by the second entrée had made his decision. Little Hony loved jewellery, and by the fish had made up hers. They were to be each others' for the six days to come on the briny.

There was no question about the success of Miss Jepps. Long before the *poulet aux champignons* Captain Russell James, R.N.R., was beginning to think a lot too much of his 9:30 date to pay proper courtesies to his other guests.

She looked radiant; she talked with a sparkle as bright as the Pommery; and she outlooked and outdressed every other woman at the table.

Mrs. Gunter Scrooge, who had on a dress three times as costly, and a face ten times as made up, glowered her enmity.

The last of the party on the 'good ship *Mesopotamia*' – one *must* use the phrase – worth talking about, were 'the Heavenly Twins,' as they were at once nicknamed, he a Yale scholar, going as a Rhodes scholar to Oxford, and she a Vassar girl going to tour Europe.

They were plum alike, and both genially nice looking; also, both well versed in the ways of the genial world.

With that we will conclude our list of the characters who set out with us on this 'Sentimental Journey.' We shall pick up others all over the world.

Dinner was over about 9:15. The Captain cut it a bit short; he couldn't hold himself, and he was nervous of the attention of others.

The company dispersed. Mr. Silverwood found himself looking moodily over the taffrail, by the side of Moss Hell. He was thinking of Miss Jepps and her captain.

'This vos a fine ship,' said Hell.

'Yes, very.'

'My brother has a fine ship, too. Mein father was the owner and he fell overboard. My brother had the presence of mind to call to my father as he was drowning, "Father, if you don't come up the third time, can I have the ship?"

'And my father, *in the presence of witnesses*, mark you, said, "Yes," before he sank. Otherwise, my uncle would have had the ship.'

And at that moment Miss Jepps was unloosening her corsets once more.

376

Two

'There is More in the Sea Air Than Salt'
– Lentory

The *Mesopotamia* slogged her path through the
Atlantic. The night had turned treacherous; the
North Atlantic squadron was somewhere in the
vicinity, manoeuvring without lights; innumerable
fishing boats drifted up through the mist; the
Deutschland and the *Admiral Veviers* must be close
behind, and the great liner was full in the highway of
the ocean, but still the Captain did *not* go on the
bridge. Duty was insignificant to the charms of Miss
Jepps.

Captain James, R.N.R., saw red – not only
stockings and *lingerie*, but passion. He would have
rammed a battleship rather than stop ramming Miss
Jepps, and he rammed her like hell. Only after the
fourth successful attempt did he call a halt.

Miss Jepps lay panting on her stateroom bed; the
Captain was still buttoning his braces, when there

came a dull boom – obviously a heavy gun fired some two miles away.

'We've run into the manoeuvres,' said the captain, fiddling with his tie.

The boom was repeated. And again, obviously much closer.

There came a rapping at the door. An agitated voice said, 'Is Captain James there, Miss?'

The Captain himself opened the door, and noting the pale face of the first officer who awaited him, hurried the man away.

'I'm afraid there's something wrong, sir,' said the man. 'I thought we had only run into the manoeuvres, but they, whoever they are, have signalled us to stop, and what's more, they've put a shot across our bows. What are we to do?'

The Captain still hot and confused from the embraces of Miss Jepps, stumbled on deck and was nearly blinded by the glare of the most powerful searchlight he had ever encountered. A shell screamed over the *Mesopotamia*. There was no doubt about it; something *was* wrong. The passengers, by now thoroughly alarmed, were streaming on deck; the officers did their best to restrain any panic.

As the Captain reached the bridge, the searchlight shut off like a turned down gas jet and a large grey vessel, like a cruiser, or a very large yacht, was plainly visible, not more than 150 yards away, steaming knot for knot with the *Mesopotamia*. Her lights blinked out the signal to heave to.

'They've done that four times already, sir,' said the first officer, 'but we didn't know where to find you. It was only Lady Tittle's suggestion –'

'Alright, alright; confound the impudent brute,

378

stopping a mail boat.'

'There he goes again, sir.'

'Heave to, or we sink you,' talked the stranger's lights to the *Mesopotamia*, and a shell sang close over the bridge.

The captain gave the necessary orders to acquiesce, and himself telephoned the engine-room to stop the engines.

The stranger curved in towards the *Mesopotamia* till both ships lay idle on the phosphorescent waters within seventy yards of each other.

There was a rattle of chains and a launch dropped from the side of the stranger. From the speed with which she approached the *Mesopotamia*, she was obviously motor driven.

Captain James stood at the top of the lowered gangway; the semi-scared, semi-curious passengers crowded the bulwarks.

The launch ran smartly alongside, and three young men, in light motor overalls, came quickly on board.

'Captain James?' said the leader, uncovering a very carefully brushed head of hair.

'Yes, sir; and what the hell do you mean by this extraordinary behaviour?'

'It's no use to bluster, sir,' answered the 'young man,' suavely; 'it's piracy.'

'Piracy!'

'Yes, sir; piracy on the high seas.'

'But –'

'You are our prisoners, sir; it is useless to protest. I have but to whistle and my guns will sink you. Look!'

It was obvious; the liners' searchlight showed up

an ugly collection of guns on the mysterious ship. Whether she was cruiser or armed yacht, it was difficult to tell from her lines, but that a little practice with those businesslike-looking 4.7 gentlemen could make the existence of the *Mesopotamia* a thing of the past admitted of no doubt.

The passengers began to get a little hysterical. Women sobbed; men blustered.

The young man took a silver whistle from his pocket and fingered it; his companions leant against the rail.

'My instructions are these. When my whistle sounds, you get a shell which, if properly aimed, removes the existence of your rudder and one at least of your screws. Before you have time to attack us – and, mind you, we have each two revolvers on us – we shall have vaulted over the side; we are all good swimmers, and our motor boat will pick us up. Then, we shall play with you until you pray for mercy. Far better save your ship, Captain.'

'What do you want?'

'What do you think? Everything of value. If you agree I shall signal for more men and we shall go through your first-cabin passengers as quickly and delicately as possible.'

His quick eye detected Lady Tittle surreptitiously placing a diamond necklace in her stocking.

'It won't do, madam. I have a female searcher in the boat below (of course I should not be so ungallant as to go over a lady myself). We mean business; it's all got to go.'

'I guess I wish we had that lady who saved the ship and the five hundred passengers,' murmured Mr. Silverwood.

Herr Kunst reflected on the happiness of his friend Schmidt's dog, and wished he was that animal.

Miss Jepps, who had just rearranged her toilet, had come on deck.

Her appearance obviously impressed the young man, and he bowed.

'Surely, Captain,' he said, 'you are not going to permit me to send so fair a flower as that to Davy Jones. Come, man, I'll only give you five minutes.'

Herr Kunst stepped forward.

'Gentlemen and ladies, der passengers,' he said, 'is it that ve all dead put are, or that ve sacrifice some little of zis vordly vealth and to Europe alive go, ain't it?'

The Captain, hectic with rage, turned to the swaying crowd.

'You are quite powerless,' said the young man, politely. 'Ah, would you!' He had detected an angular Yankee in the act of covering him with a revolver. Without a second's hesitation he whipped his hand from behind his back, and fired. The man's arm fell limply.

Consternation gripped the passengers. It was apparent to them that the pirates were quite determined.

The moments ticked on.

The young man remained unmoved, watch in hand, while the Captain canvassed the passengers.

At the end of the fifth minute he blew his whistle shrilly. Simultaneously a jet of flame leapt from his ship and a missile screamed through the air.

The great liner quivered under the impact. It was obvious that the rudder had been struck, fair and square, by a dead shell. These pirates knew something about shooting.

'Well,' said the young man, 'you see it's useless. I can sink you whenever I like. Give it up, and save your passengers'.

A general groan went up, and the Captain gave in.

More rattling of chains, and three more motor boats slapped into the water, and in a few minutes were alongside the *Mesopotamia*.

More pirates, now some seventy in all, were on the liner.

'You have done an act which the laws of God and man will avenge,' the Captain hissed, 'but I am in your power. Do your worst.'

The 'worst' was short of accomplishment. Sparing the second-class passengers and the steerage, the pirates, all young men with 'gentlemen by birth' unmistakably stamped all over them, went through the saloon passengers.

The young man remained by the gangway, and chatted affably with Miss Jepps, who seemed quite reconciled to the worst. The Captain stood by, in gloomy silence. The young man graciously spared the Captian his mails – *but*, when the majority of the pirates had returned, and Herr Kunst, reflecting that he had a considerable amount of diamonds in the rough still on him, was almost reduced to hysteria – the young man (we will refer to him anonymously throughout) made a proposition.

He *was* a pirate, he admitted, but he did not wish to become a real nuisance to civilisation. If any of the first-class passengers on the R.M.S. *Mesopotamia* would also like to be pirates, they were welcome to join his ship, and their valuables would *not* be taken from them. He would not guarantee them restoration to their proper sphere of life for upwards of two years, but he did not think he should place them in any immediate danger of the gallows.

He limited the number to twelve.

Nearly all the nice young men, all wearing motor coats, were now returned from their exploration of the ship. Heavy boxes were being lowered into the boats.

The *Mesopotamia* sagged, rudderless, in the swell, and the passengers were very nervous.

'Well,' said the young man, 'will twelve of you forsake a life of dull decorum and become pirates? I make *no* stipulation about sex.'

Herr Kunst was the first to step forward.

'If it is that my valuables so safe are, I'm with you,' he said, hastily adding, by way of qualification, 'I have in der illicit diamond buying business been; also it is that I have in prison been, ain't it?'

'Just our man,' said the young man.

'Well, after all, piracy isn't any worse than bridge, and it seems more profitable,' said Lady Tittle; 'come, Honoria. My name is Lady Tittle, of Clouds Court.'

'Exactly,' said the young man; 'I was expelled from Eton the same term as your son. Delighted, Lady Tittle, *and* your charming daughter.'

Miss Jepps made the fourth, and was received with open eyes by the motor-coated young men.

A number of passengers, confident because of the confidence of others, now came forward, but the young man exercised his discretion.

Mr. Moss Hell was picked, and his friend, Mr. Hannibal McGregor.

Half the dozen was thus accounted for, while the Captain fumed and looked in vain for the search-lights of the manoeuvring fleet.

Mr. Silverwood explained his position, and was accepted at once. It was the ivory gleam of Miss Jepp's neck did him.

Lord Reggie Cameron produced a visiting card in a delicate manner.

'Ah, yes,' said the young man, 'you were at Harrow. Do you remember Lords in '93? You know you never could play leg breaks.'

'Good God, man, it's –'

'Sh, sh, sh, Captain Kidd, or any other name does for me here. Welcome, Lord Reggie; we can't give you much cricket, but if you shoot as you used, you won't be dull, and the tarpon fishing round our little home is extra.'

The lights of the *Deutschland* swam out of the mist like a great hotel on the waves. Captain James gave a great shout.

'It's quite useless, Captain,' said the young man, very quietly. 'I could sink her, too, if I wanted to; but one's enough this trip. You get your steering gear repaired and get home. With luck, you'll get your mails in in time, and you'll save salvage. It come stiff with a big liner, you know, and I shan't worry you again. I'm not working the Atlantic for years to come. Now, then, four more.'

The Sisters Lovett, twin divinities of the music hall stage, were accepted at once, and Billy Neale, the English comedian, proved a certain starter.

The twelfth was a flapper friend of 'Hony' Tittle's, a sweet little brunette, with legs which almost rivalled those of Miss Jepps.

384

'Make it a baker's dozen, guv'nor,' said a very large young woman.

'Righto,' and they took Madge.

Madge was stewardess on the *Mesopotamia*.

A Scotch woman, she was shrewd and good-looking beyond most of her countryfolk. She rather tumbled to the fact that the pirate ship would be more genial than the old *Mesopotamia*. Besides, she was a virgin, and had some time since begun to wish she wasn't. Some of these aristocratic young pirates looked promising.

When the selected baker's dozen had finally collected their *impedimenta*, they were conducted into the boats.

Lady Tittle muffled herself into her sables, and, with a feeling of amused curiosity, watched the young man as he switched on the ignition, and the motor launch thrilled into life.

In an incredibly short time, it seemed, there was a space of black water between them and the crippled liner, now an imitation Brock's benefit of flashing searchlights.

'Bloody fool,' said the young man, *sotto voce*. 'He'll only get the Frenchman or the German back to him. They can only take his mails and send a wireless message back to Sandy Hook for help, and God help the firm when the salvage bill comes in!'

The white water stood up on each bow of the launch, and Hony Tittle had already been kissed by an elegant young pirate, who smelt of some quite delicious perfume – to the annoyance of Miss Jepps – while Lord Reggie Cameron discovered an old friend in one of the crew, who had left the army because – well, he played pool too well – and the clean-built hull of the pirate ship loomed up above them.

As the motor headlight swept the sides of the ship, Lady Tittle noted the name: the *New Decameron*. She began to be more than agreeably amused.

The young man handed her on to the gangway, and in quite a few minutes the new pirates had been escorted to the saloon, the boats swung up to the davitts, the plunder temporarily stored on deck, and the hum of the turbines showed that the yacht, or whatever it was, was under way with a vengeance.

Herr Kunst rubbed his hands with some satisfaction. He had carefully secreted his most valuable packet of diamonds up his arse, and his natural instinct for robbery coincided well with the promise of this new adventure. He had been in many things worse than piracy on the high seas, and always come out top dog – 'You don't go in for I.D.B. or running contraband of war for nothing,' he reflected.

The young man explained briefly to the assembled twelve – Madge had been given into the charge of an elderly stewardess – that the nature of the cruise would be explained to them at supper, which would presently be ready. In the meantime the men were shown to their cabins and the ladies handed over to delightfully pretty stewardesses. When Lady Tittle and her daughter – who would rather have remained with the pirates – reached their stateroom, they found Madge waiting for them.

It was a large and charming cabin: a few good water-colour drawings hung on the walls; the appointments were all perfect, and the comfort seemed absolute. Hony was charmed; this adventure seemed far better than going back to her convent in

Belgium – nor had she forgotten that kiss in the boat.

'Supper,' said Madge, 'would be ready in three-quarters of an hour,' so she had been told by a 'very nice young man, who didn't look at all like an ordinary steward.' Madge further volunteered the information that 'all the gentlemen seemed very much like gentlemen indeed.'

Lady Tittle thought a lot. Pirates or no pirates, there might be worse jobs for her daughter Hony than to marry a pirate who had a yacht or whatever it was, like this. Everything pointed to wealth. He might have been expelled from Eton; that happened to so many boys – her own son – well, Lady Tittle was a woman of the world, and she knew that 'boys would be into boys' when he came home in the middle of the term, having been discovered *in flagrante delictu* with a pretty lad who had the next room. She quite endorsed the theory of a one-time captain of Harrow – we won't mention names, but it was a very well-known one – who in all seriousness suggested to the head that, considering the epidemic of sodomy at the time existent in the school, it would be better that the elder boys were allowed an occasional whore, which, if against morality, was not against the law of the country.

The head didn't quite see the point, and the boy, having in a moment of exasperation told him to 'Oscar himself,' was incontinently removed from the school.

Still, young Lord Tittle was now quite a respected member of society, and judging from the number of chorus girls he got in the family way, he couldn't have much time, or spare ammunition, to waste on members of his own sex.

'Decidedly,' argued Lady Tittle, as she unscrewed the top of her field glasses – made to hold one pint – and had a refreshing nip of Hennessey's twenty-five-year-old (this book does not charge for advertisements, but the author can be 'got at' for the next), 'decidedly Hony ought to land that young man.

'He *may* be a duke in disguise,' she reflected, trying to recollect what members of the peerage had recently disappeared, and remembering the case of the young Duke of St. Eden, who had rattled twins out of his maiden aunt.

He, the missing duke, she knew, was tattooed down the back with a representation of a fox hunt – the fox was just disappearing up his Oscar's joy. It *might* be him. She decided to make enquiries from the elderly stewardess.

Lady Tittle was herself in evening dress, having had no time to change. Hony, of course, being young – in years – was not. Lady Tittle decided that this must be rectified. The extraordinary atmosphere of this novel situation set all the wickedness in her blood aboil. Whether there were other women on the boat besides the captives from the *Mesopotamia*, she did not know; she had seen none, but there were plainly quite a number of men. With Hony she meant serious business, but for herself – well, she was middle-aged and she could do with a bit of promiscuous fornication. After all, there was bound to be a sensation in Europe when this abduction was known, but who was going to know minor details?

Her legs twitched at the thought, and her drooping bosoms stiffened. She was a good sailor – nothing made her sick – and if she was going to have a succession of nice young pirates between her thighs, a succession of hot kisses on her still ripe, red, luscious lips, and genial dirty talk in bed – well, she was game to go on being a female pirate for ever.

Picking up her skirts, she smoothed her still well-rounded calves, and looked at Hony, envying the child her years. Hony had all the family beauty of her father's line, and the Tittles had been famous for centuries for looks.

John Manners Tittle, of Uppleford, in Devon, left early an orphan and become very dissolute by reason of bad companions, came first to court in the reign of King James I. That dirty-minded old Scotch monarch soon spotted the very handsome rough and made him a favourite. He, in common with others, had to submit to the king's caresses, and a sore arse was rewarded by a peerage. He took the family name for title, as his estates had come into the hands of the horde of Scotch money-lenders who had followed James to England.

His son became a familiar of the second Charles, and on Mistress Kate Richards, the actress, giving birth to a daughter to the king, Lord Tittle was offered an earldom if his son, then a little boy, would marry the illegitimate baby. Hence the Earls Tittle, of Casteford, an estate estreated from a Scotch money-lender by Charles II.

The union of the handsome Lord Tittle with the child of the beautiful actress produced a race that became famous for its good looks, and the last earl was no discredit to his forbears, who had fucked and fought their way from the Stuarts to the Guelphs.

The present Lady Tittle could not boast of much winsomeness herself, but Hony – Hony was a veritable feast for the gods – still, what about evening dress? Hony hadn't got one, and Lady Tittle quite appreciated the fact that the child, though tall enough to go into one of her own, must certainly show her dainty little legs.

Hony was five foot to the inch, and Lady Tittle recollected in a flash of inspiration that the Sisters Lovett, the last of the captives, were practically the same *and* were possessed of many stage frocks of an exceedingly saucy and *décolleté* nature. They would not mind lending one to the daughter of a countess.

At the bidding of Madge the sisters were summoned, both rather flustered and untidy. It was hinted in preliminary conversation that the pirates had been gallant – *trés gallant*. They were delighted to lend dresses, and presently a large basket, borne by two pirates, obviously gentlemen, made its appearance.

The Sisters Lovett appeared principally in Paris, and their costumes were – well – Parisian. Little Hony was going to make her début very, very, *very* indeed.

Lady Tittle chose a plain black silk, very low in the neck, and very high in the upwards part. It was very close cut in the waist, but Hony could go into a 15½ corset.

With the dress were delightful adjuncts of layers of frilled petticoats and the daintiest of drawers, very short, so that the open-work silk stockings had to be almost as long as tights.

Lady Tittle left the girl alone to dress. She had a mind to investigate this ship on her own. Madge had been imperiously summoned by Miss Jepps to help make her even more fascinating.

Hony undressed stark naked. She was very cute for her age, and she quite understood that she was completely in the power of these pirates. There was little also that she did not understand about the relations of the sexes. If she was going to be seduced, which she strongly suspected might be possible, she was determined that her lingerie should be faultless. Her head was choc-a-bloc with naughty thoughts as she looked at her reflection in the long cheval glass.

It was a pretty sight. A youthful Lady Godiva one might have called her – for Hony could sit on her fair, naturally curly hair, which fell over her shoulders like a shower of golden rain, swelling, it seemed, lasciviously over her semi-matured breasts. She was a twentieth-century Danaë, and Jupiter could not have resisted her.

A faint golden down curled between her thighs, and there was a little fluff underneath each of her beautifully-rounded arms. She frankly admired herself and was posturing a little before the glass, stretching her arms above her head, curving her back, altering the position of her legs, now standing with them tight together to see if any aperture showed between the thighs – and it didn't; Hony's legs were singularly perfect – now standing with them well apart, muscles taut, pleased to see how the sinews rose under the milk-white flesh. She went right up to the glass, and kissed the reflection of her own lips, thrilling with the recollection of that kiss in the motor launch. She was rubbing her stomach against the glass, pinching the cheeks of her bottom to see if they were firm, when the door opened suddenly and another girl stepped quickly into the room.

Hony jumped away from the glass with a scream, and instinctively clasped her hands over her most precious possession. Then she laughed.

It was only her flapper friend, Carrie Francks, a little Cuban beauty whom she had casually met in the Waldorf Astoria before they left New York.

Carrie was being sent to Paris to complete her education. She was not a pure Cuban, as there was a lot of Yankee blood on her father's side, but she had great, lustrous Spanish eyes, which gleamed as they fixed on the naked apparition of Hony. At the hotel, Lady Tittle having run down to Newport for the night, Hony and Carrie had shared beds for company's sake – well – well – well – to continue.

Carrie was very dark and very slight. Her figure was really too slim to be good, but there was a feline grace in it which was very tempting. Her face lacked good features, but her very full red lips, her glorious eyes, and her abundance of raven hair made up for any defects. She was a striking contrast to the pink and white beauty of golden-haired Hony.

'My, but you *do* look a peach,' she exclaimed. 'Kiss me.'

And she didn't wait; she bundled Hony into her arms and smothered her with kisses. She kissed her mouth, her eyes, her ears, her glinting hair, and descending lower, ran her tongue over each delicious little breast in turn. Hony shivered with delight and wrapped her arms round the other girl's shoulders; it was evident that she was not unused to this class of pastime, and when Carrie's right hand slipped down to the downy mount between her thighs and a deft finger was inserted into her moist little cunt, she wriggled with joy and cooed with delight.

392

'Come to the bed, dear,' the dark girl whispered. 'I *must* kiss it.'

Hony was on her back in a moment and stretched wide apart her deliciously-moulded legs; the other buried her face between them, gripped her sweetheart almost savagely round the legs, and – well, her tongue wasn't idle. Hony's lovely face took on a beatific expression, which made her look far too angelic for the occupation she was engaged in. Her fingers smoothed Carrie's raven locks and her legs, folded across her lover's shoulders, twitched convulsively with joy. It was obvious that Carrie was no mean performer. The sucking noise made by her tongue proclaimed the fact that Hony was spending copiously. Presently she pushed Carrie's head aside.

'Stop, dearie,' she gasped. 'Stop, and turn round; you know what I mean.'

Carrie slipped off the bed, stood up, and pulled her skirts up to her waist. She wore lovely underclothes – her parents were very wealthy Cuban people – and as she climbed on top of Hony the bewildering mass of *frou-frou* was a pretty sight. It was a *soixante-neuf* which ought to have been immortalised by a painter.

Carrie's firm bottom peeped, a little brown in colour, between the slit in her drawers; her legs were perhaps a little on the thin side, but delicately shaped; her ankle was very tiny and her instep very high.

Hony's white arms gleamed against the black cloth of Carrie's tailor-made costume. Her dainty legs, rose-tinted at knees and toes, were once more round Carrie's neck, but this time she was doing *her* share of the work. Only half of her lovely face was

393

visible between Carrie's thighs, and her glorious golden hair was thrown back in abandon over Carrie's befrilled Parisian drawers.

The two girls writhed in an ecstacy of lust, and a knock at the door passed unheeded, nor was the turning of a handle and the entrance of a man noticed by the engrossed *minettes*.

It was the young man. He came softly into the cabin and stood regarding the spectacle.

'I've paid a good many pounds to see this done in Paris before now,' he reflected, 'and yet never a prettier couple. Little devils!'

The young man was immaculately dressed in a slight variation of ordinary evening dress. The colour of the suit was of dark blue, with a black velvet semi-collar. The coat was cut very tight in the waist and very full in the tails. The trousers fitted perfectly over slim , but well-formed, legs. Across his breast he wore a sash, obviously belonging to some foreign order, and from a ribbon round his neck depended a glittering star. In the lapel of his coat several other orders were fixed, all of barbaric nature in design. His auburn hair was parted exactly in the centre, from the middle of the forehead to the nape of the neck. Over his arm hung a dark-blue overcoat, and in his hand was a semi-nautical, semi-military peaked cap, heavily gold braided.

In fact, he looked like a glorified Seymour Hicks.

After a moment's pause, feasting his eyes on the lust-feast before him, he walked up to the bed and smacked Carrie lightly on the bottom. Thinking that it was Hony, the girl did not stir, only her bottom moved lasciviously. But Hony lifted her eyes – and beheld the man.

394

With a scream she pulled Carrie's mass of *froufrou* over her face, and Carrie, startled, looked up.

'Well,' said the young man, 'you wicked girls, what do you think I am going to do to you? I am master here, you know. Come, get up.'

Very shamefacedly the two got up and sat on the edge of the bed. Hony hastily pulling the quilt round her naked body.

'I must apologise,' he said, 'but there was no answer to my knock and I had to see that the portholes were closed; the sea is rising. I must thank the elements for giving me the opportunity of witnessing so delightful a sight.'

Carrie stood up, suddenly pulling herself together.

'You ought to be ashamed of yourself,' she said. 'If you are a gentleman, leave the cabin at once.'

'I can quite see that "gentlemen" are not wanted here,' laughed the young man, 'but perhaps your little love affair has made you hungry. Supper will be ready in a few minutes. For the present, *au revoir*,' and he withdrew with a bow.

'Oh, Carrie, *whatever* will he think?' said Hony hysterically. 'We were caught right at it, weren't we?'

'*Right* at it, dearie,' acquiesced the dark girl, 'but it can't be helped. Besides, from what I can see, there are going to be some odd goings on on this ship. As I was coming along to see you, one of those pirates – such a nice boy – collared me, and kissed and cuddled till I thought I was smothered. Now, you hurry up and get dressed, and we'll hie to the feast.'

Lady Tittle, in the course of her wanderings on the promenade deck of the *New Decameron*, which was now rattling through the Atlantic billows, southwards, at an easy thirty knots, had drawn a sickening blank in her encounters with the various pirates scattered about the windswept deck. No one took any notice of her at all.

She swirled her silk-skirted way through the breeze, coyly scanning any man she met – it was impossible to tell whether they were officers or crew – but met with no response till, right in the stern of the ship, she was stayed by a gruff voice asking 'what she wanted'.

Lady Tittle replied (in the well-known Biblical manner of answering a question with a question) by demanding who he was.

It appeared he was the bosun, a burly, heavily moustachioed man in oil skins, who lured Lady Tittle into the shadow of a whale boat when he gathered she was one of the captives. He explained that he was Major Brander, late of the Black Watch, and that a little difference with the War Office, and, incidentally, with the laws of the country, had led him to join this adventure.

'I am the oldest of the crew,' he said, rather sadly, 'so they made me the bosun. I know nothing about "bosuning" but still this ship goes on. I remember you (Lady Tittle had introduced herself), dear lady, as the belle of the Binchester hunt ball; in the sixties, I fear it was.'

'Ah, me,' sighed Lady Tittle, 'we were children then, and love beat through our veins – eh, Major?'

'And does now, damme,' cried the bosun-major, and he boldly put his arm round Lady Tittle and kissed her.

The powerful searchlights of the *New Decameron*, sweeping the sea on all quarters, made the deck of the boat seem very dark. The major, or bosun, as we will call him, made no bones about his job. Pulling aside, with a firm though gentle hand, Lady Tittle's opera cloak, he brushed her bare bosom with his moustache. There was a hen coop just behind the pair, and on to that, despite the shrill cacklings of its inmates, he guided the amorous old lady.

It was a hard couch, but it served – and it didn't have to serve for long. Both were very randy, and the simultaneous outpourings of their sexual organs came after the fowls beneath had been terrified for but a brief two minutes.

Lady Tittle got up with a girlish simper of glee.

'Oh, *what* must you think of me?' she murmured, 'and we've hardly even seen each other's faces yet.'

'If your face is as charming as the figure I have felt, madame, I am sure it is still that of the beautiful Felicia Tittle I met years ago; besides, this ship is Liberty Hall. I should advise you to look after your beautiful little daughter.'

'Oh, Hony can look after herself; but, tell me,' whispered Lady Tittle, trying surreptitiously to wipe up the streams of semen which ran down her legs with a gossamer handkerchief, 'who is this young man who seems to be captain. He says he was at Eton with my boy.'

'That, my dear Felicia, is a profound secret; most of us know, but not all.'

'Well, I have my suspicions,' said Lady Tittle.

At that moment a loud gong, like the war gong used to call the tribes in Burma, reverberated through the ship.

'Ah,' said the bosun, in a cheery voice, 'supper at last. I can promise you, Felicia, that you will at least find that the creature comforts are well attended to on this ship.'